THE STONIMIONS AND THE BOOK OF QUANTIME

F M SHAH

CONTENTS

DEDICATION

In memory of my beloved father

The Late Syed Akbar Shah

You're still the best Dad ever!

ACKNOWLEDGMENTS

There are many people that I would like to thank for their support during the writing of this book. Firstly, my ever suffering husband, Nasir, who for the past few years only ever heard me say 'I've got to write my book'. His love and support kept me focused and determined to complete my book. Thanks for the help with the library and the idea for the pyramid. I would also like to thank my two wonderful boys Amaan & Aadil, who put up with delayed or cancelled outings so that I could finish my book. In fact it was Amaan who suggested it I write it; when I told him that I had started writing a story when I was fourteen but only got as far as the idea and one page.

My family have always been a great support; my Mum, for her constant prayers, my brother Aslam, sister-in-law Nusrat and my wonderful nephews and nieces, Hafiza, Yusaf, Saadia and Samir. Particularly a new member of the family Sufyan Ibrahim (Hafiza's husband) who on every family get together would always ask how the book was going.

There have been many encouraging words from the students I have taught at Cardinal Newman Catholic School in Luton; classes such as - Mendel, Khorana, Oxygen, Callisto and especially all the sixth form students (12XB2-you guys are great and always bring a smile to my face), and special thanks to Amy [best media student ever] for helping to create the original front cover (I hope you like the changes I made), Tia, Zayna and Niamh; Then there is Lucy and her dolphins! Zakhir, Rumaanah, Ellen, Alison, Emily, Muno, Maja & Saima). I would also like to thank the students in Archimedes class of 2016 (the inspiration for the characters in the Nevada desert).

This year I will have gone back to school and faced the physics teacher, Mrs. Daniels, and told her 'Yes I have completed it now!' I would like to thank the science department for their support and Sandra Brown for being the very first person to purchase the book on Kindle. Thanks to Tony Smailes, the tough critical English teacher, where I teach, who enjoyed the book so much he 'could not put it down', his words not mine. Those words gave me courage and belief in what I had produced. Kate & Seamus Murphy; thank you for your support and advice.

To all friends from Denbigh Juniors Luton, Denbigh High Luton (Ruth, Christine and Maria), Luton Sixth Form College (Jasbir & Chetna), King's College London (Danica, Claire, Constantine & Mirianthe), Imperial College London (Mary, Vivian, Yannie, Luisa, Claudia & Ruhana), GSK NOP; Kanwal, Candace, Lee, Lindsey, Ruhin, Cheryl & Jenny, Denbigh High School (this time as a teacher), I wish you all well. Danica, thanks for your encouraging words when I first told you about my book and your help in its formatting.

I would like to thank my neighbours Adrian and Sharon and, Theresa across the road, for their supporting words and encouragement, as well as my neighbour Pat.

If there are any well-wishers I have not mentioned – I'm sorry, but believe me when I say that every good wish, good luck and prayer (dua) is very much appreciated and gratefully accepted.

Farzana (Fuzz)

PROLOGUE

She arrived in the middle of a forest, knowing he was nearby, she could feel his evil emanating from every pore in his body. The old woman sniffed the night air like a wolf looking for its prey; treading through the forest like a stealthy predator. She knew where to look; as she headed through the forest towards the children's home.

The old woman was not aware that there was another presence here with her on Earth; a good presence that had followed her from their world, he knew that she was up to no good. As she approached the Children's home her excitement was causing her to lose control; she nearly cackled her delight into the night air. Her awareness of bringing attention to herself helped her to contain her joy.

The evil woman did not have to go too much farther, as she walked a few more steps she came across him. The old woman got closer to the young boy and held out her hand towards him. At first he backed away unsure of this strange looking old woman but then he stopped.

"Come with me child, I have great plans for you, I will take you to a place where you will rule, be respected and feared. You have much greatness ahead of you and I will serve you all the way." Her raspy voiced quivered with excitement.

Despite the hideousness of the woman the young boy took a liking to her; he had no-one here, no-one to love or care for him. He hated them all. He reached out to take her hand when he was stopped by another voice.

"Don't child, this will only lead to your doom." The man warned.

"You meddling fool!" the old woman screamed and as she did so she raised her hands towards the man.

Within a matter of seconds a fiery blaze emanated from her fingers, but the man was fast and moved out of the firing range taking refuge amongst the trees. The old woman sent out the blaze again towards a movement in the trees and as she did so there was a loud scream of pain, but the voice was that of a child and not a man. "Harvey! No!" screamed the boy who the old woman had been coaxing.

"Quick we have no time!" she said and grabbed his hand. They both disappeared into the night via the same portal she had arrived.

The man saw what happened to the young teenage boy and went over to him to try and help him, but it was too late. As the boy took his last breaths the man placed his wrist on the boys head; his wrist contained a bracelet. The bracelet pulsated gently and glowed amber in colour, but the colour seemed to originate from the man's body; the colour began to surround the boys head. A minute later the bracelet stopped glowing and the man gently closed the young boy's eyes and slowly got up whilst gently laying him down onto the ground, he turned, and he too returned via the portal he had arrived by.

STONIDIUM –THE FREE LAND

1
THE INITIATION

"Hurry up Amafiz!" "You always make us late" Dilyus said in an uncharacteristically agitated voice. Amafiz was running around trying to get dressed and looking smart for the ceremony. "It's just typical of you, you always leave everything to the last minute!" exclaimed Simsaa.

Amafiz looked at his friends despairingly. "Look, I know it's my fault we're getting late, but I was working in my Dad's shop last night and I didn't get the chance to sort this all out" he tried to explain, pointing at all his belongings that were strewn all over his bedroom floor.

At that moment there was a knock on his door and before he had time to say come in Nasami fell into Amafiz's room. "Come in why don't you Nasami" laughed Simsaa.

Nasami went slightly red at his entrance, "Sorry Amafiz, I don't know my own strength sometimes". The four friends burst into laughter but it was short lived as Amafiz's mother called to them to hurry up as they were getting very late for the 'Initiation Ceremony'.

"I really don't know what's wrong with you youngsters nowadays!?" exclaimed Amafiz's mother.

"When I was a young girl....." said Amafiz mimicking his mother.

"Cheeky young man!" she laughed. "It's true, things were different and we always made sure that we were never late for anything!"

"I know mum but times have changed and these things happen, I know it's not good but sometimes it can't be helped-we're not as perfect as you are mum!" Amafiz replied looking at his mother lovingly.

Amafiz always knew how to get around his mother, and if truth be known his mother enjoyed teasing him and loved the compliments he always paid her. "You, young man are incorrigible and a charmer, but you've won me over AGAIN!" His mother smiled. She turned to look at Amafiz's young friends and saw the excitement and fear in their eyes and gave them some words of comfort. "Don't worry kids; every Stonimion has been through this and although it seems scary you'll be fine, I promise you" she smiled with empathy.

Amafiz's mother understood the young friends' nervousness, which they were trying to disguise with their jesting, as the upcoming ceremony was the most auspicious time in the life of a Stonimion. She knew this was a very important time for him and all of his friends, going through the initiation ceremony, indeed, it was a very important time for all young Stonimions when they reached puberty.

Finally they were ready, the four friends left Amafiz's house, along with his parents and headed towards the 'Forest of the Stone'. When they arrived they could see all of the other Stonimions already waiting for them. The parents of the four friends went and stood on one side of the Initiation Stone, with the Stonimion Elders, whilst the four friends faced them. The other Stonimions present, consisting of close family and friends, stood at a distance smiling at the four young Stonimions, who were looking nervously around at all of them.

The Forest of the Stone was a beautiful, lush and green forest that was full of tall trees that looked like friendly giants looking down upon the Stonimions who had gathered there. The floor of the forest was carpeted with an emerald green grass and bordered with colourful and strangely shaped plants. The only thing missing from the forest, in comparison to Earths, was the lack of animal life, although there was plenty of movement about the forest; as the plants were mobile. The four friends were looking at the strange looking plants because they were unlike any other plants in Stonidium, some seemed to hum a soothing tune as they whooshed past the Stonimions, who stood near the Initiation Stone, and others seemed to sway as if in some kind of plant like trance.

The young Stonimions attention was diverted from the plants by a loud drumming sound that was almost like the pounding of feet on hard ground. The Elders of the Stonimions had arrived and were all looking grand in their finest robes and full battle armoury. The Stonimion armoury consisted of a large belt around the waist that contained the ancient stone of power, which was part of their own body, a cloak that provided protection from both physical and powerful energy afflictions and finally the transporter bracelet, which allowed the Stonimions to transport from one location to another. The Stonimions were not like any creature seen on Earth, they were of various heights synonymous to humans, their bodies were covered in a soft brownish coloured fur; they had large round eyes of various colours, again similar to humans. They also had hidden ears, arms with hands and legs with feet and of course their belts that they were born with containing their stone of power.

The Elders looked immaculate whilst they stood proudly next to the Initiation stone, they looked towards the gathered Stonimions as the Chief Elder stepped forward and raised his sceptre. A hush fell amongst the forest as all eyes and attention were on the Elders and the four young Stonimions standing around the stone.

The ceremony was started by the Chief Stonimion, Samaan, whose job was to oversee the entire proceedings and make sure that the Stonimions undergoing the initiation understood the laws and rules that applied to this sacred occasion.

"Welcome friends, family and all Stonimions, today we are gathered together to celebrate the coming of age and wisdom of these young Stonimions." He pointed towards Amafiz and his friends. "Our ancient traditions dictate that all Stonimions must undergo the 'Initiation', this allows them to access their powers and protect us from the enemies of our land, past and present. We're currently under threat from a heinous being 'The Evil One', from whom there is a constant threat". On hearing the reference to the Evil One all the Stonimions raised their hands towards the stones in their belts and said in unison 'freedom from evil!' Samaan continued " Once we have reached the age of puberty we not only acquire our powers but remember we are duty bound to uphold the Stonimion way of life and the Stonidium ethos 'Freedom, Fairness & Tolerance'. He looked around him and breathed in the unity of the Stonimions and their desire to fulfil the traditions of the Ancient Stonimions. "Let us begin the initiation." he said and looked towards the party to be initiated.

This was the prompt to the young Stonimions to step forward towards the Initiation Stone, by the Chief Elder. The Initiation Stone was a dark but very glassy looking oval stone that had a translucent crystal dome hovering over it. It was a magnificent sight; the young Stonimions stood staring at the beautiful Initiation stone and its dome. There seemed to be an aura of colours emanating from the dome itself and the black stone ebbed with a low energy that pulsated from it in all directions. This was where the young Stonimions would receive their powers and understand their aim in life; it would carve their paths and roles in the protection of Stonidium and of Earth.

"I think I'm going to be sick" said Dilyus, who was looking rather green around the gills.

"What's wrong?" asked Nasami, who himself was looking as bad as Dilyus. "I don't think I can do this! I'm still too young, I think I'm not ready to be initiated, I'm not good at being powerful, teleporting, fighting or BAKING!" At this point Dilyus was breathing heavily and looked as if he was about to faint. At the word baking his friends all looked at him and rolled their eyes up towards the sky, they looked towards each other and grinned. Dilyus always cheered them up even when he had no intention of doing so. As always Simsaa had some soothing words to calm him down.

"Don't be such a wuss! You'll be fine" she grinned as she took hold of his hand and gave it a squeeze. Dilyus smiled back albeit weakly but managed to calm himself down to focus on the proceedings.

The Chief Elder held aloft the crystal sceptre and with a loud 'swoosh' brought it down near the onyx Initiation Stone. The point of contact of the sceptre with the ground created a reverberation that extended throughout the Great Forest of the Stone. This was an indicator to all present that the Stonimion Elder was ready to proceed. The Chief Elder looked at the group of young Stonimions and their parents and smiled.

The ceremony had started and the parents of the Stonimions, who were about to be initiated, were asked to step forward. "Who puts forward the Stonimion known as Amafiz?"

"I do! Akjam the Brave" said Amafiz's father. He looked at his son with great elation. Amafiz stepped forward and stood next to his father; he looked up to his father and had never felt so happy in his entire life. This was a very important time for both of them and they knew it. Amafiz was summoned by Samaan to step onto the oval Initiation Stone, and as he did so he looked up into the apex of the dome, for a moment he stood mesmerised by the swirl of rainbow colours he saw covering the inside of the dome. One moment he was able to distinguish different colours moving around the apex of the dome like swirls of gases, the next moment the gases amassed into one large cloud that seemed to pulsate as a white light which then separated again.

The initiation ceremony was extremely important as it enabled the Stonimion, who was coming of age, to access his or her powers through the activation of their stone. The stone in their belt up to this point had been a grey coloured opaque stone that they had from birth. It should be noted that the belt of the Stonimion was not an accessory belt but actually part of their body. The power bestowed upon the Stonimion was given to them by the ancient Stonimions and it was based upon their name and personality, therefore, the naming of a Stonimion infant was done very carefully so that the Stonimion would have a good nature and powers that would be used for the good of all Stonimions and Humans. The colour of the stone was reflective of these characteristics as well and was acquired alongside the powers; in fact, the powers of a Stonimion are accessed because of the photon energy from the coloured stone.

"I wonder what colour stone Amafiz will get?" whispered Simsaa to Dilyus. Dilyus was slowly getting over his nausea attack from earlier.

"Forget that I'm wondering what power he'll get?"

There was crack of thunder and a bolt of lightning seemed to flash inside the dome. The noise made Nasami jump, who up until now had stood staring at the dome, he had been totally hypnotised by the colours he could see from within the crystal dome, it had a sort of a power that called to him; he could feel its energy and that of the ancient Stonimions.

A voice boomed from inside the dome and all the Stonimions looked towards the apex of the dome. "Welcome, young Stonimion, state your name and that of your father" Amafiz gulped loudly, he turned to look around at the others, worried that he may have gulped so loudly that they all may have heard. From the looks on their faces Amafiz realised his gulping had not been that loud. He mustered up all his courage and said in a loud clear voice.

"I am Amafiz son of Akjam the Brave" Amafiz was looking up towards the top of the dome as he said this.

"Amafiz!" the voice repeated his name. "So you are the protector, I know of the power to bestow upon you young Stonimion. You will have the power of defence and the gift of healing."

There was a low rumbling sound that increased to a crescendo so loud that Amafiz had to cover his ears. A bright purplish light engulfed Amafiz and he felt himself being lifted away from the onyx stone and towards the apex of the dome. The others witnessed the colour filling the dome and for a moment the young Stonimions, who had never witnessed such a spectacle, became really worried for their friend as he disappeared into the purple light, in front of their very eyes. The sound and the coloured light subsided as quickly as it had occurred revealing Amafiz standing back upon the oval onyx stone.

Amafiz slowly emerged from the dome and gently stepped off the onyx stone. His friends looked at him intensely and sensed a change in him; he seemed to have the confidence of his father and an air of knowing something that he had not known before. He looked wiser and, although had not physically changed, he seemed stronger. Then they saw the colour of the stone in his body belt. It was the most beautiful bright and deepest amethyst they had ever seen. It glowed and emanated a power that captivated them; they could not take their eyes off of it.

It was tradition that as a young Stonimion received their power they would declare what it was and would then be given their full battle armoury. Amafiz stood and announced to all his friends, family and fellow Stonimions his new

14

powers. "I have the power of defence and the gift of healing, I am the Protector!" as he said this he touched the amethyst stone in his belt and a surge of purple colour was emitted from it to his hand. At this point the Chief Elder handed Amafiz a purple cloak and the transporter bracelet. He put these on and went to stand next to his father, who was smiling so much that Amafiz thought his father's mouth was going to end up taking up all of his face.

Dilyus was next and after watching the spectacle that Amafiz just went through he was more nervous than ever. Dilyus and his father stood side by side and just as with Amafiz, Dilyus' father declared his name "I am Nalam the Helper and I put forward my son Dilyus". Dilyus was then asked to step onto the onyx stone. One by one each of the Stonimion friends went through their initiation ceremony and one by one emerged as powerful, strong and wiser Stonimions.

Dilyus had been given the power of mind control and the gift of slowing time. He had a deep green emerald stone in his belt. Nasami received the power of telekinesis and the gift of changing objects into whatever he wanted, his stone was a diamond and finally of the four friends the only female, Simsaa was bestowed the power of shape shifting and the gift of absorbing knowledge, her stone was a rich red garnet.

The celebrations had started and everyone was having a great time. The four friends were enjoying the attention from all their friends and family. There was a magnificent feast of all their favourite foods, berries, fruits and lots of fruit juices to drink. There were lots of different types of meats roasting, vegetables as far as the eye could see and some Earth foods that the Stonimions had learnt of and made. Simsaa was tucking into her favourite Earth food called lasagne, whilst one eye remained firmly on the chocolate cheesecake that was near her. The younger Stonimions always seemed to prefer the Earth foods to their own traditional foods, and enjoyed special occasions such as initiations, birthdays, for example, where Earth foods would be made in abundance.

Once everyone was fully satiated and unable to eat another morsel the food was cleared away. It was tradition that the Stonimions who had undergone the initiation would display their new powers to the others. This tradition had two reasons for being done, firstly to allow the older Stonimions to see the full extent of the new powers and also to let the young Stonimions use them for the first time under supervision, and safe conditions.

The Chief Elder used his sceptre to bring hush to the gathering and gain everyone's attention, by pounding it into the ground, as before. "My dearest friends the time has come to see the powers these wonderful young Stonimions have received today" he smiled as he pointed to the four friends. On hearing the announcement, Nasami gulped and grabbed Dilyus' arm. Now the thing with Dilyus was that he was not a very confident young Stonimion, and the day's proceedings had already drained him of any energy and bravery he did have. Nasami's reaction made matters worse, so much so, that now his knees were decidedly knocking. This made him more nervous as he thought everyone could hear them making such a loud sound. They both looked at Amafiz and Simsaa and felt slightly better when they saw the other two smiling and looking eagerly at the Chief Elder.

Suddenly Akjam stood up and made an announcement.

"Before we begin with the presentation of the powers I would like present my son Amafiz and his friends a gift". Amafiz and his friends all looked towards Akjam totally puzzled. Akjam left for a few minutes and returned with a large object that he was pushing; it was covered with a sheet of material so that it was hidden.

Akjam held the material at one end and with a dramatic swoosh removed the cover and revealed the gift, the sight of the gift caused the young Stonimions to gasp and take a step backwards. "Whoa! Akjam, I couldn't breathe under that sheet, any much longer and I would've fainted!" at the sight of the talking car Simsaa fainted.

"Wha! What is that?" asked Amafiz with eyes as wide as saucers.

"This" beamed Akjam "is Scorpicle!"

"Howdy!" said Scorpicle, looking really pleased with the effect he was having on everyone. At this point Dilyus had been helping Simsaa and had managed to bring her round; unfortunately he was also helping her up off the ground at the point Scorpicle said howdy. This caused him to drop her causing her to land with a bump whilst letting out a loud cry of "ouch! Dilyus what are you doing?"

"Wow! I've never had that effect on anyone before!" Scorpicle snorted. "What a hideous looking thing!" Nasami remarked. "What is it?"

"Hey! Who are you calling hideous?" retorted the vehicle annoyed at this remark.

"It's alright Scorpicle calm down" said Akjam. "The young

ones are just a bit shocked; I mean it's not every day they get to see a talking vehicle!"

"I guess not, they must be pretty impressed" said Scorpicle as he strutted around.

"Quite!" said the Chief Elder sarcastically. "Well anyway back to business, the young Stonimions must display their new powers!"

"Please Chief, I'd like to know what this strange vehicle, my father has given to me and my friends can do". "Can we look at it a bit longer and then show our new powers?" asked Amafiz.

"Well I never! This has never happened before, usually the young cannot wait to show their powers- Akjam what have you done?" Akjam looked a bit embarrassed.

"I'm sorry Chief."

The Chief Elder smiled "I'm only joking, let's have a look at this remarkable Er! Er! What is it again?"

The Stonimions all gathered around Scorpicle admiringly, it really was quite a strange but yet intriguing looking vehicle. Scorpicle was an extraordinary looking vehicle; it was black in colour with gold rimmed wheels, it had a spoiler that had a jagged edge which was gold and orange in colour, giving it the effect of flames coming from the car. Scorpicle's body was pretty aerodynamic, with contours going down the sides that gave it the appearance of movement. The entire colour of the car was able to change in response to light; indeed its entire body was able to scatter light in such a way that enabled it to become invisible. Scorpicle had headlights which were able to project light of different colours, but these lights did not just allow you to see objects; they also penetrated through solid objects giving Scorpicle and its occupants the equivalent of x-ray vision. Scorpicle also had remarkable features that enabled it to be very useful for dimensional travel as well as battle. Scorpicle was a vehicle that enhanced the speed of inter-dimensional travel although it was not as accurate as the transporter bracelet in terms of locality; however, the bracelet only enabled the traveller to move within the same dimension. It also had a vast array of arsenal, including; lasers, heat seeking missiles and deflector shields. Scorpicle was definitely a unique and very useful vehicle.

Whilst they were admiring Scorpicle no one had noticed that there was something else amongst them, something that was not of their kind, it was something that wanted to cause them harm and hated them with all its being.

2
THE PET

They were all stunned at the sound of the high pitched screech that bellowed across the entire forest. "What was that?" asked Dilyus nervously.

"I don't know!" Amafiz spoke as if he had been physically hit by the sound itself. Suddenly the Chief Elder announced in a loud voice "Stonimions prepare! The 'Evil One' has risen!"

"What's he going on about?" Simsaa asked looking extremely concerned.

At that point there was a loud booming voice. "Stonimions you can never succeed, Sheram the Great will conquer your precious Earth".

The Stonimions all turned around towards the sound of the voice and were horrified to see a large black horse. It was no ordinary horse; it was an abomination that had been created by an evil and warped mind. The horse stood on two legs and had strange webbed hands as its forelimbs; instead of ears it had two sharp and dangerous looking horns. Its face was long and almost rectangular in shape that ended in a large mouth and long protruding tongue.

It spoke again "You will never stop him, he will be victorious and you will be ruined". The horse rasped in a vehement manner and started galloping at a great speed towards the gathered Stonimions.

"Young Stonimions now is your chance to show your powers as we will need to work together!" The Chief Elder spoke in an urgent and almost panicked voice.

"What is that thing?" asked a horrified Amafiz.

"I am not a thing, I am Nadrog the Magnificent" hissed the horse as he continued to charge towards the gathering of Stonimions. The speed of the horse was so great that they really had no time to react. The gathering of Stonimions stood frozen unable to respond, although Nadrog was coming towards them at great speed it seemed that the weird looking horse was running in slow time motion, and as each moment passed his motion seemed to slow down even further. Nasami turned his head in slow motion towards Dilyus and saw a beautiful bright green light emitting from him. Dilyus held his hands high in the direction of Nadrog and was staring intently at him.

"What's he doing?" quizzed Simsaa to the Chief Elder.

"I believe we are witnessing Dilyus' power, the power to slow down time!"

The Stonimions all stared at the bizarre sight of this strange looking horse galloping towards them, at a snail's pace. There was then a bright flash of purple and the Stonimions found themselves encased in what could only be described as a glass wall. Amafiz was standing in front of the large group hands aloft with the purple hue emanating from his hands. His amethyst stone seemed to be pulsating and pushing out an energy that allowed him to produce a defence shield. As Nadrog approached the edge of the shield he bumped into it with an immense force that caused it to vibrate violently, however, that was all it managed to do. The force shield withheld the attack from the horse. Everyone cheered when they realised that they were safe inside the shield and breathed a sigh of relief.

The question was "what next?" Nadrog was a persistent pest and he continued to pound at the shield that Amafiz had produced. The Chief Elder knew that this situation could not continue for much longer and looked towards the other adults, not for help, but more for some sort of inspiration than actual advice as to what to do next. The solution came but it was not anything from the adults, but from Nasami; he was emitting a bright white, almost blinding, light. The Stonimions noticed the pounding had stopped, as they watched in awe, they saw Nadrog being lifted into the air and the strangest thing was he was actually shrinking in size. Nasami was concentrating hard, and as Nadrog's size decreased Amafiz removed the shield allowing the Stonimions to move closer to the strange animal. As they moved closer the strange sight of the miniaturised horse was almost comical, however, the evil in his eyes removed any humour from the situation.

Nadrog's lips were moving but nothing could be heard. There were a series of glances between the Stonimions that depicted puzzlement as to what was going on with the strange looking horse. Nasami pointed his fore finger towards Nadrog's head and a white light went straight into the horse's mouth. Suddenly Nadrog could be heard although his size was still diminutive.

"You will not get away with this!" Nadrog rasped viciously. "The Great Sheram will never allow this, don't ever think you are free, you are nothing" Nadrog started coughing violently as the effect of the power from the Stonimions was affecting him.

"You've said that already, but you forget that we are not afraid of your master and this is something he knows too well!" said Miloun, Nasami's mother.

"He is stronger and wiser than ever and he will conquer Earth" Nadrog replied.

The Chief Elder was becoming agitated with Nadrog. "You keep repeating yourself! Tell me what Sheram is up to and what gives him the nerve to say he will conquer Earth?" The Chief Elder said with great anger. "As long as there is even one Stonimion alive he will never succeed in his heinous plans!"

"I will never tell you how my master will succeed all you need to know is that he will, your good days are coming to an end and..."

Nadrog was stopped by the Chief Elder's Sceptre pounding the ground. "Enough! You pathetic, sad excuse of a pet" The

Chief Elder was usually a calm and serene Stonimion but for the first time all had seen him really angry and upset. He turned to Simsaa, "You know what you must do?" Simsaa nodded and knelt down next to the miniscule horror and held her hand over his head.

"Get away from me, you irritating little Stonimion" snarled Nadrog. Simsaa ignored his insults and continued with what she had to do. She slowly waved her hand over Nadrog, who was pinned to the ground by Nasami's power of telekinesis.

Suddenly Simsaa stood upright and looked as if she was about to faint, her face looked as if she had witnessed the most horrendous and vile thing in the whole of Stonidium. Simsaa slowly turned to face the others and said just four words "The Book of Quantime".

The sceptre that the Chief Elder was holding crashed to the ground as he stood horrified at what he had heard from Simsaa. There was murmuring of voices around the forest, the newly initiated Stonimions stared at each other and then at Nadrog. The Chief Elder quickly composed himself and began to take charge of the situation. "Akjam, this thing needs to be imprisoned immediately"

"Yes chief" responded Akjam. Akjam the Great produced a silvery orange looking cage from his amber stone, which slowly moved towards Nadrog and engulfed him like a white blood cell carrying out phagocytosis. Nadrog screamed and wriggled trying, unsuccessfully, to get away from the approaching prison. The cage seemed to dissolve, or so it looked to the Stonimions watching, however, it was definitely solid as once it had encapsulated Nadrog he was unable to escape despite his continuous efforts.

Once he had been caged one of the Stonimion elders came to pick up the cage and took it away. "That was one nasty horsey!" commented Scorpicle. The group of Stonimions turned around to look at the strange looking car. The entrance of the hideous Nadrog had taken away the surprise, and for some the shock, of Scorpicle.

"Yes, indeed and the question now is what do we do next?" replied the Chief Elder. The Chief Elder Samaan turned to Simsaa and asked her what else she had read from Nadrog's mind. "I saw an image of Earth and Stonidium destroyed and a scary looking being that looked half human and half just pure evil in a body form, standing over some humans and Stonimions who seemed barely alive, in great pain and fear". Simsaa sobbed slightly as she realised what she had described and her own fears were confirmed by the look of those around her, the horror of what she had seen in Nadrog's mind was now apparent to everyone and it had stunned them all into silence. The Stonimions knew that their lives were about to change and if they ever wanted to return to life as they knew it they would have to fight a hard battle against the evil being known as Sheram.

The long silence was broken by a timid voice that dared to speak up. "I'm sorry to interrupt Sir but what is the 'Book of Quantime'?" asked Dilyus tentatively. He was worried about what he had witnessed and did not want to add to the Chief Elder's stress by asking questions he was not supposed to. Samaan looked intently at the young Stonimion and for a moment appeared lost in his own thoughts, he finally spoke up with a heavy heart.

"My dear Dilyus, it is the one thing that I hoped Sheram

25

would never ever learn about because if he gets his evil hands on it then there will come a very dark time for Stonidium and Earth!"

3

THE FOUR GUARDIANS OF STONIDIUM

The following day Amafiz woke up and for a moment was not sure as to what day it was, slowly as his sleep and tiredness slipped away he recalled the events of the day before and was dismayed that it had been real and not just a bad dream. Today was going to be crucial for the Stonimions as the Elders were going to have a meeting to decide the steps that needed to be taken in order to stop the 'Evil One'!

As Amafiz descended the stairs he could hear his parents' talking. "I won't have it Akjam; this is not right and it doesn't make sense, what is the Chief Elder thinking of? He's just a ……." Amafiz's mother stopped in mid sentence when she saw him enter the kitchen.

Amafiz looked from one parent to the other, puzzled by their abrupt silence. "What's wrong Dad?" Amafiz queried with a worried look on his face.

"Er! Nothing, nothing at all, all I can tell you at the moment is that the Stonimion Elders are going to hold a meeting tonight and er! You and your friends who were initiated yesterday must attend" Akjam said rather nervously. Amafiz was stunned, he could not understand two things; why was his dad so nervous and why on Stonidium did the Stonimion Elders say that he and his friends must attend the meeting.

"Dad I don't understand why must we attend?" quizzed Amafiz.

"Well I do have some idea but I think it's important that for the moment we concentrate on getting ready and going to the meeting, I don't want to keep the Chief Elder and the other Elders waiting".

That was a signal to Amafiz to get ready to go, Amafiz realised that it was not worth pursuing the matter any further, as his parents' mood was unlike anything he had ever witnessed before. Something was definitely wrong and what upset him more was that his mum seemed quite concerned and sad, this was worrying because his mother was usually a happy go lucky Stonimion and it took a lot to get her into such a state, this made Amafiz even more nervous.

That evening Amafiz, his friends and all their parents were assembled at the Great Stone of the Ancient Stonimions. This was a vast mountain that contained a giant cave in which the Elders held their meetings. The outer appearance of the 'Great Stone' was not reflective of the inside, it was just a rocky mountain on the outside, however; internally it was a colourful, enchanting and hypnotic place.

The Great Stone was in two main sections; the first, was the entire floor of the cave and the second part was a centre platform that was raised. The centre platform hovered above the floor and when the visitors looked closely they could see low pulsating photon energy that seemed to connect the two parts. However, more beautiful than this were the colours from the different wavelength energies emanating from the light, they had an entrancing quality and it was hard to look away once you gazed into the light. The walls of the mountain were covered in unusual, colourful and fragrant plants that absorbed the light energy connecting the two levels of the Great Stone. If you looked closely you could see the pulsating light energy being absorbed into the plants. Alongside the plants there were strange misty wisps of smoke that entwined the plants and rocks as well as the whole mountain of the Great Stone. When these wispy smoke trails came near the Stonimions they could sense the power and strength of the ancient Stonimions, and it was then that the young Stonimions realised that these were the spirits of the ancient Stonimions. The presence of the ancient Stonimions empowered them more than ever "I feel invincible" Amafiz said to Simsaa who nodded in agreement.

"I don't think I'm scared any more" Dilyus declared with gusto as he looked towards Nasami, who smiled at his friend acknowledging what he meant.

Simsaa looked up towards the platform and saw the Chief Elder along with the other four Stonimion Elders sitting around a crystal table. "I wonder how they got up there?" she whispered to Nasami.

"Maybe they teleported with their bracelets" said Nasami.

"Or maybe they went up those steps!" grinned Dilyus pointing towards some shimmering glass like steps that they had not noticed initially. The steps were such that from a certain angle they were invisible, but could be seen when the light hit them from the side. The steps became visible when the light hitting them dispersed into the spectrum of wavelengths making up white light so the steps were not just visible but colourful as well.

The party of young Stonimions and their parents ascended the steps and stood facing the Stonimion Elders. "Welcome to you all!" said the Chief Elder standing up to greet the party. "I'm sorry to have to call you all in this way but the Elders and I have been discussing the matter of the 'Evil One' since the incident at the initiation and this seems the best solution"

"And what exactly is that?" inquired Salani, Amafiz's mother, with a tone of disparagement. The Chief Elder raised his hand in a gesture to try and calm down the obviously upset mother.

"Please, Salani, I can understand your concerns but..."

"Can you really?" interrupted Miloun. Samaan looked at the parents of the four young Stonimions and understood their concern but realised that he would have to explain everything to them in great detail in order to convince them of his plans. Samaan turned around and stood for quite a few minutes with his back to the others, but to them it seemed like a lifetime until he turned around. There was a long silence that made the group of Stonimions feel uneasy; they all looked from one to the other and waited in anticipation as to what the Chief Elder would say next.

Amafiz impatiently turned to his father and asked "Dad, Why have we four been called here, when something so serious is happening, what's the significance of us being here? Akjam knew that the answer to this question was going to be revealed when Samaan decided to explain to the youngsters exactly what was going on.

"OK kids sit down and let the Chief Elder explain to you the seriousness of the problem and let us find out how and why he thinks you can be of help." Akjam smiled at them reassuringly.

The four friends were intrigued; they had just been initiated and for some reason the Elder Stonimions seemed to think that they could help, despite being novices to their new powers. "This should be interesting!" whispered Nasami to Amafiz, who nodded in agreement.

"Dear friends the appearance of that monstrosity and its threats tell us one thing, that the 'Evil one' is planning a serious assault on Earth, why now we don't know? But it does mean that after a long time of peace things are going to become rather difficult and uncomfortable" The Chief Elder addressed all those present in a serious demeanour, he had lost all the jovialness from his eyes, the young Stonimions had never seen him in such a serious mood.

"I have a feeling that he has gained new knowledge through the only other evil source in the whole of Stonidium, Imfalin "the heartless one" All but the Elders looked puzzled at the mention of Imfalin. "Before you ask she is an evil woman born without a heart, she possesses the looks of the people of Earth but is not of any place that we are aware of as she has no pulse, no heart, nothing to show that she is alive!" The Chief Elders eyes were protruding as he said this, adding emphasis to the horror story he was telling about this most hideous creature imaginable.

One of the other Elders spoke at this point "Some say she has come from another dimension where all who are evil, and those who have done evil in their lives, reside. No one knows how she got here but she has always caused trouble in the past. About one hundred Earth years ago there came a dark time when Imfalin and her hoard almost succeeded in destroying Earth, but the powerful ancient Stonimions were victorious and banished her to the 'place of no return'."

"So you're saying that this Imfalin came back from the 'place of no return'? Is that supposed to be funny? As I'm really not finding this at all funny and I'm going be honest I'm quite scared!" Simsaa remarked nervously. Her friends all turned to face her and looked at her shocked at her interruption, but understood that her fear had to be quite substantial for her to speak up like she did.

Samaan looked her intensely and replied with no humour in his voice whatsoever. "It IS the 'place of no return' which means that she has practised and become empowered with such an extreme evil power that we cannot even begin to imagine its strength or effect!" This last remark silenced all of those who were present, as each Stonimion took a few minutes to absorb and comprehend the intensity of the words spoken by Samaan, but in truth none of them could really understand the potential outcome of the rise of Imfalin and Sheram.

The silence was soon broken by Amafiz's father "I still don't understand" interjected Akjam "What does this have to do with these children? I mean, this is a job for the army of Stonidium and..."

"Yes indeed it is and they will be manoeuvring and preparing to protect Stonidium, however, there is the matter of dealing with Sheram directly and the issue with the Book of Quan-time!" The Chief Elder explained.

Dilyus gulped and mustered up all his courage to ask a question that was on the mind of most the Stonimions present "Sorry to interrupt Sir, but what is so important about the Book of Quantime? He asked nervously.

The Chief Elder turned to Dilyus and spoke in a sombre tone. "It is the most powerful book known to all in Stonidium and any who are aware of it, it has the power to allow time travel and in the wrong hands it can be used to completely change life as we know it."

"How come we've never heard of it?" questioned Nasami.

"It was supposed to be a well kept secret but obviously not well enough" continued the Chief Elder. "Somehow, and I believe it's mainly down to Imfalin, Sheram has found out about it and I can guarantee you that he will not rest until he has got hold of it"

"So what do we do now then?" asked Nalam,

"Well Nalam, the army of Stonidium, as I said earlier will be on standby to protect our land, but we also need to send a group on the quest to retrieve the Book of Quantime before Sheram gets hold of it."

At this point he turned to the four friends and gestured to them to come towards him. One by one they went and stood next to the Chief Elder, they all stood facing the other Elders and their parents. "What I am about to say goes against the grain, I know, but when I explain why I have come to this decision I believe that you will all agree with my thoughts"

The Chief Elder cleared his throat and took a deep breath as if he was getting to ready to give an important speech to the Ancient Stonimions.

"I have lived a long life and have initiated many young Stonimions; indeed, all of you parents present here were initiated by me!" Samaan made a sweeping gesture with his hand as he scanned a glance over the four young friends and their parents who were stood facing them. "I think you will all agree that, therefore, I have witnessed many a powerful Stonimion and the extent of their powers, but I have to say that what I witnessed yesterday was beyond anything I have seen in my life time". He paused allowing them to start to take in and slowly digest his words; none of them said anything giving Samaan his cue to continue with his thoughts and plans. "What we saw yesterday, dear friends, was not just a show of the abilities of these young Stonimions, but something more intense!"

"They showed an immense connection, to each other as well as a great natural control of their powers". Samaan paused; he was almost breathless with the excitement of finally being able to tell his plans, and at the thought that he was lucky enough to be the one who first became aware of these special young Stonimions. "The co-ordination they demonstrated, if you compare it to practised and experienced Stonimions, could be classed as very good, but in terms of the fact that they had used them for the first time, under such stressful circumstances, and in such a confident way leads me to believe one thing!"

"And what is that?" interrupted Salani.

For a moment Samaan looked almost too intimidated to

answer, but answer he did and with great conviction. "I believe these young Stonimions to be the ones known as the 'Four Guardians of Stonidium!' One of the Elders spluttered and coughed into his sentence.

"Samaan, I know you told us these children were special but I had no idea that you were thinking along those lines, they're a myth, Samaan for Stonidium's sake!" Samaan looked hurt that his fellow Elder doubted him, especially in front of the young Stonimions.

"I don't believe this!" started Nalam as he stood upright. "You mean to say that you want our children to carry out the duty of adults because of some myth you've read! That is preposterous; I am not waiting around to hear anymore, Miloun, Dilyus lets go"

Nasami's father Maraj who had been listening quietly spoke up "Nalam wait, Samaan has not been our Chief Elder for such a long time without good reason, he is wise and knows our history very well, I would like to hear what he has to say."

"I agree" said Zarani, Simsaa's mother.

"Thank you Maraj and Zarani" Samaan said humbly, he turned to the other parents and looked at them with great intensity and understood their concern but at the same time felt duty bound to ensure that he did not let this opportunity slip by, he knew that if anything happened to Earth or Stonidium he would never forgive himself. "The legend states that there will be four young Stonimions who will be the ultimate guardians of Stonidium, their bravery, wit and expertise in the use of their powers will be known throughout the land". Samaan paused and looked towards the party gathered at the

Great Stone as if he was expecting another interruption, but none came.

So he continued by taking a deep breath, not so that he would not run out of breath, but almost as if he was bracing himself for an onslaught of negativity once he had completed what he wanted to say. "The legend states that these Stonimions will arise at a time of great danger and peril, their bravery and skill will become infamous, they will be victorious in their quest and free Stonidium and Earth". Samaan looked around him, there was utter silence from the stunned and almost sullen faces of the Stonimions; some were almost hypnotised by Samaan's words, others were trying to absorb his words and make sense of what he was saying.

Samaan continued with his explanation " You see it cannot be just a coincidence that Sheram is on the rise and these young Stonimions have just been initiated, they way they handled themselves instantly brought to mind the story of the 'Guardians' and this made me look into the book of Stonidium to find out more". At this point Samaan produced an old ancient looking book, it was quite large and dusty looking and as Samaan opened it the others saw that the front of the book had a picture of the Initiation Stone and battle armoury of the Stonimions. He tentatively turned the pages, as if he turned them any faster they would disintegrate, as the others watched with anticipation they too felt as if the ancient pages were going to fall apart. Indeed, they were very old looking however, the book was also very strong and protected by ancient Stonimion power so that no harm could come to it.

When Samaan arrived at the page he was looking for he cleared his throat and began to read "There will come a dire time when evil will rise with such ferocity and devastation that Stonidium and those it protects will be under grave danger. Chaos will thrive and endanger the very fabric of life and time, but there will be salvation in the form of four brave and unique Stonimions who will endeavour in their quest to overcome the evil and save Stonidium and Earth." He looked up at the others and finally saw that they had understood the significance of what was written in the ancient book and how it could not just be a coincidence that on the very day these 'four' Stonimions were initiated, the incident with Nadrog occurred and that they were given the news that Sheram was readying to attack Earth.

There was a silence amongst the group of Stonimions that seemed to last for a long time, it was finally broken by Maraj. "The question is what do we do next? How do we find this 'Book of Quantime'?"

Samaan simply replied "Farmoeen the Oracle" and closed the ancient book of the Stonimions.

Samaan was relieved and almost close to tears with relief that finally his message had been understood, that the young Stonimions and especially their parents had realised that this was a very serious time for all, that something had to be done quickly and that it was to be done by them.

The other Elders stood up and looked at Samaan, "Well it is obvious that the story about the 'Guardians' is not a myth but a significant part of Stonimion history and legends", said Luman the Chief Elder's assistant "Chief, we need to contact Farmoeen, but how? No one knows how to get to her, she only allows herself to be found if she wants it!"

"I know how to get a message to her and I'm sure that when she gets it she will contact us for a meeting, herself". Samaan looked positive and a bit like his old smiley self again, he turned to the young Stonimions and their parents and told them "I will let you know as soon as I have managed to contact Farmoeen and arranged for the young Stonimions to see her, but for now it's time you all went home and rested. Thank you for coming and understanding my plea, I know it can't be easy but believe you me I would never put your children at any risk if I truly thought that they would be in danger". Akjam stood up and walked closer towards Samaan holding out his hand, he took Samaan's hand and said

"My dear friend we know you and trust you, you have our full support" Akjam turned and looked at the other parents. They all stood up and smiled in unison as if to show their agreement and solidarity in this time of unrest. "For freedom and Stonidium!" remarked Nalam

"For freedom and Stonidium!" they all repeated.

As the young Stonimions and their parents trudged back home, weary from the events of the past few days, each Stonimion was deep in his or her own thought. Thoughts that were full of excitement, trepidation, fear and most of all horror at what could happen to them and those they protect if Sheram was to succeed, however, none of them were actually sure as to what his plans were. Amafiz turned to Simsaa and asked "Do you think Sheram wants to take over Stonidium and Earth?" Simsaa turned to him and said gravely.

"If that's what he's planning then we're okay! What if he plans to destroy us completely?"

Akjam who had been walking close behind them put his hands on their shoulders and said "Then children, we will all work together to make sure that he does not!" he smiled at them as he said this but Amafiz knew his father too well and he could see the worry in his eyes. Amafiz decided that he did not like to see his father upset and worried and in his own mind promised himself that he would do whatever it took to help his people and those of Earth.

4

THE ORACLE

Back at the Great Stone of Stonidium Samaan asked the elders to return to their homes and sat down to begin his telepathic link to the wise and intelligent oracle Farmoeen. It had been a long few days and Samaan was not as young as he used to be, so the task ahead of him seemed like a monumental one, however, he knew that despite his fatigue he had to try without any further delay.

He sat down at the table of the 'Great Stone' and carefully placed his hands on the table; Samaan cleared his mind and began his telepathic link to his old friend Farmoeen. Farmoeen had always been a special child, even when they were young she had immense powers and always knew what was about to happen, he knew even then that she was no ordinary Stonimion and that she was meant for greater things. He pushed away the thoughts of his past, any thoughts of the present and thoughts about what was to come in the future, but it was not that easy. His mind was in turmoil and he was under immense stress, "Come on Samaan concentrate" Samaan spurred himself on to try and contact Farmoeen. Slowly he managed to control the thoughts that were dancing around like butterflies in his mind; the deeper he concentrated the more control he had over his thoughts and the more easily he removed them from his mind, until all he had in his mind was the image of Farmoeen.

"Farmoeen are you there? I need to communicate with you as a matter of urgency", he waited repeating the thought over and over again, yet there was no response, He continued as he knew the link would take time to establish. After what seemed an eternity to him and continuous repetition of the same thought he suddenly felt as if someone had entered into his mind.

"Samaan is that you? Your thoughts sound foreign, are you alright?" finally Farmoeen had been contacted.

"OH! Farmoeen, I thought I wouldn't be able to get through to you!" Samaan said with relief. "What with the news of the rise of Sheram I thought he may have used some of Imfalin's magic to create some sort of barrier to stop any telepathic communication in Stonidium"

There was silence, Farmoeen did not respond; Samaan began to panic again, "Farmoeen are you there? What's happened?"

"It's alright Samaan I'm here, I was mindful of what you were saying, unfortunately I had sensed there was something wrong and for the last three days I have been searching to find out what has been happening and I'm afraid to say that things are quite serious." Farmoeen's thoughts were sombre and serious, Samaan knew that there were hard times ahead as usually

Farmoeen would reminisce about their childhood and talk about happy times but today there was nothing of the sort.

"So what have you found out?" Samaan asked nervously as if he knew what the answer was going to be but was hoping it would be something else. "Well it seems as if Sheram has been planning this for a long time, I was watching the initiation and saw Sheram's pet launch the attack, I also saw the response of the four young Stonimions, Samaan correct me if I am wrong but these young ones are the 'Guardians' of Stonidium, are they not?" Samaan was not surprised at the revelation of Farmoeen's knowledge and he simply replied

"Yes Oh wise and intelligent oracle!"

"Sheram is ready for a full attack on Stonidium and Earth, he has been fully prepared by Imfalin, and my searches have revealed that he is aware of the book of Quantime!"

"I know Farmoeen". Samaan was not happy that the more he spoke to Farmoeen the more his worst fears were being confirmed.

"Farmoeen I have contacted you to ask you if I can send the 'Guardians' to you as they will need help in preparing for their quest against Sheram" Samaan came to the point, as he knew that time was precious.

"I will do all in my power to help these young Stonimions, Samaan, bring them to me tomorrow, waste no time and come by the power of the bracelet" Farmoeen replied.

"Indeed - for freedom from evil, good night to you dear friend"

"Good night to you, be safe Samaan".

The telepathic link between the two had now been severed and Samaan sat quietly contemplating the journey and task ahead, for the first time in his life he truly felt scared a feeling he thought he would never experience.

The following day Samaan left his house and headed towards the town and the homes of the 'Guardians'. His eyes were bleary and his body weary from the events of the last few days, but the reason behind his exhaustion was more down to the communication with Farmoeen, not so much the telepathic link but more the realisation of the troubles to come. He reached the house of Nasami; he knocked on the door and patiently waited for someone to reply. A few minutes later Nasami's mother Simoo answered the door.

"Good morning, Chief" she said with a forced smile on her face.

"Good morning Simoo, may I come in?" Samaan knew she was not thrilled to see him and he could not blame her either.

"Of course, please do", Samaan stepped through the threshold and into the simple but beautifully kept home of Maraj and Simoo.

As Samaan sat down after being offered a seat, he saw Maraj followed by Nasami descending the stairs from the first floor of the house. Samaan rose to greet Maraj who immediately took his hand and gently placed his forehead on it, greeting the Chief Elder with the respect one would give to one's parents.

"So Nasami are you ready?" Samaan addressed the young Stonimion directly, "Yes Sir I am, er if that's ok with Mum &

Dad?" Nasami said quizzically looking towards his parents; his father laughed and said

"Nasami you're going to have to make your own decisions now, you and all of your friends!"

"But Dad, how will we know that we've made the right decision?"

"Don't worry son, the Chief Elder would not have given you kids such responsibility if he did not have faith in you to do the right thing, and I think you all proved yourselves on the day of your initiation".

"Nasami its time to leave" Samaan turned to Nasami's parents and said "I will be collecting the others and taking them to Farmoeen, she will then advice the children on what they are to do, we will be back soon." Samaan stood up and left with Nasami. Nasami's parents stood at their doorway and waved good bye to their son; they had heavy hearts but knew that their son would be fine; he and his friends had proved themselves quite capable of looking after themselves.

One by one Samaan gathered the young Stonimions and took them back to the Forest of the Stone. "Ok children, we will be going to see Farmoeen the great oracle, she will guide and advice you on the next step"

"How are we going to get to Farmoeen Sir?" asked Amafiz.

"Well young man, I think now is the time to use your teleporter bracelet don't you?" Samaan's sarcasm was not appreciated by Amafiz much to the amusement of the others, Amafiz turned around to look at his friends and found two of them smiling inanely and the third (Dilyus) was pulling a face indicating that Amafiz was not very intelligent, accompanied by "DUHHH!!!!!"

Samaan gave Dilyus a stern look, although he too did find Dilyus' action quite amusing. Samaan wasted no more time and held aloft his arm and asked the Stonimions to do the same, "Now, there are two ways of using the teleporter, you can think of the place you are going to or if you are going to see someone then repeat their name in your mind several times, as Farmoeen's location is a secret we will need to all repeat her name continuously." "Is that all we have to do?" asked Simsaa.

"No, whilst you are thinking of the place or repeating the name you then also need to touch the bracelet and rotate it once around your wrist".

The Stonimions all stood in a circle in the forest and simultaneously raised their arms and held their bracelets. "Ok everyone are you all ready?" the young Stonimions nodded in unison, Samaan began the repetition of Farmoeen's name and the others followed suit. Suddenly the forest seemed to melt almost as if it was dissolving from around them, the Stonimions saw the colours of their bracelets emanate from them and combine around them enveloping them completely. Then it seemed as if the colours, the forest and even they themselves blended into one great mass of images. The Stonimions experienced a feeling of pull from within their core as if their centre of gravity had shifted and they found themselves moving with great momentum through space. Their speed was such that it felt as if they were travelling through a vacuum where no particles were stopping them. For a split second Dilyus had a frightening thought that, indeed, they would never stop, however, this was short lived for as quickly as they moved they came to a halt.

They stood in the same position as if they were still in the forest, yet they were not, "Welcome, dear young ones and you Samaan!" The Stonimions all turned around and smiled at the vision in front of them, "Good to see you again Farmoeen!" smiled Samaan.

5

THE CRYSTAL

Farmoeen was an elegant and beautiful Stonimion with an air of serenity, wisdom and simplicity; she seemed to emanate a quiet power and knowledge unlike any other. She smiled at the young Stonimions and said "Welcome Guardians of Stonidium, it is an honour to meet you". The four friends stood with their jaws wide open, shocked at Farmoeen's comment.

"Are you joking?" quizzed Dilyus "You are the wise oracle Farmoeen and you're saying it's an honour to meet us, I think you've got that the wrong way around!" he smirked.

Simsaa dug her elbow into his ribs, "Sorry Farmoeen, Dilyus seems to have lost the connection between his mouth and his brain, it must have been the effect of the teleportation!"

"Hey!" Dilyus objected but managed a smile when all the others laughed at Simsaa's comment.

"Come children let's go and have something to eat, I'm not sure about you but I'm famished after that teleportation"

Samaan said rubbing his stomach. He ushered the four young friends to follow Farmoeen into her home.

The inside of Farmoeen's house was as immaculate and smart as she was, they walked into a large central hall that consisted of a sparkling white alabaster floor, walls that contained precious stones of different colours and on the ceiling, there was a chandelier in the centre that was made of the most clearest crystals they had ever seen. The materials and decorations gave the hall a gentle atmosphere of light and colour which seemed to give the impression of dancing misty figures around the hall. The young Stonimions stood in wonderment, of course, Nasami could not resist. "Nice décor Farmoeen, did you do it yourself?"

"Nasami, don't be so cheeky!" Simsaa looked embarrassed at Nasami's comments.

"Ha! I like it!" said Farmoeen "A sense of humour is always good"

"Yea, but not when, it's not funny!" remarked Dilyus,

"Don't hate, at least I have some kind of sense of humour!" said Nasami. "Come now children, we're supposed to be friends are we not?" Samaan stepped in eager for them to get back to the reason as to why they were all here.

"Sorry Samaan" they said in unison, the youngsters felt a bit embarrassed after all they were here because Samaan thought them to be the Guardians of Stonidium and instead of being serious and responsible they were arguing for no reason. Samaan looked at Farmoeen and said "I think we should tell them as much as we know so that they can be as prepared as they can be", Farmoeen nodded and signalled to them all to follow her. She led them through the hall and into a large room that was decorated with mirrors and a large table that was set in the centre of the room, Farmoeen gestured for them to all sit down. "Please be seated" as they were taking their seats the young Stonimions noticed the appearance of different dishes on the table, fruits, breads and sweet delights.

"Wow, I didn't realise how hungry I was until I smelt the food" commented Amafiz, the others nodded in agreement. "Well Samaan did say he was hungry and I thought we would all feel a lot better after eating".

After they had finished they all looked a lot happier and relaxed, Farmoeen clicked her fingers and the table was cleared as quickly as it had originally been filled. She then turned her attention to the young Stonimions and said "So young ones what do you need to know about Sheram and the Book of Quantime?"

"Well the question is what do we NOT need to know? And the answer is NOTHING!" Dilyus answered dramatically. Farmoeen smiled and started from the best place possible, which was the beginning,

"Well from all the information I have on Sheram, he seems to have appeared in Stonidium at least one hundred years ago, where he came from I have been unable to find out as the magic that surrounds him is very powerful, however, I do know that he is under the protection of Imfalin" Farmoeen stopped for a few seconds and then continued, "What I have told you is knowledge known to Samaan and the other Elders as well, but what I also know is that Sheram has created an army, consisting of spies that are searching for the Book of Quantime, he seems to have established an understanding of its power and it is becoming apparent that his intention is to use it to control the future of Earth.

They all sat in silence for a few minutes and suddenly Simsaa spoke "What do you think he is going to do with the book of Quantime, what I mean is how do you think he's going to use it to conquer Earth?" she asked. Farmoeen took a deep breath and began to explain, "Well, the Book of Quantime allows the controller to travel in time, whether it's to the past or to the future, there is no limit to how often the controller can do this, however, the controller will be able to affect present events and ultimately change the future, the Book of Quantime can affect any place in any dimension".

Samaan interjected at this point "The question now Farmoeen, is, where it is?"

Farmoeen replied "Not just where Samaan but also how will the Guardians get to it?"

Farmoeen explained to them how the Book of Quantime was kept in a secret location known to no-one, but it was possible to find its location by the use of a deep strong power. The young Stonimions were interested in how the Book could be used, however, this was not really important at this time as the onus was on retrieving it before Sheram did. "When it is necessary young Stonimions then I will inform you about how to use it" smiled Farmoeen. This comment pleased the young ones as they were excited to hear about such a power, it was something they had never even dreamed of. "What you do need to understand is that it is extremely powerful and needs to be handled with care, when you do get to it don't try to open it as it will not, and any force used to try and open it will lead to the Book retaliating and using severe ancient forces to free itself from your possession." Farmoeen explained

"So how can it be opened?" Amafiz asked intrigued.

"It can only be opened with four keys but..."

"Let me guess, the keys locations are also a secret!" smiled Samaan, Farmoeen smiled back and replied "Indeed".

Farmoeen got up and gestured to the others to follow her; she took them into another part of her house. She stood in front of a wall and then turned to face Samaan and the young Stonimions, she pointed towards the wall and said "This is a hidden portal to another part of my house that is protected, come and stand close to me so that we can enter together. She slowly lifted her arms and murmured something under her breath; slowly they found themselves no longer staring at a wall but a thin sheet of glass, or so it seemed, they soon realised that it was not glass as Farmoeen gently stepped towards the glass sheet and walked through it and it was then that the others noticed the fluid property of the gateway into the secret part of her home. They all followed Farmoeen and felt a strange sensation as if they were walking through a thick translucent liquid.

As they emerged on the other side Simsaa turned to Amafiz and said "That was weird I felt as though I had been drifting for days!" He nodded in agreement and swayed a little, "I feel a bit giddy" he said to Samaan who was looking at him rather concerned.

"You've gone a funny colour my dear boy!" Samaan turned to Farmoeen looking worried "What's wrong with him?"

"It's alright Samaan; although the journey through the portal is short it can sometimes have strange effects on you especially if you are not well". They all turned to look at Amafiz who sheepishly explained that he had been unwell. Satisfied that there was nothing seriously wrong with Amafiz they all continued with the task in hand, which was to find the location of the 'Book of Quantime'.

As they walked towards the centre of the room there was a strange humming that seemed to encase them in a hypnotic and euphoric trance. Once they arrived to the centre of the room a large crystal rhombus appeared amidst them. The crystal glowed pearlescent colours that rotated through the colours of visible light; Farmoeen carefully placed her hands on the rhombus crystal and spoke to the others. "Can you all place your hands on the Crystal of knowledge, one by one please?" They all did as she asked and one by one placed their hands gently onto the pulsating crystal. As each of them placed their hands on the crystal they could feel a connection with it and each other; the crystal was enhancing its own power through them and vice-versa, however, it also made a telepathic connection with and between them all.

The young Stonimions jumped slightly as they 'heard' the voice of the crystal speak to them directly. "What can I do for you Guardians of Stonidium?"

Farmoeen spoke to the young Stonimions telepathically "The Crystal of knowledge has spoken to you directly children you must communicate with it" Nasami mustered up his courage and said- in his mind. "Wise and knowledgeable crystal we wish to find the 'Book of Quantime'." There was a quiet sniggering in their heads as Dilyus expressed his amusement at the way Nasami had spoken to the crystal.

"Dilyus, you find Nasami's request amusing?" the crystal asked him.

"Er! No, sorry I didn't mean to interrupt" Dilyus' face was rather red with embarrassment as he expressed his thoughts to the crystal.

"The answer to your request is simple - you need to stop looking for it!" They all stood in silence not quite sure how to respond to what they had just heard from the Crystal of knowledge.

"I'm sorry crystal, but that does not make sense to us, could you elaborate?" asked Samaan tentatively.

"Samaan and Farmoeen you need to cast your minds back to your youth" at this point Amafiz was tempted to remark with 'that would be going back a long way' but sensibly controlled his thought considering the situation, however, he could not help but smirk at his own humour. The crystal continued "... there were many parts of Stonidium that you had been told about but had never been to; it is in these hidden parts of Stonidium you will find the Book of Quantime"

At this point Amafiz decided enough was enough and said quite aggressively "look crystal, I don't mean to be rude but we really don't have time for riddles and puzzles we need to find the Book of Quantime as soon as possible." There was a sharp intake of breath from the others as they heard Amafiz's thoughts; there was a common concern surging through them all as they were waiting for the repercussion of his comment to the crystal. What happened next was totally unexpected. The crystal started to change colours at a rapid speed and pulsated as it did this, "I have located the Book! But you will need your vehicle Scorpicle to reach it in time because Sheram is closing in on its whereabouts. It is surrounded by ancient powers but his evil magic is getting stronger." The crystal stopped for a moment but then continued "There is one more thing that you need to know, the Book of Quantime can only be opened using the four keys of light."

"Thank you Crystal, Farmoeen has informed us about this but we are not sure about their location" Simsaa explained. The crystal was silent and then answered her

"Simsaa the four keys of light are not within our dimension, they are hidden on Earth and their exact location can only be found once you have the Book in your possession or..." the crystal stopped in mid sentence, they all waited for it to continue but it did not.

There was an atmosphere of uneasiness from them all, which was eventually broken by Samaan. "Crystal what would we need to do if the book was not in our possession?" again there was silence, a long agonising silence, finally the crystal communicated again "Someone would have to enter the mind of the person who had possession of it and they would need to manipulate them in order to get the book from them!" Nasami nearly choked as he entered the telepathic conversation.

"You mean if Sheram was in possession of the book we would have to enter into his warped little mind- nice!"

"But that's so dangerous!" exclaimed Amafiz.

"This is why we need to make sure that we get to the Book before he does!" Farmoeen explained.

The crystal communicated with the group again "It's important that you are successful in your mission, however, if Sheram was to obtain the Book I'm sure he will manipulate events on Earth which you can imagine will not be good for any of us, as the Guardians of Stonidium our futures will depend upon your actions."

The Crystal ended the telepathic communication with the group by reducing its light until it had diminished and disappeared as quickly as it had appeared. Samaan, Farmoeen and the four young Stonimions sat in silence pondering on the conversation they had just experienced. "Well, that was interesting!" Dilyus and his strange sense of humour released the tension from the air and resulted in them all bursting into laughter. Unfortunately it was short lived as reality hit them once more about the mission ahead.

"First things first, we need to get you back to your homes, get you packed and get Scorpicle briefed for the quest ahead of you all!" Samaan informed them standing bolt upright with such speed and fervour that the others all jumped. "You're absolutely right Samaan, we've no time to waste, come on children it's time to go" Farmoeen ushered the young Stonimions back through the room, its unusual entrance and into the main part of her house.

She turned to Samaan and smiled but her eyes told a different story, she was concerned as there were many questions whizzing through her mind about the quest ahead, whether or not Sheram was going to find the Book of Quantime, what might he do once he had control over time and would they ever be able to overcome any changes that could occur. These were questions that she could sense were in the minds of every single being in Stonidium as news was spreading about Sheram and the incident that had occurred at the initiation just a few days ago.

Samaan and the young ones said their goodbyes to Farmoeen, whilst Farmoeen promised that she would keep them informed about any new news that she would come across. The mentally exhausted party returned the way they had arrived "I don't think I'll get used to this mode of travel!" exclaimed Amafiz as he looked as woozy as he had when he had arrived at Farmoeen's house. Samaan took each of the young Stonimions to their homes and explained to their relieved parents that he would return the next morning to explain what had happened and the next steps that they would be taking.

As Samaan returned home he sensed that something was not quite right, as he entered his house he was stopped by a sound that was definitely not human. Samaan froze because as he heard the noise there was also a voice in his head, "Get out Samaan, you're in danger!" It was Farmoeen who had made a sudden telepathic link with him. Samaan immediately backed out of his house and used his turquoise stone to produce a protective shield around him. As he slowly backed away from his house he saw the evil Nadrog emerge from the doorway, snarling and hissing his hatred as he had a few days ago. "You!" gasped Samaan.

"Yes, it's me!" rasped the animal. "Did you really think that you could cage me for that long, now I will get my master's revenge and rid him of you once and for all Samaan!"

Nadrog began to charge towards Samaan but as swift as he was Samaan was faster, Samaan created a vortex in front of

Nadrog as the animal charged towards him. It happened so fast that Nadrog did not even get the chance to slow down. He went screaming into the void and at that moment Samaan closed the vortex, "Good riddance" he said to himself and wearily walked into his house, closing the door behind him.

6
THE EVIL ONE

At the moment Nadrog disappeared into the vortex, in a hidden part of Stonidium, there was a horrendous scream that was so malevolent, hideous and shrill that it could have destroyed an entire galaxy.

"He has gone Sire, our pet that we raised with such effort and love!" wailed Imfalin. There was no reply from Sheram but a long stony silence that created an atmosphere of such hatred, anger and evil that the air around them seemed to turn poisonous.

"No! No! It can't be, not my Nadrog! Who was responsible for this?" Sheram asked in a deranged tone that ended the sentence in crescendo. He looked around the room like a crazed loon ready to attack anyone who got in his way, and it was for this reason that Imfalin and his minions, known as Mangra's, kept low, out of sight and more importantly kept absolutely silent. Slowly Sheram began to calm down, but those that knew him well knew that did not guarantee safety from his wrath.

Eventually Imfalin mustered enough courage to go closer to him; she gently placed her old withered and warty hand on his shoulder. "You know that Nadrog can never be retrieved, he is untraceable as he has entered into a dimension to which none of us have access and you also know that there is only one Stonimion that can create a vortex to a different dimension." Imfalin stepped back as Sheram turned to look at her and stood up. There was a low rumbling sound that erupted into a scream from Sheram "Samaaannnnn!!!!!!!"

Sheram was breathing heavily, almost panting as he spoke to Imfalin. "I will get him and those young Stonimions who took part in the capture of my pet, I will make them pay." He shook violently as he spoke and was foaming at the corners of his mouth, Imfalin mustered up all of her courage to speak up. "Don't worry my dear, revenge will be ours but more importantly we will be victorious too!" Imfalin's pep talk was not well timed and this was a risk that she took, because her relationship with Sheram was that of a carer and the 'looked after', so she did not suffer the brunt of Sheram's anger. He turned to look at her, his eyes blazing with such vehemence that Imfalin and all the minions present winced at the intensity of the pure evil that they saw in his eyes.

When Sheram became angry someone normally had to pay and on this occasion it was two of the minions that had the misfortune of being the closest to where he was standing. Sheram raised his hands into the air and a low ebbing noise began to pulsate around the room, Imfalin and some of the other minions realised what was about to happen and began immediately to back away, however, the speed with which the energy bolt was released was such that none of them escaped without some kind of injury. The two Mangras that were the closest to him were obliterated and turned into two piles of dark grey ash. The Mangras were a strange creature, they were many in number but they were clones of one parent Mangra that had acquired the ability to clone itself by mitotic cell division, this parent Mangra was a dark grey in colour, quite small in stature, it had a round body and even rounder face, big blue eyes and it was covered in short fur and feathers, so although there were many of them and easily replaced there was one problem with them, when one felt pain they all did. The Mangra's were not just telepathically linked but also to a certain extent they were physically linked as well. So when two of them were vaporised they all felt the anguish of the two who had perished. This phenomenon resulted in a simultaneous scream of pain from the surviving Mangra, which ended up in irritating Sheram further. "Get away from here you wretched creatures!" Sheram screamed at them, at which point they scurried away still wailing with pain.

Once the room was empty Sheram turned to Imfalin and asked "What of the Book of Quantime, have you come any closer to finding its location?" Imfalin knew he was still seething with anger so she chose her words very carefully, so as not to anger him any further.

"Yes Sire, I am closer to it, but it will take more time than I anticipated because it is surrounded by very powerful protective incantations." For once he did not react angrily; he nodded wearily, turned around and left her. Imfalin stood in silence understanding his reaction, he was exhausted emotionally, Nadrog had been a pet but also a companion to Sheram and she knew that he would not rest until he had sought revenge, for which he needed to recuperate his powers.

Imfalin returned to her own room to continue the search for the Book of Quantime. The urgency to find it had increased and her parental love for Sheram meant that failure for her was not an option. The relationship between the two was an extremely strange one, and one that even she did not understand. Imfalin was from a dimension not known to any one on Stonidium or on Earth, her anatomy was different from theirs in a major way- she did not have a heart and her brain was void of feeling true empathy, sympathy or any understanding of others emotions, yet she had a great devotion and loyalty to Sheram that even confused her. Imfalin turned her thoughts back to the mission in hand, finding the Book of Quantime.

Imfalin sat at a small square stone table in the middle of her room, the table had on it a small black candle, that burned but did not seem to get any smaller, a small glass crucible that contained a purplish red precipitate and a map of Stonidium. There was a small misty vapour rising from the crucible which increased in intensity as Imfalin began chanting and murmuring verses that only she knew the true meaning of.

As the intensity increased Imfalin was surrounded by the purple mist and her chanting became more frenzied, finally it stopped, Imfalin had broken out in a sweat and was panting as if she had been running. "At last I have found it, but wait who is this? Who has entered my mind? No, Farmoeen, not you!" Imfalin was shocked that within seconds of her locating the Book of Quantime Farmoeen had intercepted her thoughts. This told Imfalin that Farmoeen, and obviously the other Stonimions, were aware of the fact the Sheram was after the Book of Quantime, this made their mission to get to it even more urgent.

Imfalin blocked Farmoeen from her mind and headed straight to Sheram's room. She rapped the door vigorously "Sheram! Open the door it's me Imfalin, hurry!" Sheram quickly opened the door and for a moment looked panicked and confused; he quickly composed himself and asked "What's wrong Imfalin, it better be worth it for you to disturb me like this!"

"Oh! Believe me it's very important" Imfalin firstly gave Sheram the news he had been waiting for, and it had been a long time coming but Sheram's joy was short lived as Imfalin nervously told him about Farmoeen's invasion of her mind.

Sheram exploded with anger, he was livid "You careless old hag! You know how strong our enemies are, how could you be so neglectful of the fact that we're being watched?" "Don't you understand the importance of keeping our enemies from our plans?" Sheram was spitting out the words at her with such ferociousness that for the first time Imfalin was scared for her life. "Sheram I know that it's important for us to keep our plans hidden for as long as possible but you have to understand that Farmoeen is extremely powerful she must have already been tracking me and as soon as I found the Book she became aware of it!" Imfalin was as close to tears as it could be possible for her as she did not have any true understanding of being sad. "Well the damage has been done; we now have to think how we can stop them from getting any more information on us" Sheram stopped and turned and looked at Imfalin more intently. "Did Farmoeen see the location of the Book as well?" Imfalin panicked as the truth was she was not sure and she knew that it was no use lying to Sheram because he could find out from her by probing her mind and the consequences of lying could be worse than telling him the truth, so she did. Surprisingly, he was quite calm about it; Sheram was obviously more concerned about getting to the Book first.

The Mangra were all waiting in the 'Room of Malevolence', as soon as they had been telepathically summoned by Imfalin. There was a hushed murmur amongst them as they were wondering what was going on, they were still frightened from their previous encounter with Sheram. Sheram entered the room and a silence fell amongst all present, along with the Mangras, there was Imfalin and Sheram's hoard of strange creatures. There were creatures of flight that looked like hybrids of frogs and emus; there were creatures of land and water that looked similar to piranha with four hairy long limbs. These strange concoctions of Sheram's warped mind made his pet Nadrog look quite cute.

Sheram took centre stage in the room and raised his hands in order to address his minions. Sheram was wearing his most impressive robes, these consisted of several long layers of material that were black in colour but each layer shimmered with different colours, and this was an indicator to everyone that he meant business and was ready for victory. "Hail to the Evil One- Ruler of Stonidium and Conqueror of Earth". Sheram's minions knew how to suck up to him, they had learnt the hard way in how to make sure that his ego was well and truly fed. Sheram smiled and waved to his hideous creatures and looked at them affectionately, like a proud father.

"My dear friends" Sheram's voiced echoed around the large room, on hearing themselves being addressed as friends there was a murmur of excitement and happiness, for this meant

63

that Sheram was happy, which also meant that at long last he was close to succeeding. "The time has come when we shall no more have to be the second class citizens of Stonidium, but indeed, we shall be the rulers". There was an enormous uproar of cheers from the room at Sheram's announcement. This enthusiasm pleased Sheram even more than before. He beamed from ear to ear and continued in his address of his hoards.

"Tomorrow I shall be setting off to claim the Book of Quan-time, which will seal our victory over the vile Stonimions and Humans". On hearing the name of the Stonimions and Humans the cheers changed to boos and hisses and chants of 'death to the Stonimions and their filthy friends'. Sheram lowered his arms and turned his back on his minions and exited the room, the others waited in silence and once Sheram had left they too quietly left the Room of Malevolence as they knew they had to help their master prepare for the journey and quest that was ahead of him. They all knew their individual tasks and each of them did not want to be the reason for Sheram failing, so their preparation was of paramount importance.

The only one left in the Room of Malevolence was Imfalin, who stood, deep in thought about what was to come. She was inwardly nervous, excited and somewhat, in disbelief, that they could be so close to succeeding, a conquest that Imfalin was beginning to think was impossible. It had been such a long time coming, and it had taken her what felt like thousands of years instead of the few centuries that it actually had, to find the perfect specimen to help her in her plans, a specimen that harboured the same hate and despise as she did for the Stonimions and the Humans that they protected. Finally she was close to succeeding, and yet her joy was masked by her anguish that had led her to this moment, the history of her existence and her hatred was not even known to Sheram. However, what did frighten her about the situation was that her puppet had become much stronger than she had ever anticipated and she knew that he was no longer under her control as he had been when he was young.

Suddenly, there was an interruption in her thoughts, it was Sheram. "Where are you Imfalin, there is much work to be done and no one knows where you are, are you trying to escape from working?" Sheram sounded annoyed "Sorry my dear I was just on my way, where are you? She replied trying to sound as motherly as was possible for a woman without any feelings of love. "Well hurry up, I'm in my chamber!" Sheram hissed at her.

When Imfalin arrived at Sheram's chamber she found him rummaging through his various vials and containers with a look of extreme anxiety on his face. On Imfalin's entry into the room he addressed her without even looking up at her, "Have you seen the empowerment elixir?" he asked her. "What do you need that for? You have enough of your own powers". Never has anyone regretted uttering anything so quickly as Imfalin did at that moment for the look of pure annoyance and anger that was on Sheram's face was enough to destroy a whole planet. "How dare you question my needs?" "Sorry Sheram I didn't mean to question you, what I meant was do you really need it?"

"Imfalin if life has taught me anything it is to be cautious, I know I have powers but I need to make sure that I am empowered more than my enemies, never under estimate any of them!"

Imfalin understood his concern and desire to win at all costs, so without any further discussions she began to help him find the most powerful concoctions they had produced and place them into his bag.

The following day Sheram was ready to set out on his journey to acquire the Book of Quantime. Imfalin had pinpointed the book to within a ten mile radius but could not get any closer than that, she hoped that this would be sufficient enough for Sheram to get to the book before the wretched Stonimions.

Sheram's hoards were ready to see him off, and the chosen few to accompany him were nervously waiting, excited at the prospect of being with their leader at the time of his victory, yet on the other hand extremely anxious to be in his presence if things did not go according to plan. Sheram stood at the entrance to his dominion and turned to face Imfalin and his minions, "I will return to you all victorious, and together we shall destroy the Stonimions and conquer Earth." There was an enormous uproar as they all cheered at the thought of being on the side of those who would be feared and in charge.

Sheram and his minions set off on their journey, the only guide being the information that Imfalin had given him, but unknown to Imfalin, Sheram had a little trick up his sleeve. During the night he had manufactured a device that used light energy to create a virtual map of the location they were going to and it would also be able to pick up energy pulses. Sheram knew that the Book of Quantime contained immense power and energy that would emanate from it, so his device would be able to detect it quite easily. Sheram was not just evil but he was also a genius, which made him very dangerous indeed. As they set off Imfalin called to Sheram, "Make sure you do not waver from your mission, Samaan and his troops will try to stop you by old Stonimion powers, don't let them into your mind!"

Sheram turned to her and looked her square in the eyes and said "You need not show any concern, for my want is greater than yours and I will not let anything ruin this victory." With that he turned and began to lead his minions away from his home, admirers and the closest thing he had to a mother. Sheram remained quiet for the main of the journey, as night time got closer he knew that he too was nearing his prize because when he was nearing it he began to feel the power of the Book of Quantime. "I did not need my map!" he thought to himself, "my own powers are tuned in to the power and energy of the book- it belongs to me" at this point something rather strange was happening to his face that lasted only for a few seconds and quickly passed; Sheram smiled with actual happiness.

7

THE SEARCH FOR THE BOOK

In the heart of Stonidium there were others who too were preparing for the war that was imminent; their trepidation was obvious as they held meetings to ensure that every last detail of the mission for the young Stonimions was reviewed and that there was no chance of the hideous Sheram getting to the Book of Quantime. Farmoeen had immediately informed Samaan of the moment she had made a telepathic link with Imfalin and the fact that Imfalin had pinpointed the location of the book. This information had increased their preparations tenfold as the urgency of what could occur, rose; the elders gave the four young Stonimions additional knowledge about the Book of Quantime. "It's important that once you have the Book of Quantime you are able to protect it, this is a special cloth, wrap the book in it and press it against the stone in your belt and think it invisible" Amaran, the elder who was known to make gadgets of power, often used in battle, was always inventing useful new tools. Simsaa took the cloth from Amaran and placed it into the inside pocket of her cloak, she turned to Farmoeen who had arrived to their village in the early hours. "Farmoeen, if we did need to use the Book of Quantime, what would we need to do exactly?"

At that point Samaan interjected into the conversation "I'm sorry to interrupt but I believe that all of the young Guardians need to hear this" "You're absolutely right Samaan" Farmoeen smiled and waited for Samaan to gather the others together. Farmoeen looked at the four friends and for a moment wondered if the Stonimion elders and, indeed, all of the Stonimions were doing the right thing as these 'Guardians' were really very young and inexperienced, however, the doubt was only for a moment as she knew from Samaan's account of their initiation, there was something very special about them.

As the Stonimions were reinforcing the protection around their main village and various parts of Stonidium, Farmoeen sat down with the four young friends at Dilyus' house and explained to them about the true power of the Book of Quantime and how it could be acquired. "There are four keys that are needed to open the book; these are called the keys of light, the keys need to be placed into the book in the correct order. Firstly the primary keys, one is red, one green and one blue, this is the order they are placed into the book, the final key is the secondary key which is made up of three colours; yellow, cyan and magenta. Once these are all in place the white light of time will allow the book to be opened and used to travel back or forth in time." The four friends sat in silence. "Wow, this is like a science lesson!" they all turned towards the window to see Scorpicle grinning at them.

Farmoeen turned to look at Scorpicle and said "Sorry Scorpicle, I didn't mean to exclude you from this meeting, please join us!"

"Thank you I will!" he smiled and reduced his massive size so that he could enter into the house, Farmoeen continued. "The keys to open it are hidden all over Earth and it will take a lot of skill and power to find them all successfully"

"Hold on, Farmoeen" remarked Nasami "If these keys are needed to open the Book of Quantime then what are we all worried about? Even if Sheram gets to it first it's of no use to him because he doesn't have the keys!"

"I'm afraid it's not as simple as that, if Sheram does get it, he has access to incomprehensible evil power that will allow him to open the Book of Quantime." Farmoeen continued "…and if it is forced open the consequences could be vey dire"

"How dire?" Amafiz asked with concern.

At this point Samaan explained "The Book of Quantime is very powerful but has always been used for good, however, if it is used for evil then the devastation it could cause would be phenomenal and its effect could resonate throughout Stonidium, Earth and maybe into other dimensions as well." "I know the consequences, I saw a glimpse of it in Nadrog's mind" Simsaa added in a heavy voice.

At that moment the enormity of the mission became more apparent and created an extremely sombre mood amongst the four young friends, but this mood did not lead to negativity and thoughts of losing this important quest, instead it made them even more determined to succeed.

Later that morning, Samaan, Scorpicle and the Guardians of

Stonidium were at the 'Great Stone', Samaan had decided to empower the Guardians as much as was possible. Inside the Great Stone they were all gathered around the Waters of Wisdom, this was a grey circular stone that seemed to have an endless supply of water; however, there was no obvious source point to indicate where the water came from. Samaan turned to the four young Stonimions and spoke slowly and gently, as if he wanted to make sure that they understood the importance of what he was saying by using dramatic dialogue. "These are the Waters of Wisdom" he said whilst looking each of them in the eye.

"We know- you'd already mentioned that when we came here!" exclaimed Nasami.

Samaan glared at Nasami, which made him squirm and look down at his feet feeling slightly embarrassed. "..As I was saying! These are the Waters of Wisdom and it's important that you drink from these as they have the power to enhance your Stonimion powers and abilities tenfold, which with your immense abilities means that you will have phenomenal powers, and believe me you will need them to overcome Sheram and his plans".

"I have a question Samaan" Amafiz stated, "When you say that these waters will enhance our powers is that our abilities that are within us from our birth stones only or does it also enhance the powers of our weapons?" he quizzed the Elder. Samaan simply replied "the latter my dear boy, in fact, whilst you are driving Scorpicle the power of the waters will also transcend from you onto him as well!"

"Hey! Now that's what I'm talking about" remarked Scorpicle with a massive grin on his metal face.

One by one each of the Stonimions drank from the powerful water source, as they were drinking Simsaa turned to Samaan and asked, "Samaan, sir, if these waters are so powerful then why do the other Stonimions not drink from it, especially now when they all need to protect Stonidium?" "I knew one of you would ask this of me and the truth is that although these waters give immense power, they can also cause enormous pain and maybe even death if..." before Samaan had the chance to finish his sentence Dilyus, who was at that moment drinking a great gulp full of the water of wisdom, spurted out the water so fast that it made a hyperbola projectile whose trajectory would have been admired by any mathematician.

Dilyus stared at Samaan in total disbelief, with drops of the water falling off of his chin "I'm sorry sir but I don't think our parents will approve of you giving us something that could kill us! I mean really it's..."

Samaan raised his hand signalling for Dilyus to stop what he was saying "I would never put you in danger, young man, if you would let me finish, as I was saying, these waters would only cause pain or death if the Stonimion or anyone, for that matter, drinking it, did not have the inner strength to cope with the water, with you four I knew there would be no problem, however I did verify this with Farmoeen and she carried out an incantation to check that you would be able to cope. The thing is we can only do this with those Stonimions

that we know will not be affected negatively and with the situation of Sheram's threat we only have enough time to let those that can cope to drink it. People like your parents, the other Elders for example who have known to show great power and strength in their times can drink from it, and, indeed will do so in the following few days."

Once they had all drunk from the waters of wisdom Samaan led the four youngsters to the inner chambers of the Great Stone. This part of the Great Stone contained old scriptures, scrolls, books and weaponry that had been safe guarded by the Stonimion elders during the history of Stonidium. "Alongside your own powers and arms you have at your disposal all of these" as he said this he pointed to the array of items in front of them. Their eyes nearly popped out of their heads at the sight of the entire armoury and, more importantly, old Stonidium wisdom at their fingertips.

Amafiz turned to Samaan and looked extremely serious "Do you think we're going to be able to overcome Sheram, because it looks to me as if you all don't think we've got the capability?"

"Amafiz, there's no harm in being prepared, we all want to give you children the best fighting chance because Sheram will not look at you and think awwww! They're just children I won't do anything to them!" Samaan shook his head with great vigour, "If anything that heartless monster will happily use you all as a way to get to us, so we cannot afford to give him any chance of getting the upper hand."

Samaan left the children for a while giving them time amongst the old artefacts, time to look and choose carefully. He trusted these children explicitly, and he found this to be a strange feeling, as there were some adult Stonimions who would not be able to instil such trust in him as these young ones had. He felt safe in their hands and this is why he knew that they were the 'Four Guardians of Stonidium'.

Samaan looked at the four Stonimions and asked "What items have you chosen then?" Each of them showed Samaan what they had chosen; Amafiz had chosen a glass globe that changed colours every so often, the globe had the power to enhance Amafiz's defence system, Simsaa had chosen an old parchment that was able to absorb information and this would help her power of acquiring knowledge, Dilyus had taken a small monocle that allowed him to penetrate deeper into the minds of others to enable him to place instructions to control them in the future without him having to be present, and finally Nasami had found an object that looked like a miniature telescope, this enabled him to not only move inanimate objects using his telekinetic powers but also helped him to operate them for his own use.

Samaan looked at the four children and smiled "I believe it's time for you to go!" They looked at each other with excitement, trepidation and pride, whilst carrying the weight of great responsibility on their shoulders too.

"Simsaa looked sadly at Samaan and said "I wish you could come with us, I feel safer with you around"

"Funny that, because I feel safer with you guys around!" he replied.

The Stonimions returned home to say their goodbyes to their families, it was a hard thing to do for all of them but they knew it had to be done. Akjam looked intently at his son and then turned to Scorpicle. "My friend I am entrusting my child and, indeed, all of these 'our children' to you, be there for them as you have for my ancestors as this is probably the most serious battle you will have ever been in".

For the first time, in a long time, Scorpicle was quite serious "Akjam these are my children and my worlds, both of them!" within that sentence there was an exchange of looks between the two that Amafiz noticed, a look that suggested an important piece of information that only they knew about.

Samaan and the parents of the four friends stood along the edge of the Stonidium village, they called home, to see off the 'Guardians'. As they were waving them off Samaan called out to them, "Children you need to hurry, I've just had a message from Farmoeen, Sheram is almost there, he is very close to the 'Book of Quantime', you need to be careful, make sure you use the map that I gave you!"

"We will and don't worry!" they all said at the same time. They took out the map that Samaan had created, it was a map of the whole of Stonidium however, it was empowered to locate objects of great energy and power, in fact it was not dissimilar to Sheram' s map! The only problem was that there were numerous objects of energy dotted around Stonidium, including items at the Great Stone, however, the four friends and Scorpicle had an idea that there was a chance of the book being in the unchartered areas of Stonidium and so headed towards them.

Initially the four friends had thought about starting their journey on foot, but as time was of the essence they decided against this and sat inside Scorpicle to help speed things along. Scorpicle was a vehicle that was able to travel at extremely fast speeds and the usefulness of this was that whenever, they thought they had spotted the 'Book of Quantime' due to pulses of energy showing on the map, he was able to transfer to the location due to his inbuilt mapping system and take them straight there at the speed of light. This was all well and good but Stonidium was a vast place, so even with this method it was not a fast mission that they were carrying out.

Soon it was nightfall and they were no closer to the 'Book of Quantime' or so they thought. "Something is not quite right!" exclaimed Scorpicle. "What's wrong?" asked Simsaa.

"Well if you look at my mapping system its indicating that there is an object of immense power nearby but if you look out there you can't see anything for miles" Scorpicle explained.

"It could be underground." Nasami interjected.

"I had already thought of that and checked a twenty mile radius in all directions, but there seems to be nothing or nowhere that the book could be, yet I'm still getting the energy pulse!" Scorpicle said extremely confused. "Well we have two choices; we can stay for a bit longer and figure out what is going on or we can move on" said Amafiz.

"Let's vote, all of those in favour of staying raise your hands" said Dilyus, no sooner had he completed his sentence then they had all raised their hands, including Scorpicle raising his right front wheel. "Well that's unanimous then" exclaimed Dilyus with a grin.

Unbeknown to the young Stonimions they were in the right vicinity, for they had arrived to the right place and that Sheram was already here, hidden using his powers of camouflage. The only fortunate thing was that Scorpicle, being the wise vehicle that he was, too had turned on his invisibility protection as they had approached the area, just to be on the safe side, so neither party could see the other, however, their power senses were all on alert and knew something was not quite right.

The Stonimions and Scorpicle were not able to see any of the natural surrounding foliage, rocks and the like, because Sheram had not only camouflaged himself and his minions, but he had also changed the appearance of a key part of the area to look like a deserted part of Stonidium without any forms of life being noticeable, so to the Stonimions the area looked barren and uninhabited.

Scorpicle was carrying out several examinations of the area using all the instruments he had in his possession. "Oh! Oh! I think I know what's happened!" they all looked at him with anticipation "Sheram!"

"What do you mean Sheram?" queried Simsaa nervously.

"He's changed the environment, what I mean is that he has disguised the area to look different and that can only mean one thing, we're in the right place!" said Scorpicle excitedly.

"Yeah! And so is he!" commented Nasami.

"Why did you have to say that?" Dilyus asked almost in tears.

"Dilyus you really need to man up, stop getting scared at every situation we come across, we've got a lot to face up to and there are two worlds relying on us!" Amafiz said totally exasperated at Dilyus' fear of everything.

Dilyus looked embarrassed and commenced to apologise profusely, "It's alright Dilyus, we're all a bit stressed and worried, but don't worry we'll be okay" Simsaa told him reas- suringly.

"It's lucky that Scorpicle had already hidden us from others otherwise we'd already be exposed and in serious trouble" said Nasami.

"Hey with me around it's not luck but just sheer genius!" gloated Scorpicle. They all rolled their eyes towards the sky and grinned, it did not take long for Scorpicle to stop being serious.

Whilst they had the protective shield that kept them hidden, they had the chance to try and figure out where Sheram was, but time was against them for two reasons; they knew that Sheram was getting closer to finding the book but also that he too must now be aware that someone else was in the area and was probably trying everything in his power to ascertain who they were and more dangerously pinpoint their location.

They sat for a few minutes trying to figure out how to tackle this enormous problem, when Nasami turned to the others and said "I think I've got an idea!" They all looked at him with great anticipation, as they all knew that Nasami's ideas were usually very good and productive. "Simsaa can shape shift into an object that will blend into the surroundings and I can transport her to the outside where she could then try and absorb information from the environment to try and locate the book or Sheram or both!"

Amafiz spoke up "That could well work, well done Nasami, the only flaw I can see is getting Simsaa out of Scorpicle without giving us away!"

"That's easy, I'll move nearer to those trees that we can still see and then you can transport her from there, I'm sure she won't be noticed then." It was decided that this was probably the best plan considering the situation they were in. Simsaa placed her right hand on her stone and closed her eyes; the stone began pulsating, a red hue emerged from it and surrounded Simsaa and in front of their very eyes she changed from the Stonimion they knew into a large round boulder. Dilyus grinned and of course could not resist making a remark in connection with what Simsaa had changed into, "How apt, a big round, lumpy object!" the others glared at him with horror because they knew Simsaa would make Dilyus pay for that comment, the boulder shook slightly and it was at this point that Nasami thought it would be a good idea to continue with the plan, before Simsaa changed back and walloped Dilyus.

Nasami concentrated on the boulder and as he did so a bright white light emerged from his eyes, the others watched as he swiftly transported the boulder from Scorpicle through his side window and out onto the ground outside.

At that point they carefully watched and as they stared at Simsaa the boulder, they noticed a slight red mist around it which gave the boulder the appearance of trembling. "I think she is getting the information we need" said Scorpicle. "How will we know when she has finished?" enquired Dilyus.

"Asks the one with the power of reading minds? Honestly Dilyus you scare me sometimes!" laughed Amafiz. As usual Dilyus grinned sheepishly at his own lack of thought, he then commenced in trying to communicate with Simsaa when all of a sudden he looked scared, really petrified. The others too looked scared and asked him what was wrong. He turned to face them and said "She is going to kill me for the lumpy comment!" they all laughed at him because they knew Simsaa was going to give him a very hard time. "Okay in all serious-ness, Dilyus has she managed to get the information we need?" asked Scorpicle.

"Yes she has" said Dilyus reluctantly. Nasami took this as his cue to transport her back into Scorpicle.

Once Simsaa was safely back inside Scorpicle she transformed herself back and glared at Dilyus. "I will deal with you later; don't think for a minute that you're safe because I will get you, but at the moment we've got more important things to do" she turned to Amafiz and winked at him.

"Well asked Amafiz what did you find out?" "Sheram is defi-nitely here, I could sense his evilness and his knowledge of the Book of Quantime and it's a good job I went out there because the strength of the force field that's disguising the area is really high and impenetrable so trying to attack it would have been useless."

"Is he near it?" asked Scorpicle.

"Well it seems as near as we are! I was able to absorb his panic at not knowing exactly where it was but I do get the feeling that he is getting closer" said Simsaa.

"Well at least it gives us a bit of time I suppose" with that Scor-picle began searching through the virtual map he had created of the area trying to locate any intense energy pulses that could be the book.

Whilst Scorpicle was doing this the others too were trying to locate the book by forming a link with each other that would allow their senses to be enhanced and maybe form a link with the book. However, this technique back fired, as during their 'astral' like journey through the area they came face to face with Sheram.

Sheram stared at them and they could feel his evil eyes penetrating deep into their souls and every cell of their being. They were shocked that even though they were only in front of him in astral form he could see them so clearly; he raised his outstretched arms towards them and with a malicious grin on his evil face he hurled a black blue coloured bolt of light towards them. It was only their fast reflexes and sharp instincts that saved them as it all happened with lightning speed but they were faster. Their astral forms disintegrated in front of Sheram's eyes as they had broken their link with each other but in the split second they broke the link Sheram realised that they were escaping and as they were getting away they witnessed his rage which sent a tremor of true fear through them.

They sat back in Scorpicle panting heavily as if they had physically been there and had to run to save their lives. Scorpicle was shocked by their panicked appearance, "What happened?" he asked them unsure about what could have caused such a reaction.

"He knows we're here, he's seen us and to say that he's unhappy would be an understatement!" explained Amafiz.

"We're going to need to work faster and move from here because if he knows we're here then..." Scorpicle did not complete his sentence because his detectors pinpointed an immense power surge heading towards them. He transported them all in milliseconds from one side of the area, where Sheram was, to the other, "It won't take him long to find us again, but don't worry I think I've found the Book of Quantime!"

Scorpicle headed towards an area that was as deserted as the entire area, he stopped by a tree and produced a pulse of black and orange energy that destroyed the tree. Once the debris and smoke from the explosion had dissipated into the surroundings, the four young Stonimions saw that the tree had been replaced by a small cave which was glowing with a brilliant white light. The blast had destroyed the disguised area so that the true environment could be seen and so once the blast disintegrated the magic that had been used by Sheram the cave had been revealed. The four friends stepped out of Scorpicle who then reduced his size so that he could enter the cave with them. They slowly entered the cave with great trepidation and anticipation, the cave was quite deceptive as it was small looking on the outside but as they walked in it turned out to be of a vast size. In the centre of the cave was a crystal pedestal on which they saw the Book of Quantime.

"Wow! I can't believe we've found it, it's so magnificent!" said Nasami with eyes wide open.

"It's amazing, so beautiful and it seems to have an aura of serenity" said Simsaa. As they drew closer one of them stayed behind, they turned to see Amafiz hesitating in coming towards the book.

"What's wrong Amafiz?" asked Scorpicle.

"I'm not sure but something does not seem right, I mean first of all we were having such difficulty in finding it then all of a sudden it's there in front of us." Amafiz explained and as he did so the others too picked up on his feelings of doubt. They too felt uneasy and started to edge away from the book and it was a good thing that they had because at that moment the Book of Quantime exploded. There was a horrific scream of pure joy as the cave around them disappeared and they found themselves surrounded by Sheram's hoards. His nasty looking minions parted to reveal Sheram standing in front of them whilst holding something aloft.

"Looking for this?" he asked whilst waving the object. Scorpicle and the Stonimions stared in horror as they realised that Sheram was holding the Book of Quantime. When he knew they had realised what had happened he raised his free hand and waved it around himself and called out "Now Imfalin" and disappeared. He left without any dramatic smoke or whoosh, but just with an eerie silence, unfortunately for the Four Guardians and their vehicle, though he left on his own leaving behind his minions who were now slowly closing in on all five of them.

THE QUEST

8

THE BOOK OF QUANTIME

Farmoeen woke up with a start, something was terribly wrong and she knew that she had to act fast. She established a telepathic link with Samaan immediately and explained to him that all was not right and she believed that the young Stonimions had not been successful in getting hold of the Book of Quantime, "I'm going to look into the Crystal of Knowledge to find out exactly what has happened." Samaan summoned the Stonimion Elders and the parents of the young Stonimions for an emergency meeting.

"I'm afraid I don't have good news, in fact I don't have definite news of any sort all I know is that Farmoeen has sensed something is wrong and she believes that the children were not successful in getting to the Book of Quantime before Sheram, and as soon as she tells me more I will let you know."

"Where are the children?" asked Akjam with trepidation, almost as if he did not want to hear the answer. The others all looked intently at Samaan and when there was no response they knew that their young children were in trouble.

"I knew we should not have let them go, anything could have happened to them, we have no idea where they are and in what state!" screeched Zarani in a total state of panic. Akjam raised his hand in a gesture of calming her down.

"My dear nothing will happen to them, trust me I know!"

"Do you really?" asked Maraj cynically.

"Look all I know is that sitting here blaming each other is not going to help" Akjam protested, he turned to Samaan and said "You need to re-establish your link with Farmoeen and find out exactly what's happened and then let us know if there is anything we can do?"

Samaan returned to his house and made no delay in communicating with Farmoeen. "What's happened Farmoeen?" Asked Samaan; dreading the answer.

"I'm afraid the children have not been successful in intercepting Sheram, he has the Book of Quantime!" Farmoeen revealed with a heavy heart. For a few minutes there was absolute silence, Samaan had been literally stunned into silence. "Samaan are you there?" asked Farmoeen concerned at the lack of reaction from Samaan.

"What about the children, what's happened to them?" Samaan's telepathic voice sounded distant and vacant. "I'm going to try and make a link with the children to find out what's happened to them." And with that Farmoeen broke the link with Samaan.

"Dilyus are you there?" Farmoeen was trying to get through to the children but it was proving to be a fruitless exercise. Farmoeen was not one to give up so easily even though she was now becoming really worried. "Dilyus can you hear me?"

"Farmoeen is that you? Sheram has the book, we failed everyone!" Dilyus sounded tearful as he mentally spoke to Farmoeen.

"We'll worry about that later are you all okay?"

"Not really! Sheram has gone but we're surrounded by his minions and they're closing in on us!"

Farmoeen knew that she must not panic the young Stonimions, "Listen carefully Dilyus, you all need to work together and fast, think back to the day of your initiation and how you all used your instincts in using your powers."

"Okay Farmoeen, we will" Dilyus replied trying to sound brave, as he telepathically relayed Farmoeen's message to the other Stonimions.

As Sheram's hoards came closer Nasami remembered a science lesson where he had learnt about the human body's defence system, he turned to the others and said three words "Antibodies and phagocytosis!" They all looked at Nasami and Dilyus exclaimed "Poor Nasami the stress of our predicament has caused him to lose the plot!"

"No, he's absolutely right" said Amafiz, and with that he pressed his stone from which purple coloured shimmering ropes appeared.

The ropes descended onto the different minions, changing

shape and size to fit around each one precisely, as each one became tied up the loose ends of the ropes slithered like snakes in the air and came together bringing each of Sheram's little pets into larger groups that were now clumped into a few large masses. At this point Simsaa knew that this was her opportunity to try and extract some information from these strange looking creatures. She initially penetrated into the mind of one of the Mangra's and was astonished to hear the thoughts of all of them, she realised they must be connected in some way. Simsaa then tried to read the minds of some of the other hoards, but with all of them she did not get very far because all she managed to find out was how much these strange creatures admired their master. She also understood that these creatures were of no use to her as they did not have any knowledge about anything that Sheram could be doing next.

The hoards were struggling and wriggling trying to escape from Amafiz's ropes and the little Mangra's startled to wail, the wailing began to crescendo, it was then that Dilyus realised that this wailing was an attack mechanism and not just a protest at being tied up. Dilyus became covered in a pale green hue as he entered into the minds of the Mangra; "Stop the noise! Stop it right now!" the authority and fierceness of his voice inside the Mangra's minds brought their wailing to an immediate and abrupt halt. It was then that Amafiz displayed his true powers of defence and created a giant amethyst stone which enveloped Sheram's hoards, as they all disappeared from sight and became trapped inside the giant stone, it vanished taking the hoards with them.

"Where have they gone?" Nasami asked Amafiz.

Amafiz turned to Nasami with a big grin on his face and replied "Back to where they belong, their master!"

Simsaa looked at the others intently, a look they all recognised as one which acknowledged their failure and defeat. Scorpicle looked at the four of them and spoke "We tried our best but this is not over, we need to get back to the village, if Farmoeen knows about our defeat then your parents must know and will be worried about you all."

"I'll take us back, quick time, climb in and let's go" Scorpicle tried to sound cheerful in order to keep up the children's spirits but he knew that their failure would have dire repercussions for all on Stonidium and Earth.

As they returned home, in a hidden part of Stonidium there was an almighty crash as Sheram found himself pinned down under his hoards. Amafiz had attached an instruction to the stone to home in on the one that the hoards loved the most; he knew it would be Sheram.

"Imfalinnnnnnnnnn! Come here now mmmmm!" came the muffled scream from Sheram. "Coming, Sire!" Sheram heard the panicked voice as he was smothered by the weight of his minions. Imfalin looked horrified as she saw her master disappear under his own hoards; Imfalin raised her arms and thrust her hands forward in a gesture of throwing, and indeed, she threw an enormous energy bolt at the hoards, being careful not to aim any of the energy bolt at Sheram. The minions scattered like diffuse light being reflected from an uneven mirror in a fun house, they were strewn all over the Great Chamber, were Sheram had been perusing over ancient scriptures about the Book of Quantime. As soon as the hoards got over the shock of their unceremonious dispersal they fled from the

91

Great Chamber before they could be subjected to anymore pain or humiliation. Sheram's normally dark slicked back hair was strewn all over his pointed face. His dark eyes were large with shock and his usually sallow skin showed a tint of colour as his anger at his situation started to escalate.

"What do you think happened?" Imfalin asked Sheram nervously.

"What do you think, it's those blasted Stonimions; it's probably their idea of a joke!"

"Sire, if they can send your hoards to you then they could find you too!" "Highly likely but they wouldn't dare, they're not that ignorant that they would think that I don't have some sort of defence or alert system in place. They wouldn't risk being caught, especially now that I have the Book of Quantime, they know my security will have intensified." "I'm not worried about them now, for I have what I wanted, my mission now is to access the book and carry out my heart's desire!"

"Heart sire?" questioned Imfalin.

"If you had one then you'd know about it!" he hissed at her. With that Imfalin left as she knew that staying in Sheram's presence any more than was necessary would only lead to pain and trouble for her.

When she left Sheram turned his full attention to the book, he stared at it for some time, as if looking at it would reveal its secrets to him. He wondered how such an ordinary looking book could hold so much power, how it could change the destiny of worlds, the more he thought about it the more he realised that the book itself was truly not the powerful tool that everyone thought it to be but like any vehicle or tool it was only as good, useful or powerful as the person operating it. With that thought in his mind he went back to trying to find the way of opening this useful tool, the tool that would allow him to fulfil his main purpose in his, otherwise, empty life. Sheram was searching through the ancient scriptures, when he came across the secret of opening the Book of Quantime and when he realised that searching for the keys would be a long winded mission he let out a shrill scream that summoned Imfalin.

Imfalin was in her room and when she heard her name being called in such a manner, she let out a tired sigh, "Here we go again!" she said to the little Mangra that was with her working on potions and elixirs to help with future battles or ailments that they may encounter. The Mangra grinned at her for really that was the only reaction it knew to any new situation, it thought this was the safest reaction around Sheram and Imfalin, but it could never be more wrong; for usually grinning at the wrong time caused a lot of pain and anguish to the Mangra, but being the creature it was it could never remember this fact. However, for the first time ever it seemed to have got it right, because there was no painful repercussion because of the grin.

When Imfalin arrived, the Great Chamber seemed to be heavy with Sheram's rage "Oh No! What now?" she thought. "Sire, what's wrong?" she tried to sound concerned but ended up sounding really sarcastic and almost as if she was making fun of him. His reaction to this was unpleasant, to say the least. "You withered old hag, are you making fun of ME?" roared Sheram.

"No Sheram, why would I do that? I am concerned that you

are not happy even with the Book of Quantime in your possession." She bit her tongue as soon as she uttered the words for she knew that she had irritated him further and they were going to go through the same routine again.

It was obviously a sign of the times and things changing for them because despite Sheram's built up rage he did not explode as usual instead he spoke in a calm voice, which if truth be known was more unsettling than if he had been angry. "Imfalin, the ancient scriptures talk of the 'four keys of light' being the only way of opening the Book of Quantime"

"Well, we shall have to search for them then Sheram"

"No, it would take too long for they are hidden on Earth and protected by ancient powers" Sheram looked at her intently when he spoke. "What then do we need to do Sire?" Imfalin asked like an obedient servant.

"We need to use other means to open it, although the scriptures talk of undesirable consequences if the wrong sort of force is used".

"Undesirable?" Imfalin asked.

"Yes but the question is undesirable for whom? I believe it would only be good for us." Sheram replied. Sheram set Imfalin the task of finding incantations that would open the book whilst he tried various physical means of trying to open it and so this continued for some days, by which point Sheram was becoming extremely frustrated.

Their victory came by surprise, to them both, for they had got to the point of giving up when it seemed that one of the incantations that Imfalin had produced had some kind of effect on the book. The incantation that Imfalin had produced was partly from her world and partly from Stonimion ancient scriptures. She had come across the Stonimion scriptures when she had first arrived in Stonidium and had managed to infiltrate the Stonimion elders by befriending them, after she had gained enough knowledge and revived her powers she had revealed her true self to them.

The Stonimion elders had banished her, but unknown to them Imfalin had 'acquired' some of their secrets and knowledge of force, secrets that were now being used against them. As she read the incantation over the book it began to vibrate as if every molecule in it was being given an immense energy and as the vibrating grew in intensity they both saw beams of white light emanating from the edges of the book. They looked at each other with great excitement, but it was short lived as the effect of the incantation quickly wore off and the book became silent again. "We're almost there Imfalin, you need to work on perfecting the incantation; I can feel victory upon us, go don't waste any more time."

Imfalin returned to her room to continue with her task and Sheram looked greedily at the Book of Quantime, he felt like a child who was standing in front of a sweet shop with a key to the door and he could feel it about to open up to him for his enjoyment. In her room Imfalin stood in front of the mirror, admiring her intelligence, for now there was no beauty to admire, once there had been, she had in her youth had beautiful long blonde hair, blue eyes, rosy cheeks and an enchanting smile, but as she had grown and her true intentions of her life and hatred of others came forth, her beauty too disintegrated. She looked now and saw a woman who looked withered; her hair was straw like in texture, her eyes were a dark grey and blood shot and her skin looked liked old meat that been hung to dry and mature. However, to Imfalin this was of no consequence, her thirst for her victory over those she hated far outweighed her desire to be attractive or to look kind; that was for those who had no purpose in life. Imfalin did not understand that true beauty came from within and that her outer appearance was a consequence of her evilness.

9

THE LAIR

The four young Stonimions were not expecting such a 'heroes' welcome on their return home for in their eyes they had been anything but heroic. However, their parents and family were so relieved to see them in one piece that they had not given any thought to their failing in the mission for which they had left. Their parents ran to them and hugged them until the fur on their bodies became matted. Zarani held Simsaa's face in her hands and stared into her daughter's round brown eyes and smiled. She stroked the fur on her face, from the tip of her cheeks to her pointy chin, "My child I was so scared for you!"

"I know Mum but you don't need to be, really!" Simsaa replied.

Zarani was now thinking about the question that was on every Stonimions' mind, which was, what next? There was a general meeting in the village square, led by the Elder Stonimions, "Stonimions it is clear that Sheram has enhanced his powers and trickery to such an extent that he was able to acquire the

Book of Quantime, it is obvious that he will go to any length to access it's powers and to use it for his own evil purposes, the question is how long will it take for him to access the Book of Quantime?" Samaan announced to all who were present.

Simsaa raised her hand to speak, Samaan acknowledged her by nodding. "Amafiz was able to send Sheram's hoards to him, I know it's dangerous, but I was wondering if…"

Akjam interjected "Sorry to interrupt you young lady but I think you know that although in theory your idea would be sound, but the reality is that Sheram would have reinforced his defences so it would be fruitless to even try to attempt anything!"

"I believe that we would be better off increasing our own defences and reassessing the next step that the 'Four Guardians of Stonidium' would have to take, but I also think that we need to try and get the book back!" The Stonimions all turned towards the voice and were stunned to see Farmoeen in their presence again so soon. Farmoeen the oracle very rarely entered public places, if anything, if there were any problems or difficult situations the Stonimions would go to her.

"Farmoeen, it's an honour to see you, we need you to guide the Guardians, whilst Samaan and the elders help us with Stonidium's defences." Faraan did not mean to state the obvious but a combination of his nervousness and excitement, at seeing Farmoeen, resulted in him doing so. Farmoeen simply smiled and nodded her agreement with Faraan.

Samaan led the elders and some of the other adults to the Great Stone, where they gathered additional weaponry, old scriptures and mystical objects from the ancients, basically anything they thought would help in protecting the main parts of Stonidium, including their village.

The Four Guardians followed Farmoeen back to her house, where they proceeded to consult with the Crystal of Knowledge. The Crystal confirmed their suspicions that Sheram had enhanced his protection, but it also told them that Amafiz's tracking mechanism could take them to a safe enough distance so that they could then try and infiltrate his lair.

"The only thing is that Amafiz was able to use the homing mechanism to send the hoards to the thing they loved the most, but we don't have anything of Sheram's now to do the same again." Dilyus explained.

"Yeah, but there is a way around that, the incantation I used will have left an essence of memory behind in my stone if I tap into that memory then we may be able to follow Sheram's minions."

"It's worth a try" said Simsaa.

Amafiz stood up and touched the stone in his belt; there was a gentle wisp of colour that floated out from his stone, the purple smoke formed a circle in front of Amafiz. He closed his eyes and murmured the incantation he had used before. "Ancient powers of Stonidium take these creatures to their loved one." As he repeated the incantation the others saw a trail forming that started at the centre of the purple circle and seemed to extend into nothingness. "What do we do now?" Nasami asked Farmoeen.

"Well I think you should all follow the trail, but please be careful, it won't take you to exactly the same spot, luckily! But we don't know where you will end up so be prepared to defend yourselves!" she replied.

Scorpicle and the four young Stonimions stepped through the circle with a slight apprehension and were immediately whisked away, with the circle of purple smoke closing behind them as if it had imploded or disappeared into a black hole. Farmoeen was left standing alone in her house; she thought that she should inform Samaan and the elders that the Four Guardians had left to try and get back the Book of Quantime, as she was about to make the telepathic link she felt a jolt within her, as if someone had sent an electric shock through her soul. She heard the voice so clearly she could have been standing in front of her.

"Farmoeen, it is I Imfalin, I know you very well and I am contacting you to warn you, don't send those meddling Stonimions after Sheram, for if they are caught their fate will be too abhorrent to think about!" By the time Imfalin had finished Farmoeen had gotten over the shock of the contact and composed herself to reply.

"Imfalin firstly don't ever tell me what to do! Secondly don't under estimate the Four Guardians of Stonidium!"

There was an anxious silence between the two women, finally Imfalin responded. "What did you say?"

"You heard me! These are no ordinary Stonimions that you are dealing with; you'd better run to your master and WARN HIM that he is not going to get an easy ride in trying to rule the Earth or Stonidium!" This unusual outburst from the usually serene Farmoeen severed the link between the two women; Farmoeen then turned her attention back to contacting

Samaan. Once she was in contact with Samaan she informed him of her conversation with Imfalin, for the first time ever the wise and intelligent oracle seemed a tad embarrassed that she had lost her 'cool' but Samaan reassured her that her reaction had been justified and it was good that she had told her about the Four Guardians of Stonidium, as this would make Sheram take them and their threat a bit more seriously. Farmoeen also informed him about the 'Guardians' following the trail to Sheram's lair, Samaan expressed some concern but realised that sitting around doing nothing was more dangerous in these times.

Samaan told Farmoeen to return to the village to help the other elders enhance the protection that they were all preparing. He emphasised the urgency of this and also asked her to bring along the Crystal of Knowledge; they needed all the help they could. When Farmoeen arrived, she saw that the Stonimions had posted lookout barricades around the circumference of the village and, on speaking to some of the elders she found out that there also some around the outermost parts of Stonidium that were under their authority and possession. At the point she met with Samaan he was instructing the some of the elders to create a giant force field from one end of the village to the other. He turned to her and said "Farmoeen, good I see you have bought the crystal with you."

"Yes, but I don't know how the crystal will help in the defence preparations Samaan, I'm intrigued." Farmoeen smiled at him.

"Watch, CRYSTAL!" Samaan summoned, the crystal began to pulsate different coloured lights and telepathically connected with Samaan.

"Samaan it's an honour to speak with you, how can I help you?"

"Thank you Great Crystal of knowledge, I need you to guide us on the most effective incantations, protective forces and armoury to use against Sheram and his hoards, he has managed to get hold of the Book of Quantime and we need to prepare for the worst." Samaan explained.

"Unfortunately I am aware of this and if I know that evil being he will not stop until he has control over the book. This means any incantations we perform need to be ones that will not be affected by alterations in the fabric of space and time." The crystal explained. This statement confirmed Samaan's suspicions and with that he teleported to the Great Stone to look through the ancient scriptures for the appropriate tools needed to ensure the protection of Stonidium.

The five of them landed with an almighty thud that sent them reeling in all directions, but luckily they had not landed inside Sheram's lair but in the woods that surrounded it. They gathered themselves and looked up in awe at the gargantuan building in front of them. "That Sheram is really warped!" Scorpicle exclaimed. Sheram's lair was made out of a red coloured rock that had layers of black, grey and gold circling it from top to bottom, as if it had been carved from a giant sedimentary rock mountain. The building itself was a cross between a castle and a glass office, something that was extremely alien in Stonidium but a sight that maybe would not be as unfamiliar on Earth. The four young friends stared at the monumental structure in front of them. "It's ugly!" was the only remark that Dilyus could muster up.

"I'm surprised that we've never come across it before, it's so big you can hardly miss it!" Nasami remarked.

"There's probably some sort of protection in place that creates a camouflage so that if anyone comes near they would be guided away from it." Amafiz explained, and as they stood there they witnessed an example of Amafiz's explanation, they saw a baroo, a small animal that had a round plump body, covered in fur with limbs that had fish like scales, coming towards them. For a moment it looked as if it was going to walk straight into them but as it got to just a few feet away from them it turned to its right and carried on as if they and Sheram's large home were not even there.

"He's clever!" said Simsaa, "Yes, and so is Imfalin" added Scorpicle. "She is involved fully with everything he does; we're going to have to be alert and on our guard more than ever, you need to realise that our presence may already have been noticed by them inside there!" Scorpicle continued as he pointed his headlights towards Sheram's lair.

They carefully started to move further in towards Sheram's home as well as skirting around the edge of it, they were looking for a safer area from where they could try and get inside. As they moved further in towards the lair, their apprehension grew, they could sense something in the air; it was putrid and laden with hatred, it clawed at their throats, as if trying to strangle them. Dilyus turned to Amafiz and spoke with great difficulty. "I'm finding it hard to breathe; I don't know what's happening, I feel really weird!" he sounded really upset but what Amafiz also noticed was how Dilyus sounded really distant despite the fact he was standing right next to him. After the shortness of breath the four Stonimions began to hallucinate; Nasami looked at Amafiz and looked horrified. "Amafiz why do you want to hurt me? Put that sword away please don't, noooooooo!!!!" Simsaa slapped Nasami hard; Nasami stared at her as if he had just come out of a trance.

"Sorry Nasami, I didn't know what else to do?" Simsaa explained, looking embarrassed.

"It's okay you can may be explain to me later what happened, I feel a bit dizzy at the moment so I don't think I really want to know!"

Scorpicle, however, knew exactly what was happening. "I think we should back track our steps and try around the other side" they all turned around obediently and went back the way they had come. They arrived back at the spot they had appeared at initially and they all drew a long deep breath, as if they had been holding them breaths for a very long time. "Whoa! That was unpleasant to say the least" Simsaa said taking in deep gulps of air "What happened?"

"There was a very strong magical incantation placed at that spot, it was designed to interfere with us both physically and mentally, that would explain why you were all finding it difficult to breathe and why Nasami had that funny turn." Scorpicle continued "I think it may be safer if you guys sat inside me as I can make sure I can protect you from anything in the air, it will be more functional than having a protective field around us from your bracelets."

Once sitting safely inside Scorpicle they slowly went around Sheram's lair to find a weaker spot than where they had originally landed. Scorpicle suddenly stopped, "I think this may be a slightly safer spot." The four Stonimions stepped out of Scorpicle and stood facing Sheram's lair. Amafiz stretched out his hand towards his stone and muttered under his breath "Oh Stone of the Stonimions show us the safest route into Sheram's lair!" As soon as he said this then the purple light emitted from his stone and formed a circle on the wall in front of them, Amafiz moved from side to side allowing the light to trail across the wall slowly. As the light was sweeping across the wall they noticed a dark patch in the centre of the light about four feet above the ground. As they looked closer at the dark patch it became apparent that it was darker in colour because it was an opening in the wall. Scorpicle used his laser lights to increase the size of the hole, so that they could fit through, the effect of the laser light was temporary as the size of the hole returned to its normal size once they had stepped through it. They walked through it with their protective cloaks draped over them and Scorpicle, who had reduced his size.

Dilyus turned to look at the opening as it went back to its original size, "That does not make me feel safe!" he declared.

"I know but we can't let it stay large as it may be noticed by Sheram" Scorpicle explained.

"How do we know that Sheram will not already be aware of our presence?" he asked Scorpicle.

"We don't!" he replied. "I did place an enchantment over our cloaks that would reflect any powerful incantations that may be around to detect intruders." Amafiz said, so hopefully they would not have detected us yet. Amafiz was right because there was no disturbance or commotion amongst any of Sheram's hoards on guard duty.

The five of them slowly crept along one of the many corridors that were woven around the lair, like strings of spaghetti slopped onto a plate. The presence of pure evil was all around them, they felt it in every pore of their being; it seemed to penetrate into every single one of the cells in their bodies, it was as if the evil had combined with the haemoglobin in their red blood cells and was being delivered into to their cells instead of oxygen. Scorpicle, being the mechanical vehicle that he was and not living tissue, was not affected by whatever was present in the air. "I feel strange!" Nasami said.

"Yeah I know what you mean it feels as if Sheram is being absorbed within our very being!" Dilyus said shaking violently as he spoke.

"It's the essence of Sheram that's trying to embed itself into anyone who enters his lair; it's a case of if you can't beat them make them join YOU!" Scorpicle said flippantly.

Simsaa looked at him sternly "Scorpicle, why is everything a joke to you? You need to take things a bit more seriously, we are in grave danger and so is our world as well as Earth!" Simsaa sounded exasperated at Scorpicle. Scorpicle, for the first time since the children had met him, went quiet and did not retaliate with any smart comment. Amafiz glared at Simsaa, and she looked at him with the expression of 'What?' Amafiz turned to Scorpicle and said with absolute sincerity.

"Scorpicle I think Simsaa did not mean what she just said! We know that your jesting is just a way to keep our spirits up and to help us to stay positive, as I've said to you before and we appreciate what you're trying to do, but I think that before we go any further we need to recalculate our bearings and see if we can locate the Book of Quantime."

Dilyus took out the monocle that he had take from the ancient Stonimion artefacts at the Great Stone. He placed it on his eye and swivelled his head around whilst at the same time turning a full circle. He looked a strange sight; as if he was looking for something he had lost but was not quite sure if he had lost it on the ground or in the air. Suddenly he stopped moving and froze on the spot; the others stared at him as his face contorted into a look of horror. "I've found Sheram and I think we're too late, from what I can sense he is ninety nine percent close to opening the Book of Quantime!"

"We need to move fast, Dilyus did you get a feel for where he is?" Simsaa asked him, looking more concerned than usual.

"He seems to be on his own in some kind of large chamber; it could be his own quarters."

Scorpicle knew that he would be able to pinpoint Sheram due to the fact that Dilyus was able to point him in the direction of his room. He used his scanning system to locate Sheram and then focused his headlights in the direction of Sheram's room. The colour of his headlight changed from the normal white light into green, then blue and finally purple, at that point where the light hit the wall the Stonimions noticed that it started to change and where a moment before there was solid wall, they could now see straight through it and as they stared at the 'hole' in the wall they all gasped when they laid eyes on The Evil One!

They saw Sheram standing in his room with the book in his hand; they saw the book shaking and white light appear at its edges. They knew that Sheram was almost there, he was just one step away from his success and their doom. "We need to get hold of the book or cause some kind of interruption; we've got to do something!" Dilyus said with his voice ending in a crescendo.

Scorpicle looked at Nasami and said "Do you think you could use your telescope to get the book?"

"I could but I need to get closer as from this distance I don't think it's possible."

As part of his defence power Amafiz had the ability to produce maps of areas that they were in, the maps would then be able to show them the safest route to their destination by avoiding their enemies and other forms of danger. Using his bracelet Amafiz produced a map of Sheram's lair; it initially appeared as a wisp of light which slowly formed into a more solid looking piece of paper. As it manifested into a solid map it started to float towards the ground but before it touched the ground Amafiz caught it. They all gathered around it and saw it showed the key areas of the lair; "Map, show us how to get to Sheram's room please" Amafiz requested of the map. In front of their eyes a purple line started to appear on the map, it started from where they stood and finished at Sheram's room. "Okay kids let's go!" Scorpicle said.

The Stonimions sat inside Scorpicle and he turned on the invisibility system that covered his body; this system consisted of a special element similar to silver, which had the ability to reflect light, the element had been embedded into Scorpicle's paintwork in such a way that once Scorpicle activated the system the element particles were able to rearrange themselves in the paintwork to reflect light allowing Scorpicle to become invisible.

Scorpicle slowly moved towards their destination, for he may have been invisible but there was still the matter of noise. As they moved through the lair they all saw the immense size of the lair, the hundreds of strange creatures that belonged to Sheram and most of all they could feel the unpleasantness of the entire place. As they got closer to Sheram's room Scorpicle stopped suddenly; there was a room on their right that seemed to heave pure evil. Scorpicle moved closer extremely cautiously and as they passed the room they heard something rather abnormal. For a moment Scorpicle stopped outside the room and they all looked into the room. There they saw the strangest sight; they saw a haggard old woman sitting on the floor surrounded by weird little creatures that were prancing around her, there was also a circle of light and flames that emitted from the floor. As the creatures danced around the old woman the Stonimions stared at them, they saw that these creatures resembled toads with bird's wings and dogs legs; whilst they were dancing around her they were also chanting the same verses as she was and laughing hysterically.

"Who is that?" Simsaa asked to no one in particular.

"That must be Imfalin, Samaan mentioned her; the woman without a heart!" Dilyus said in a monotone voice that seemed empty and far away, for he was mesmerised by the scene he was watching.

"When you say woman you mean she's human, but how can she have no heart?" Nasami quizzed Dilyus.

"I don't know but that's what they call her." He replied.

"Let me explain" said Scorpicle "We use the term woman to really mean that she is what would be described on Stonidium and Earth, as a female, but she is thought to be from a different dimension to ours and her physiology is such that her physical internal anatomy is also different to ours and to that of humans."

"She sounds repulsive." Simsaa said with a shudder.

"She is Sheram's force; her evil intent is only known to her, however, together their intent seems to be to conquer both of our worlds!" Scorpicle exclaimed.

They watched and saw the light and flames intensify as the chanting and dancing increased in pace. Imfalin was swaying in a circular motion which also increased in pace; she was also breathing heavily, her chest was heaving as if she was finding it difficult to breathe. Suddenly they all stopped and Imfalin turned and looked directly at them. "Oh Oh! I think she's seen us!" Nasami said in a loud voice that made them all jump.

"No, I don't think she can but she has sensed us, we'd better hurry Scorpicle!" Amafiz said urgently.

Scorpicle doubled his pace, not because he was scared but just to get away from the gaze of the wretched old woman, she gave him the creeps, and he shuddered, even though he had no skin with hairs he felt as if he had goose bumps. As they moved further away from Imfalin and closer to Sheram's room the air seemed to thicken and although the Stonimions were sitting inside Scorpicle they felt a cloying sensation at their throats as if some toxic gas had penetrated into Scorpicle and was trying to kill them.

"What's that in the air? I'm finding it hard to breathe!" Simsaa gasped. Amafiz understood that this was obviously another of Sheram's defence mechanisms, he produced a protective casing around them that was semi permeable; it allowed air into them but would detect and stop any particles that were associated with any unfamiliar form of evil magical incantations. Slowly the air around them cleared and they could breathe easily again.

They finally reached their destination and were ready to retrieve the Book of Quantime from Sheram. Scorpicle stopped outside of Sheram's room; he scanned the entrance to the room to make sure that there were no nasty surprises awaiting them, it was clear. He slowly rolled into the room, it was empty; but they could all hear a muffled noise from a chamber within the room. Scorpicle turned towards the direction of the noise and cautiously headed towards it. "I think you guys should get out and be ready!" the Stonimions stepped out carefully; they were armed with their cloaks, bracelets and stones poised to produce the appropriate response that would defend them. However, there was no attack; there was nothing but the muffled noise and a white light that was filtering into the part of the room they were in. Amafiz stepped forward and carefully opened the door to the chamber from whence the noise and light was coming from. The five of them took a step back because of the sight that confronted them; they knew at that moment that once again they were too late, as they stood staring at Sheram and the opened Book of Quantime.

10

THE VIOLATION

Farmoeen stood upright with such a jolt that she nearly tipped over the dining table. "What's wrong?" Samaan asked as he went towards her, arms outstretched, to catch her if she happened to keel over. Farmoeen's eyes were wide like saucers and her breathing was fast but shallow; she looked as if she was going into hyperventilation. The other elders all stood up, there was something very wrong and they knew it.

"He's done it, that evil being has opened the Book of Quantime by force!" Farmoeen looked drained as she spoke, the usual elegant and poised oracle with her auburn long locks, rosy cheeks and deep brown eyes look decidedly dishevelled as if she had not slept for weeks. Despite her current appearance Farmoeen was still majestic in her demeanour, for her kind were very rare; their outer body may have been similar to that of humans but they were a special form of Stonimion who had changed form because she had been initiated to the ultimate level of power and granted the position of oracle, one with powers that were destined for only the use of good against evil.

When the news spread about the Book of Quantime there was pandemonium for a while, many of the Stonimions were angry, some confused but the majority were concerned about the current situation. The question on everyone's mind was whether or not they had made a grave error in thinking that those four young Stonimions were actually the 'Four Guardians of Stonidium'. Samaan heard the whispers that were going around and became very angered and upset that the Stonimions had questioned and doubted his authority and ability. He would defend his decision and actions to the death for he knew he was not wrong, he needed to make the Stonimions understand that Sheram was powerful, more than they had imagined and that he would stop at nothing to carry out his evil deed. It was imperative that they as a people now came together and reassembled their forces and renewed their tactics for the next step in the battle.

There was an emergency meeting, again, held in the village square, there was a gentle murmur of noise amongst all present, each involved in a conversation that had its own thoughts and conclusions about what was actually going on.

"We have to prepare for the worst!" Samaan was straight to the point; there was no time to sugar coat the situation; on hearing this statement the noise amongst the crowd increased.

"Exactly what do you mean?" asked one of the Stonimions "We have prepared our defences and their children are dealing with Sheram I'm sure" he said pointing with some sarcasm towards the parents of the 'four guardians'.

"If it's true that Sheram has accessed the Book of Quantime then it's not just a case of being under attack by his hoards, he will use the book to change events in the past and there is no knowing what he will do exactly and what will be the effect of this on our world or Earth." Samaan looked extremely solemn as he spoke.

"The Stonidium that we know the Earth that we know and protect could be no more, could be very different, we don't even know if any of us will be affected, some of us may not exist anymore!"

On uttering this Samaan turned to the other elders and took them inside the village meeting room. He explained to the elders that they needed to leave written parchments as instructions for whoever still existed or any new Stonimion that would then exist because of changes in space and time. Without any delay the elders started on the task set by Samaan, they ensured that alongside the old scriptures of the Stonimions they wrote down all of the current events, about the Book of Quantime, the 'four guardians' and what Sheram had done. Once these had been created Samaan took the new parchments to the Great Stone and placed them carefully with the other ancient scriptures. He walked outside of the Great Stone and stood in front of it and raised his arms; slowly a pale blue coloured vapour appeared from Samaan's stone. It rose slowly and encased the whole of the Great Stone; Samaan had a fine bead of perspiration on his furry forehead as he had to use a lot of energy to create this powerful incantation. The pale hue combined with the mountain's colour and the Great Stone's colour changed slightly and it now glowed with a tint of mauve. Samaan had made sure that whatever the future would be like the Great Stone and all the knowledge of the ancient Stonimions would be safe and accessible to the Stonimions. The protection was such that changes in time and space would not change or affect the contents of the Great Stone in any way.

Samaan returned to the village and informed them all of what he had done. His revelation helped them all to breathe a sigh of relief, because at least now there was a glimmer of hope that even if Sheram did succeed in changing history and their worlds, there was a chance that those in the new present would be able to rectify Sheram's evil actions.

Farmoeen took Samaan aside and spoke to him out of ear shot of the elders and other Stonimions. "I'm worried about the children; I'm unable to make any form of contact with them!"

"They're probably inside Sheram's lair which means that there will be powerful forces preventing any telepathic communication, they are dedicated to their mission and are probably trying to stop Sheram as we speak." Samaan was trying to console Farmoeen but was doing a poor job because inwardly he too was worried about the 'guardians' and how they were dealing with Sheram and the opened Book of Quantime.

For a moment time seemed to have stood still, it was then that the four guardians realised it actually had, it was the effect of the book. Sheram looked at them intently; he shook his head as if to say 'why did you even bother?' There was a deep rumbling sound that originated from the book; it started to shake violently in Sheram's hands. Dilyus turned to Amafiz "What's happening to the book?"

"It's being opened using force and evil force at that, the book's reaction is something that no one has experienced before, but it can only be bad." Scorpicle advanced towards Sheram; he instantly raised his hand towards Scorpicle signalling him to stop.

"Don't even think about it!" he warned him, the Stonimions decided to follow Scorpicle's example because they were not going to be intimidated by Sheram.

Sheram knew that if he delayed any further then he could be under attack and even if they did not succeed in stopping him he did not want to prolong his victory any further.

Without a word of warning Sheram screamed "nineteen twenty one here I come!" and stepped onto the book; Sheram disappeared into the white light and as he was disappearing Nasami saw Sheram's hand still poking out of the book it was ready to grab the end of the book but with lightening speed Nasami closed it shut.

"That was quick thinking and excellent reflexes!"

Nasami looked at Amafiz and said "Thanks!"

"Yeah well done, if Sheram had grabbed the end of the book he would have taken it with him and caused more mischief." Scorpicle said. "Now that he's gone we'd better get back to the main village as Stonidium may change or could be more dangerous."

The five of them turned around to leave the room and Sheram's lair when they froze on the spot. At the door way stood Imfalin; she stared at them, her rotten old worn out face was twisted into an obscene looking grin. "You're doomed!" she cackled like a mad woman possessed and with that she raced towards them poised to attack, with her little creatures and many of Sheram's minions following suit. Amafiz touched his amethyst stone and produced a force field that stopped them in their tracks. They rebounded off the shield as if they were rays of light being reflected off a mirror, as soon as there was a moment they got back into Scorpicle who then disappeared from vision.

They needed to get to a safe spot as soon as possible to teleport away from the lair, Scorpicle was unsure if Sheram's absence would mean some of the defences and force fields that did not allow them to teleport would still be in place, but it was worth a try; just to get away from that hideous place. The invisible Scorpicle, along with the 'four guardians' drove out of Sheram's room and retraced the original path they had taken; they were almost back to their starting spot when they were confronted by an awful sight. There in front of them stood a huge abomination; it had eight limbs, two heads that resembled frog's heads and a giant jelly fish body, it lumbered towards them ready to engulf and destroy them.

Scorpicle knew that it was now or never; he did not need to get to a high speed to teleport as he was not going into another dimension or world, so he just activated his teleporter and vanished from Sheram's lair, leaving behind the bedlam, noise and evil that were celebrating their current victory.

The five of them arrived back in the village to find the Stonimions scurrying around, each busy with something to do. Samaan saw them and took them all to the main hall where the Stonimions parents were helping with new incantations. Samaan explained to the four guardians what they had been doing because of their fears of things changing due to Sheram's activities.

It had been a long day and all of them were exhausted, the four guardians because of their encounter with Sheram and his hoards and the rest of the Stonimions were shattered due to the preparation of the protection needed from Sheram's 'new future'. They all went to sleep that night and slept soundly, not because they had no worries but because of sheer fatigue.

11

THE BEGINNING OF THE END

Sheram landed unceremoniously in the dark alley; for a few minutes he was dazed and unsure where or when he was. He rose slowly and gathered himself; he was disappointed when he looked at his empty hands he had been so close in bringing with him his prize, but those incessant nuisances had intervened again. "Never mind" he thought he would still be able to carry out his plan, if he was not able to get back to Stonidium or Earth in the future, if his device to contact Imfalin was not successful, he knew exactly what he was going to do to affect their future.

Sheram headed towards the east end of London, he walked down one of the many dingy dark streets, his target, an old man who was to him a very important pawn in his plan. Sheram knew no mercy; all he knew was that for him to succeed in his plans the old man needed to be eliminated. He understood fully the ripple effect in time and space and after carrying out many researches using all his powers he had made a list of those that would affect his plans. Sheram knew all too well that killing too many people would be extremely risky and bring him unwanted attention; so he had pinpointed the most effective killing to ensure that everything else would then fall into place. Getting rid of him would mean that further down the line he would be able to enter into the world of politics and influence the way the world existed. His desire to rule had no limits and neither did the actions needed to achieve those desires.

He arrived at his destination; it was an old dilapidated terraced house, he could hear laughter coming from nearby, it sounded like the maniacal laughter of a crazed old woman. It grated on his nerves and caused him such a distraction that he forgot why he was there, all he could think about was stopping the annoying laughter. He raised a hand towards the direction of the laughter and started to squeeze his outstretched hand; as he was doing this in mid air the sound of the laughter began to change, there was a gurgling sound which turned into a choking noise. There was a scream from a male voice, a scream of fear, shock and helplessness as he watched his beloved choking and dying in front of his eyes. Suddenly it stopped, and the woman was breathing again, Sheram could hear her taking in large gulps of air as she tried to get her breath back. If it had not been for his ultimate plan, Sheram would have finished her there and then, but it occurred to him that if he did not stop then maybe the alarm would be raised for help and he may not be able to get to his true victim. It was vital that he was removed tonight.

Sheram knocked at the door, as casually as if he was a family member paying a quick visit. He waited for what seemed like an eternity and then he heard a voice. "I'm coming, just wait!"

The door opened slowly and an old head cautiously peeped around the corner of it. The old man looked at Sheram, not quite sure what to make of him; he was an odd looking stranger, who looked as if he had not been fed well and was suffering some kind of deficiency disease. "Yes, can I help you?"

"Hallo, I'm looking for Frederick Stephens; I'm from Nelson & Nelson Solicitors" Sheram lied.

"Oh yes! And what would I be wanting with solicitors?" asked the old man. "I ain't got no estate that I'd be wanting to leave to anyone!" he snorted with a laugh.

"Actually it's the other way around, may I come in to explain in more detail?" The old man was intrigued; he was financially in a grave situation and the thought of getting some money was too inviting to ignore. Little did the poor old man know that he had invited his own death into the house; as he looked at the street outside, to ensure that no-one was looking, he closed the door with a smile on his face which was immediately removed as soon as he turned around and saw Sheram's arms raised ready to attack.

The removal of this human was far too easy for Sheram; humans had no powers of defence and all it took was a single blast of energy from his hands to obliterate the old man. Sheram looked at the pile of dust that was left behind. Frederick Stephens did not know why this stranger had attacked and killed him so violently, he did not realise that a single comment he would make in passing to a complete stranger would, in the future influence British politics. The comment would be passed on like Chinese whispers and would eventually reach the ears of a young influential businessman; causing him to enter the world of politics and so on. The ripple effect would lead to certain decisions being made that would shape the future of the Earth, however, with one gesture from Sheram's hands everything had changed, the old man was no more, his casual comment had never been made to the stranger in the pub, there was no passing on of the comment, no entering into politics of the young businessman; the future Earth's new path had now been established.

Sheram did not want to arouse any suspicion so he created a simple note stating the old man was fed up with the landlord's threats about eviction and had left with his few belongings to try and start a new life elsewhere. Sheram left the house as calmly as he had entered it, no remorse, regret or embarrassment at his actions. In fact it was another of those rare occasions where he had a slight smile on his evil face; it was a sickening sight indeed.

Time passed and so did the years pass but Sheram stayed the same; he did not age but quietly watched the repercussions of his action and waited patiently; he waited for the right moment to 'enter' into the world and execute his wicked plan. Sheram soon incorporated himself into the world of power, where he ascended in rank, removing anyone that got in his way. There then came a time when Sheram knew he could trust some of the humans who had become very close to him and were fully involved in his evil plans; the time came to invade the rich countries, where there was oil, copper, natural gas and other resources that would provide wealth and ultimately power. The political structure of Earth had changed dramatically compared to before Sheram's interference; most of Europe, the Americas and the Middle East were under a new regime's power, that of Sheram's or as he was known to the humans 'Samuel Watson'. Sheram's business accolades meant that he influenced those countries that had wealth; he controlled the major businesses in the world and enslaved those that opposed him and for many the enslavement that they had to endure was worse than death; indeed, Sheram was not just hated by those who had not joined his evil forces, but also feared.

Sheram was the ultimate dictator, whereby, he did not just ensure that he had the wealth of different parts of the world, but also total control over the lives of the humans who were resident in those countries. Slowly his power became so supreme that he had possession of ninety five percent of the world's land mass and wealth, his statues, pictures and emblem of his political party were prominent everywhere. The dictatorship was such that any opposition would inevitably lead to death if enslavement did not break those against Sheram, but despite his success he had still not revealed himself completely to the humans; they still thought of him as just another over-bearing controlling clever businessman with an overt interest in politics.

Sheram was truly happy but not completely, for there was still the question of Stonidium and, its conquer, then and only then would he be truly happy; the question that remained on his mind was how to get back and reign Stonidium and get vengeance on those who had been against him.

Sheram knew that there would have been some changes in Stonidium, as the different dimensions of the Universe were connected and changes to one world and dimension would have an effect on others. He was not going to have true peace of mind until he had conquered all that had been against him, their pain would give him pleasure; torturing them would reduce the pain and anguish he felt at being rejected and isolated. Sheram was a twisted soul who had been unloved by all who encountered him, including his parents. It is unclear whether those that encountered him came to dislike him because of the evil they could sense in him or whether their behaviour led to his evil nature. It was unfortunate that Sheram had never learnt how to forgive as this led to a lot of bloodshed on the new Earth.

Whilst he was in authority, Sheram made sure that those who had caused him grief before had been eliminated; for Sheram had returned home to Earth. Those that had known him, albeit as a child, lived only for a short while to regret having crossed Sheram's path.

12
THE SIGN OF THE TIMES

The morning seemed like any other, there were the usual dew drops on the grass of the forest floor, twinkling like tiny diamonds that seemed to have been scattered all round, the small creatures of the forests were stirring and the Stonimions still existed. However, things were not as before, the structure of the land had changed, those in charge had changed and the Stonimions were the not the free beings they had been before. For many of them this was normality, this was the life they knew and they did not know any better. There were, however, some who remembered everything, from before Sheram had stepped back into Earth's past.

The Stonimion village was now overrun with the Mangras; they lived in small sections within the village area, where each group of Mangra's had built small barricades to stop Mangra's from other groups entering their territory. They were very strange creatures, indeed, for despite having such a close mental connection, they were extremely unsociable. Further out, on the outskirts of the ex-Stonimion village the remainder of Sheram's hoards resided; these consisted of the strange creatures that Sheram had created whilst he was in Stonidium, they had remained, despite the absence of their creator, for one reason only; Imfalin.

Imfalin knew that there would be serious changes and reper-cussions due to Sheram's return to the past and, similar to the Stonimions, she too had placed powerful incantations to protect Sheram's hoards and herself; she knew she could not afford to lose any of them as then any success in the conquering of Stonidium would become too difficult.

The reality of the situation was that in Sheram's absence Imfalin had managed to succeed in conquering more of Stoni-dium than he had; but on closer inspection her success was not entirely her own, for the changes that had occurred amongst the Stonimions because of Sheram and the Book of Quantime played a crucial part in the present state of Stonidium.

The Stonimions did not have any powers; the changes to Earth had infiltrated into Stonidium and brought about many changes one of which was the loss of the Initiation Stone. The legend was that it had not been destroyed but had been hidden by an evil force; the evil that had done this, the one and only Imfalin. During ancient times there was the Great battle of the Stone, where the Great Stone had been attacked; the ancient Stonimions had managed to save the Great Stone, however, the Initiation Stone had been captured. Imfalin knew that for complete victory over the Stonimions taking the Initia-tion Stone would mean that future generations of Stonimions would not be able to access their powers, this would mean that the 'Four Guardians of Stonidium' would not exist making Sheram's success easier. Imfalin had hidden the Initiation Stone deep within Stonidium and had placed a protective incantation around it so that it could not be found.

The absence of the Initiation Stone had been a terrible loss and had created many generations of Stonimions who had no understanding or knowledge of power. This had led to them becoming over powered by Imfalin and the 'evil ones' hoards and for many Stonimions this led to a life of enslavement and misery.

Despite all the things that had gone wrong for the Stonimion race, there were a few who had managed to escape the effects of the present Stonidium. Samaan, the elders and Farmoeen had managed to create a form of protection from everything that had happened and of course Scorpicle being made of non living material was not affected. The only problem was that the strength and intensity of the protection was not enough to enable them to protect any more of the Stonimions.

They were all inside the Great Stone sitting at the table of wisdom; they knew it was around the right time to gather the Stonimions and reveal the past. It had been far too dangerous to do this before as they had all been vulnerable and suffered a lot at the hands of Imfalin; all this time they had been waiting for the right moment, the time when the 'Four Guardians' had come of age.

"We need to use all the devices we have within the Great Stone to locate the Initiation Stone and empower the 'Four Guardians of Stonidium'. The others all looked at Samaan as he spoke. Farmoeen stood up and turned to the crystal of knowledge that she had summoned just prior to the meeting. "We also need to inform the other Stonimions about our search; they need to understand the urgency of what we're doing and how important it is that we all pull together in this search." Farmoeen was about to turn to the crystal of knowledge, when she was interrupted by one of the elders.

"Is that wise?"

"Is what wise?" Farmoeen asked.

"Telling everyone else about the Initiation Stone!" she explained. Samaan looked at the elder, "Why do you think it wouldn't be wise? They need to know what we're looking for and why; it's time now for everything to be out in the open!" he exclaimed.

"I'm not sure what their reaction will be, for many generations the Initiation stone has been missing and the Stonimions have been without their powers, many of them don't know of the original past that existed and that the Stonimion race was a powerful one; I don't think they will be happy about the fact that the Initiation Stone could have been taken back many generations ago and that they may have suffered unnecessarily at the hands of Imfalin, when they could have had the powers to stop her!"

For a few minutes they were all quiet pondering the comments just made by the elder. Samaan spoke up "Tarim, you have a valid point, but I think you underestimate the honour and self respect of the Stonimion race; I believe that if we explain to them why we hadn't revealed the possibility of getting back the Initiation Stone then they'll understand completely."

Scorpicle had been listening intently and despite his high levels of intelligence he too had not quite worked out why

Samaan, Farmoeen and the other elders had not tried to retrieve the Initiation Stone sooner.

"Forgive me Samaan but I was wondering as well, why you didn't try and get the Initiation Stone back sooner, Tarim is right, the Stonimions will want answers!"

Samaan turned to Scorpicle and understood fully his remark. "My dear Scorpicle the answer to this dilemma is simple, we will tell the Stonimions the truth, and the truth will always prevail.

Tarim spoke again "And what is the truth that you will tell the Stonimions?"

"Simply that we could not risk trying to get the Initiation Stone and failing, and that only the 'Guardians of Stonidium' would have the best chance of retrieving the Stone, I'm afraid that they will have to accept and understand our decision, because it was by far means not an easy one." Samaan replied in a slightly irritated voice.

The next day the elders cautiously went to the houses of the Stonimions that were hiding in the various parts of Stonidium; the message was simple, to get to the Great Stone as soon as possible. Samaan and Farmoeen had decided that they would go in person to the homes of the 'Four Guardians' and they took Scorpicle with them.

The first house they got to hidden in a far corner of the forest was that of Simsaa. Samaan nervously knocked on the door and then courteously took a step back as they all waited patiently. It seemed like a very long time until anyone answered the door, but eventually someone came. Faraan very cautiously opened the door and left it ajar as he stepped out onto the threshold; he looked at the group at his door and became very nervous. He could not understand why the Chief Elder and the Oracle were at his house, accompanied by the strange mechanical being known as Scorpicle.

"Hallo Faraan, we've come as a matter of urgency, may we come in?" Samaan stepped forward towards Faraan as he spoke. Slightly bewildered Faraan could only smile and reply "Of course you may, please do." With the verbal welcome Faraan showed them into his home. Simsaa and Zarani were sitting at the dining table, wondering who had interrupted their evening meal.

As the visiting party walked into the dining area Simsaa and Zarani stood up; Simsaa was taken aback at the sight of Scorpicle, letting out a slight gasp. Scorpicle turned to Samaan and said "This is like déjà-vu!" and grinned. Samaan knew exactly what he was talking about and smiled back at him. Faraan gestured to them to take a seat and as if obeying an order they all dutifully sat down, except for Scorpicle of course, who just stood next to them.

"I'm not sure where to start, so the best thing to do is to start at the beginning!" explained Samaan. "This life that you have is not the true life you had before; there was an evil being in Stonidium called Sheram who managed to get his hands on a powerful device that enables its owner to travel in time and in any dimension; it's known as the Book of Quantime." Samaan paused to allow them to absorb the information so far; he continued "When Sheram got hold of the book he went back in time on Earth and whatever he did there had an effect on Stonidium as well.

At this point Zarani interrupted Samaan. "I'm sorry Samaan,

that's all well and good and thank you for explaining to us how we got to our current predicament, but why are you telling us?"

"Sheram was close to being stopped from his hideous plans by the 'Four Guardians of Stonidium, but he proved to be too conniving and cunning; however, if anyone can reverse what has happened it would the 'Four Guardians' and we need to help them by getting their powers back."

Faraan was the one who interjected Samaan this time. "I'm sorry Samaan but this still doesn't make sense as to why you're all here to tell us this, if this Sheram is as powerful and as dangerous as you say there's nothing we can do!"

"Yes there is, the Stonimions are a powerful race, look at your belt and your stone, it may be just a plain looking piece of rock, but that's because Sheram's number one side kick stole and hid the one thing that could give you your powers 'The Initiation Stone', so once the 'Four Guardians help to get the stone back everyone else can get their powers too. This brings me to the key reason as to why I am here with Farmoeen and Scorpicle today."

At this point Samaan stood up and faced Simsaa. "Simsaa, there's only way to say this and that's to be direct, you are one of the 'Four Guardians' of Stonidium."

No sooner had Samaan finished his sentence than Simsaa and her parents all burst into laughter. They were in stitches and continued for a few minutes until they realised that the guests in their house were not laughing and that this comment from the Chief Elder had not been some kind of joke. It occurred to them that their reaction had been rather immature and they all looked rather embarrassed.

Faraan spoke up "I'm really sorry Samaan, we did not mean to be so disrespectful, but what you just said was a bit of a shock and just seemed like a bit of a joke."

"Samaan please tell us more, how do you know this and who are the other three guardians?" asked Zarani.

"Well, the 'Four Guardians' are mentioned in the ancient Stonimion scriptures; their story is quite clearly given, that there will be four Stonimions who will display an unusually high ability in their powers, they will be the ones to defeat the 'Evil One' who would cause great problems in Stonidium and on Earth."

"Okay, but what makes you think that Simsaa is one of them?" Faraan asked reiterating his wife's question.

This time Farmoeen spoke up, "We know because before the Book of Quantime was taken and the Stonimions still had their Initiation Stone, Simsaa and her three friends; Amafiz, Dilyus and Nasami underwent their Initiation and the acquisition of their powers. It was during this ceremony that an incident showed Samaan that these four were the Guardians of Stonidium and indeed, they had been on a mission but unfortunately the evil force they were up against outwitted them."

What makes you think that my friends and I can be successful now, if we failed before?" Simsaa spoke for the first time since the visitors had arrived.

"You will succeed, you have to!" Samaan simply replied. He then explained to her parents that they were gathering as many of the Stonimions as possible to get their help in locating and retrieving what was rightfully theirs. "We need to get moving now Faraan, Zarani as we've got to explain to the others about all of this and get the Guardians ready for their quest that's ahead of them."

With that they left Simsaa's house, leaving them all with a sense of confusion, dread, excitement but most of all hope that things were going to change. They soon arrived at Amafiz's house and the convincing started all over again. As they left Amafiz's house, Amafiz and his parents stood at the door to see off their guests. Akjam looked intensely at Scorpicle and said "Did you know about this?"

"What you mean about Amafiz being one of the Four Guardians? Yes but I couldn't say anything to you until the time was right, I'm sorry." Scorpicle said looking upset at having to lie to his friend all these years.

"I understand Scorpicle please don't feel bad." Akjam replied.

Scorpicle looked at him with great fondness and said "I hope the 'Four Guardians' are able to reverse everything so that we can get back all the years we enjoyed as a free nation."

With that he turned around and rolled away quietly, sighing deeply at the loss of all the good times they had enjoyed. Scorpicle who was usually very laid back and bore no animosity towards anyone or anything, at that moment truly disliked, abhorred and even to an extent hated Sheram for what he had done to the land he had called home for such a long time.

Once they had visited the homes of the remainder two guardians, the now tired party returned to the Great Stone. Samaan turned to the other two and said "I think we should try and rest now, tomorrow is going to be a busy day and we will need to be alert and full of energy." They all said their good nights and entered into their temporary quarters that they were residing in inside the Great Stone.

In her room Farmoeen sat down at table that was set in the centre of the room. It was a brilliant cobalt blue stone that sparkled in the light of the electrical precious stones that were dotted around the room. Stonidium's connections with Earth had given them many benefits, such as, electricity. She was tired but she could not sleep so instead she summoned the Crystal of Knowledge.

"Hallo Farmoeen", no answer "Farmoeen?"

"Oh I'm sorry Crystal; I was away with my thoughts"

"The recent events have caused you a lot of distraction." The crystal replied.

"Are you surprised?" said the exhausted Farmoeen. The crystal pulsated gently and gave off a shimmering light that constantly changed in colour.

"How can I help you Oh wise oracle?"

"My dear friend I need as much insight as possible into the kind of places Imfalin could have hidden the Initiation Stone, it's our only hope to try and get things back as they were!"

"Give me a little while, Stonidium is quite vast and Imfalin is bound to have placed some kind of incantation around the Stone to stop it from being found too easily." The crystal said.

"Of course, and I too will start my own search as well, thank you Crystal."

Farmoeen ended the telepathic link with the crystal and started her search for the Initiation Stone. Her first port of call was her map of Stonidium; she laid it out on the table in front of her and closed her eyes, slowly she moved her hands across the map of Stonidium. Her intention was to try and sense any large surges of energy in any places where they should not be; as she was moving her hands over the map she detected energy pulses around what had previously been the main village within Stonidium, this was as expected as Imfalin and her minions now resided there. She also sensed a huge energy surge where the Great Stone was situated and also in a hidden part of Stonidium. She assumed this to be Sheram's old lair; Farmoeen was not sure but it seemed likely from Scorpicle's description of the surrounding landscape of the lair and her knowledge of Stonidium. This was a place where the Stone could possibly have been hidden, but the question was would Imfalin hide it there because it seemed obvious not to?

Farmoeen carried on throughout the night, searching carefully every nook and cranny of their world, the inhabited areas as well as the uninhabitable places; places that contained unimaginable creatures that could harm, maim and kill at the blink of an eye. She had finally come to the end of her search and found seven areas that were possible hot spots as to where the Stone could have been hidden.

Samaan was in his house when the telepathic link from Farmoeen established itself. "Hello Farmoeen, is everything ok?

"Yes, Samaan I thought I should let you know that I have found seven possible sites for where the Stone may be hidden."

"Samaan, I was wondering; if I was able to 'possibly' locate the Stone without too much difficulty then why didn't we do this before? Did we make a mistake?"

"I know Farmoeen, it's a good question, but I think we both know the answer to that, I don't think we would have any chance of getting to it without enormous casualties because Imfalin would have it heavily protected. He paused for a moment deep in his own thoughts and then continued "I still believe that our only chance are the skills of the 'Four Guardians'; even without having their powers activated they will be successful because they have shown enough skill and innovation, where I think they will be able to get the Stone back, with Scorpicle's help of course!"

The next day the four youngsters arrived at the Great Stone with their parents. Samaan greeted them and took them inside; he gestured to them to take a seat, and reflected for a moment about the fact that this was definitely strange going through this whole process all over again. However, he knew that it had to be done, so once again he explained to the four young Stonimions and their parents about the incident with Nadrog; that Farmoeen had mentioned. Samaan also told them that the 'Guardians' had been very near to success and that the restoration of their powers would ensure that Sheram's mischief would be undone.

He again, asked the youngsters to choose from the powerful devices, as they had done before, and as he expected they chose the exact same powerful devices; this told him for certain that they were going to receive the same powers and knowing this convinced him even more that this time Sheram would be defeated.

As they left the Great Stone, there was an eerie silence; the creatures that normally inhabited the surrounding forests were silent, even the plants of the Great Forest were silent; it was as if nothing existed anymore, not even the air. Samaan turned to the others and said something but all the others saw was his mouth moving and no sound was coming out; there were no particles the entire place was like a vacuum, in fact as they started to move further away from the Great Stone their breathing was becoming more laborious. Simoo who was slightly ahead of the rest of the party, dropped like a stone; one second she was moving the next she just fell to the ground. The four youngsters sprang forward and grabbed her by the arms and rather unceremoniously dragged her back towards the mountain.

"Quickly we need to get back inside the Great Stone!" Samaan said as he herded them all back into the mountain. It took them a few minutes to get their breaths back; Samaan checked them all to make sure they were fine and gave Simoo some medication, which was an elixir extracted from a flower that grew on the sides of the Great Stone, a flower that was able to change its scent and colour once every hour. "Here drink this, it's the juice of the rungscent flower, make sure you drink this water as well as the juice can make you very thirsty too." Samaan cupped her head in one hand whilst he gave her the medicine.

Nasami who had been quietly watching his mother being tended to suddenly spoke with such vehemence in his voice the others became startled. "This is the doing of Imfalin isn't it?" he seethed through gritted teeth. "I will not have my family, friends or people placed in danger." He looked at

Samaan and said "We need to get the Initiation Stone back now!"

Samaan understood the young Stonimions anger, hurt and helplessness, and he was right they had to do something fast as Imfalin seemed to be getting stronger and more powerful each day. Somehow she had found out that they were at the Great Stone, highly likely it was her nasty little minions that scurried around Stonidium like the vermin that they were.

Samaan went back to the inner part of the Great Stone and found an old cloaking apparatus that would shield them from any magical and physical afflictions. The apparatus looked very similar to a useful tool on earth – the umbrella, but this was not to protect from rain, the skyla, as it was called, once opened looked like a giant mushroom; which then cocooned them all when they stood underneath it. Once safely inside the skyla, they slowly walked out of the Great Stone; the skyla was transparent so vision was not a problem, however they could not hear anything.

They were almost near the Great Forest of the Stone, as it had been known when the Stonimions had had possession of the Initiation Stone, when there was an enormous juddering sensation, running through the skyla. Akjam turned around and saw a small army of Imfalin's minions running towards them, throwing weapons of various forms, like stones, knives and spears. "We need to run!" screamed Akjam, which resulted in the entire party running as fast as they could, with the intention of getting inside the forest which would hope-fully provide some kind of temporary shelter. The moment they stepped into the Forest of the Stone, there was an enor-mous flash of light that blinded them all, causing them all to fall over into a big heap. The sound of the minions running towards them had become deafening as they all lay upon the ground.

"What happened?" Miloun asked to no-one in particular. She was holding her head as it buzzed with the effect of the light, fall and the stampeding minions.

"Where are they? Simsaa asked as she looked around where they had landed. The others looked around too astonished that they were on their own.

"That's strange they were there just a few seconds ago, how could they have disappeared so instantaneously? Dilyus quizzed.

"It was me! I was tracking Imfalin and her minions and realised that she had sent them to the Great Stone I knew they would try something like this; I was ready for them but needed them to be near enough so that I wouldn't miss. They all turned around to see Farmoeen standing nearby; she seemed to glow with an iridescent light that emanated in all directions around her giving her the appearance of an ethereal body. She looked exquisite.

Samaan stood up and slowly walked over to his friend; he put his arms out and laid his hands on her shoulders. "You're amazing Farmoeen! And your timing is impeccable." He smiled gratefully at the wise oracle. Samaan looked at the rest of the group and said "we'd better get back to their homes and start the search for the Initiation Stone straight away." Farmoeen took that as her cue and transported them all back, for her powers were different and not activated as the Stonimions' powers were; her powers were active from birth.

Back at their homes the four young Stonimions, their newly acquired instruments of self defence and Scorpicle were ready to set off on their mission. Farmoeen had handed them her map with the seven locations, where it was possible that Imfalin had hidden the precious stone, showing; the possible locations in red. "Each time you go to one of the locations it will then turn blue, which will not allow you to double back to the same location twice, which will hopefully save time; something that we're extremely short of!" explained Farmoeen, "You must go carefully as each of these locations could also be a trap because I'm sure that Imfalin knows that we'll be searching for it."

"Don't worry! Farmoeen we may not have our true powers yet, but, I think that we are pretty well prepared and believe me we've understood that we shouldn't take anything for granted after what happened at the forest." Amafiz said. Farmoeen smiled and nodded her understanding and essentially her acknowledgement of their ability to succeed. She bid them good bye and left them with wishes of good luck.

13
THE SEARCH FOR THE STONE

The five of them began their journey with a heavy heart because a lot of hopes were depending on their success and the four young Stonimions were dubious about their success because from what they could gather from Samaan and the other elders, they had not been successful the first time around. Scorpicle knew that the youngsters were nervous and setting out on this difficult mission with great trepidation, he knew that it would be up to him to help them as much as he could to ensure that this time they would succeed.

They said their goodbyes to their parents and left their homes in a rather sombre mood. Scorpicle was not going to have this, he decided that if these children were going to have any chance of succeeding they would need to change their mental attitude and if it meant corny jokes then so be it.

During the first hour or so of their journey, they were on foot with Scorpicle slowly rolling beside them, as each moment passed Scorpicle became more and more uneasy in terms of the atmosphere amongst the young Stonimions, so he decided to cheer them up. "Do you guys remember the first time you saw me! Man your faces were so funny, and you Simsaa, you fainted!" he snorted. They all stopped in their tracks and looked really puzzled. "I don't remember Scorpicle, you've always been there, I mean our families have always known you." Amafiz said.

"Wow your memories are terrible, come on! The first time you all saw me was at your initiation in the Forest of the Stone." He beamed at them all. Dilyus looked at him with a serious look on his face and simply said "What initiation?"

Scorpicle could have kicked himself, instead of cheering them up he had made it worse, for now they were probably feeling like they had lost out on getting their powers- which they had and worse still had no memory of life as before.

They continued with their journey and eventually stopped as night had fallen. They had all been walking but Scorpicle advised them that to be safe they should take refuge inside him and he would use his invisibility device to hide them all from their enemies and potential attack. They obeyed Scorpicle without any arguments and settled down for the night.

The four weary Stonimions were at the start of their journey but were already mentally and physically exhausted. Each in their own thoughts, each one could not understand their state of being. Scorpicle knew! He knew that they were feeling like this because of the immense negative energy that was surrounding them; the evil that penetrated throughout Stonidium was bound to affect them, however, he knew that the intensity of the evil had increased; almost in anticipation of the pending conflict to come, the conflict between good and evil, the conflict that would finally decide the fate of Stonidium, the Stonimions and the Humans.

"Aaaaaaggghhhh!!!!!!" the scream startled Scorpicle who jumped, or to be more precise, his wheels jolted. To all intense and purposes he had nodded off, but the truth was the conscious mind that existed in his electronic software had switched off. The Stonimions woke with a start and for a few moments sat and stared at each other, not knowing where they were or why they were there.

They looked out the windscreen and saw their parents, but the sight of their parents did not fill them with joy, as they were being tortured by hideous looking creatures that seemed to have no solid form. The torturers were slipping and sliding between their parents, leaving trails of a luminescent teal coloured slime, slime that scalded and burned the fur and skin of their parents. The scream they had heard was of their parents' pain and agony every time a fresh bit of slime caressed their pain stricken bodies.

"How did they get here? And what are those things? Amafiz asked horrified.

"I don't know, but I'm not waiting in here and watching them being hurt like this, it's time we fought back- powers or no powers. As he said this Nasami was about to open the door when Scorpicle shouted. "Wait!"

"It's a trap!"

"How do you know?" asked Simsaa.

"Why have your parents been brought right to this spot? How do they know we're here?" Scorpicle replied.

They had no reply, but were not totally convinced by his argument. Scorpicle continued "This is very strong magic and the environment is filled with hallucinogenic incantations that will tap into your thoughts and use them against you!"

To prove his point he emitted a grey coloured smoke towards their parents and the slimy creatures that were afflicting them with excruciating pain, as the smoke covered them the four friends saw the strangest sight unfold before their very eyes. Their parents and the creatures seemed to merge into one entity that pulsated; the image swirled around and around until it imploded into nothing. There was an eerie silence within Scorpicle and their external surroundings.

"What just happened?" Simsaa asked no-one in particular. "A lot of what is to come by the looks of it, and something we have to be prepared for!" Amafiz replied. With that he produced the map Farmoeen had given them, he studied it for a few moments, then spoke "This area is one of the spots that Farmoeen marked as a possible site for the Initiation stone, so I'm thinking that if there are powerful incantations here they could be to hide something important!"

"How did we know to come here?" Simsaa questioned.

"I believe the map is not just a visual guide but also a physical one, it's literally dictating to us where to go!" Scorpicle replied.

"I'll scan the area and you Dilyus search the area for any undesirables from Imfalin's mob that may be lurking!" Scorpicle instructed. Dilyus nodded and took hold of the monocle he had chosen at the Great Stone, and placed it carefully over his left eye. Dilyus stared intently out of the windscreen for any signs of other beings when his demeanour changed; his breathing became deep and laboured. Suddenly he stopped his deep breathing and started short sharp intakes of breath, his breathing became dangerously fast and the others began to worry that he may faint; Dilyus had had his head hung down towards his chest but in one swift movement he straightened his head, so that he was staring ahead at nothing in particular, and had also raised his arms in front of him. "There!" he said, "I can see you and I can control you" Dilyus spat out the words with such vehemence that the others sat back in shock. They had never seen the timid and docile Dilyus display such hatred and anger, which made them realise that something was not quite right.

Slowly Dilyus turned to look at them all; his eyes were black as the midnight sky and showed a rage that was alien to the good natured Stonimions. "Get out all of you!" Scorpicle screamed, the Stonimions, except for Dilyus, did not need to be told again and at Scorpicle's instruction they scrambled out of the vehicle with such haste that they stumbled over each other and fell out of Scorpicle.

They stared at each other as they lay sprawled over the ground. "What happened to Dilyus?" Nasami asked looking as if he was ready to be sick.

"I think Dilyus has been possessed" Simsaa replied nonchalantly.

"By what?" he asked. That was the question that frightened them all the most.

Inside Scorpicle the atmosphere was becoming more and more putrid. As Dilyus breathed heavily a nasty pungent green coloured gas was pouring out of his mouth and nose, a gas that was filling up the inside of Scorpicle and penetrating through his circuitry and very soul (his conscious being). Scorpicle shuddered and spluttered as the fetid gas diffused through him and knew that he would have to act fast otherwise he too would be infected as was Dilyus.

Scorpicle searched his data bank of powerful incantations, ones that Farmoeen had programmed into his system; within seconds he had found the one that would be the best in this situation. Scorpicle addressed the being that had possessed Dilyus by saying "You are in danger if you do not vacate this body straight away!"

"Hah! What do you think you can do to me? You pathetic tin can" Dilyus hissed at Scorpicle,

"Don't say I didn't warn you!" Scorpicle said and with that he started the invocation "I ask you once, I tell you twice, leave this body or else pay the price!"

Dilyus laughed hysterically. "What absurdity was that?" "You enemies of Imfalin are ridiculous, why she thought you might be a threat is beyond me?"

Scorpicle felt a rage and hatred that he had never experienced before, but he also realised that this entity was stronger than he had anticipated and mere invocations would not be enough to remove it from Dilyus. He was also outraged that this foreign being had invaded this innocent young Stonimion and then had the nerve to mock him and his friends. Scorpicle knew that he would have to be brave and not hold back, but he desperately hoped that what he was about to do next would not permanently harm Dilyus. Scorpicle mustered up all his energy and channelled it into his antennae; he aimed the antennae into his body and straight at Dilyus. "I'm sorry Dilyus I hope this doesn't hurt too much but I have no other choice" Scorpicle said apprehensively. The last thing Scorpicle, and the other Stonimions standing outside watching with great anticipation, heard was an overwhelming pulsating noise that seemed to crescendo into an unbearable booming sound, followed by an evil laughter that quickly changed into an agonised scream.

The silence that followed was more frightening than the initial boom and scream they had been exposed to. The three Stonimions looked at each other not quite sure what to do next; they looked at Scorpicle and were horrified to see an acrid, dense smoke, which was changing through a medley of colours, emerge from him. They took a step forward and then hesitated still unsure of what to see or expect. As they inched forwards towards Scorpicle there was a sudden noise and a strange looking being fell out of Scorpicle. They gasped at the strange sight but as it dawned on them as to what they were looking at they each began to smile, smiles which eventually turned into smirks and giggles of laughter.

"What's so funny?" the strange looking being said to them. Amafiz took the creature by its arm and showed it Scorpicle's wing mirror. "Aaagghhh! That's not me!" It screamed.

"I'm afraid it is Dilyus!" Nasami laughed.

"Nice hair style!" Simsaa giggled.

"Scorpicle what have you done to me?" Dilyus screamed

"I'm sorry Dilyus, I had no choice. Look at it positively at least you're alive!" Scorpicle beamed sheepishly.

To say that Scorpicle's surge of electrical energy had left Dilyus slightly singed would be an understatement. Dilyus looked as if he had been unceremoniously estranged from his fur, placed in a hot oven and basted for a good few hours; he was not a pretty a sight, but as Scorpicle had quite correctly stated, Dilyus was lucky to be alive.

"Don't worry Dilyus, we'll find some plant ointment in this nearby forest which will help with your healing, my mum's quite a good herbalist and she's taught me a lot about some of the natural healing properties of the plants in Stonidium." Amafiz said trying to sound as positive as he could whilst staring at Dilyus.

"I hope you're right Amafiz, and stop staring at me!" Dilyus said unhappily.

"Sorry Dilyus" Amafiz apologised.

"Scorpicle, is it safe now? There aren't any more beings around that might attack or possess us are there? Amafiz asked.

"I've already scanned the area and there's no undesirables around that must have been the only one here, and that's the one that must have been showing as a power source in this area, well one down six to go!" he replied.

Amafiz walked into the forest looking for a small plant that his mother had once showed him that had phenomenal healing properties. He remembered he had managed to severely burn the back of his hand and his fur had singed so much that his skin was showing, he also remembered how when she crushed the plant with water and applied it to his hand within a matter of minutes his hand had completely healed, so much so, that his fur re-grew and there was no pain either. He knew that for them to complete their mission successfully they all needed to be in the best of health, but also he could not bear to see his friend in such a bad state.

Amafiz had searched for about twenty minutes when he finally spotted what he had been looking for. He ran over to the small plant that was wedged in between two large smooth stones that looked like enlarged pebbles. The plant itself was rather strange but very beautiful at the same time. It had a long thin stem which had square shaped leaves which were perpendicularly placed on either side of the stem at regular intervals. The flowering part of the plant was truly the most amazing looking feature of it and it also contained the true healing properties he wanted. The flower consisted of a brick orange square base from which protruded a multitude of petals that had the appearance of birds' feathers. They showed the colours of the visible light spectrum, from the red to violet wavelength, however, each one was not just one colour but intermittently changed colour and glowed iridescently.

Amafiz carefully picked three of the plants and took them back to Scorpicle. He placed them into a container that resembled a mortar, but was made of glass and was oval in its shape. He slowly ground the plants with a metal pestle and as he ground the flower he slowly added water until it turned into a smooth purplish looking paste. Amafiz turned to Dilyus and said "This may sting initially but within seconds the pain will go, the chemical properties in this plant not only heal wounds but also numb them."

Dilyus looked horrified "If you think that I'm going to put that horrid purple mess all over me just to experience some more pain, you've lost your mind!"

Dilyus you'll be fine!" Nasami said trying to sound reassuring.

Scorpicle interrupted "You have no choice Dilyus, unless you like looking like a chicken whose had an argument with an open fire and lost!"

Dilyus looked defeated and submitted himself to being covered in the ointment. He soon realised, after the initial squeal of pain that it was working and his pain soon subsided, as well his hideous wounds, which started healing up, and to his joy, the return of his fur.

Dilyus' possession and recovery had exhausted them all, so they decided to settle down for the night and resume their quest for the Initiation Stone the next day. Stonidium could be described as Earth's twin, where its days and nights were similar to that of Earth's, the nitrogen level in its atmosphere was on par with Earth's giving it the same beautiful blue sky and it too had a magnificent star that provided energy for the sustenance of life, albeit, some organisms being rather stranger than others, they all depended on the energy provided by their 'sun'.

Luckily for the Stonimions and Scorpicle the darkness that had fallen had no new surprises for them, allowing them to get a peaceful night's sleep. They awoke the next morning refreshed and ready to continue with their quest, however, there was the question of breakfast before they could even contemplate setting off. Nasami volunteered to find breakfast from the forest, as he had often gone into the forests with his father on camping expeditions. His father had taught him all about the most nourishing of forest plants that could be eaten. Nasami soon returned to his hungry friends laden with a huge variety of foods to eat. The four friends tucked into the tasty fruits and other edible plants and it was only once they had started eating did they realise how truly ravenous they were.

After breakfast, Scorpicle looked at the map he had scanned into his computer system, Farmoeen had coloured the various locations that they were to investigate, red, and their current location, was now blue; he also drew a line through it signifying it being crossed off. He looked at the four Stonimions and simply said "Time to move on!"

The map they were following was a paper version of a satellite navigation, thanks to Farmoeen's powers. She had installed a system where, the map would direct them, as they had discovered from the first location they had come to without even realising it was one of the hotspots. It felt as if they had been travelling for days as they had reached an extremely barren looking area of Stonidium. It reminded Scorpicle of tundra's on Earth and as he mentioned this to the others a question arose from Dilyus – "How do you know?"

"Erm well, I'm a well travelled vehicle you know!" Scorpicle replied, the others all looked at each other, they knew he was hiding something but they could not work what or why. Scorpicle came to a halt near a large shrub, the only one that was around for as far as they could see. The Stonimions stepped out gingerly, almost ninja style, looking around them, fervently ready for any form of attack that could occur. There was nothing, not even a breeze, nor any sign of life, animal or plant, except for the tree.

They stood still back to back looking three hundred and sixty degrees all around, the eerie silence was unnerving but they stood their ground, the lack of noise was not going to scare them. Scorpicle scanned the area for energy sources that may have been hidden in this vast vacuum; there was nothing, not even any areas of heat energy let alone any other type of magical or more powerful energy. "Nothing, not an iota of energy anywhere, this is truly the dead zone" Scorpicle exclaimed. "The question is if there are no energy pulses then why did the map bring us here?" Scorpicle continued.

"Is that where we are? I've heard about this place, nothing exists here, but how come there's that single tree?" Amafiz quizzed Scorpicle.

"That's a very good question, let me check my databank to see if there's any information on this tree" Scorpicle answered.

Whilst Scorpicle searched through his databanks the others dared to venture further into the area known as the dead zone, but they had only gone a few feet when Scorpicle called out to them. "Guys, hurry back we've gotta get outta here!" They all hurried back to Scorpicle and as they climbed into Scorpicle they heard a wailing that started to crescendo into a scream. Scorpicle went into light speed mode and left the area in a split second, and if he had not done this they would all have been shattered into tiny atoms that would have simply dissipated into the surroundings.

They ended up many miles away in another part of Stonidium, Scorpicle, once again, crossed off another of the locations. "Well we won't be going back there again!" Scorpicle retorted in his usual humorous manner. They sat in silence too shocked to ask what had just happened, so Scorpicle decided to enlighten them anyway. "Children, we have just had the pleasure, and I use the word very loosely! Of witnessing the reason why the dead zone is DEAD! That was the 'Screaming Shrabny' a strange plant that produces energy pulses replicating a scream, but one that causes molecules to vibrate at such high speed that it causes living matter to explode."

"Two questions Scorpicle! One if it sends out pulses of energy then why didn't you sense the energy on your radar and secondly, why did Farmoeen send us here? Simsaa asked shocked at the thought that they could have been completely obliterated.

"Well, Farmoeen obviously had this place on the map because of the energy waves she picked up, she probably had some idea about the Shrabny but we cannot overlook any possible area and as for me, the Shrabny was not giving off any energies until it started the wailing and it was at that precise point I had found out what it was and when the energy being generated registered on my radar I realised what was about to happen."

"Whoopee do yaay for the fast thinking Scorpicle!" Dilyus' sarcasm was duly noted by all. Scorpicle was used to sarcasm and knew how to respond "That's okay you can thank me later!"

"Sorry Scorpicle I think it's the shock, I'm not having a good day so far!" Dilyus apologised realising he was being unduly ungrateful. No-one was annoyed with Dilyus' attitude as it was too hard to be angry at someone who still looked such a mess.

"Well at least we didn't have to waste too much time at the dead zone!" Simsaa commented.

"Always the optimist!" Nasami grinned. He turned to the others and gestured for them all to exit Scorpicle.

"Where are we going Nasami? I don't think we're in a hot spot at the moment!" Amafiz questioned Nasami's decision to get out of Scorpicle.

"I think you'll find it is" Nasami replied as he turned back and pointed in the direction of the map, which was showing a pulsating spot. "Am I right Scorpicle?" he asked the vehicle.

"You are indeed!" Scorpicle smiled "and the energy pulse is pretty close by" he added.

"Well let's hope its third time lucky, but knowing our luck we'll find the Initiation Stone in the last place, it's like when you're looking for something in a pile if you start at the top it's at the bottom, but if you start at the bottom its near the top! Amafiz exclaimed.

Simsaa giggled "Is that why you're always late for everything?"

"Ha Ha very funny!" Amafiz retorted.

The four Stonimions and their vehicle walked slowly ensuring that they did not overlook any area and miss the possible location of the stone. They scanned the vicinity but after a while realised that there was nothing to hint a possible energy source. "I think the maps broken!" Dilyus said looking completely serious. Scorpicle snorted as he laughed at Dilyus' comment. "Don't be silly Dilly!" this made the others smirk but Dilyus did not look very pleased about his new nickname.

They were about to admit defeat and go back to look at the map again when an unusual noise stopped them in their tracks. "I don't like the sound of that!" Nasami exclaimed even before they had turned around to see what was making the hideous noise.

As they turned the atmosphere around them thickened and they all looked at each other in slow motion. "Whaaaaat isssss gooooiinnng oooonnnn?" Simsaa asked, surprised by the sound of her own voice, for not only were their movements slow and sluggish but her voice was the same, she sounded like an old cassette tape being played really slowly.

During this strange phenomenon only Scorpicle seemed unaffected by whatever was obviously affecting the rest of them. Scorpicle realised that the entity making the noise was also causing this strange affliction and that it did not affect non-living materials like him!

Scorpicle realised that the Stonimions reduced speed   left them exposed to attack, but before he had time to warn them or think about how to protect them, they had become surrounded by a thick orange cloud. He watched in horror as the four friends collapsed around him and started to slowly shrivel, as if all the water was being drained from their bodies. Scorpicle knew he did not have much time; the state of the young Stonimions was such that they were of no use to him or themselves. Escape was not going to be quick enough and even if he managed to get them away from here   the effect of the orange cloud could still be present and essentially killing them. There was only one answer; to destroy the source of the cloud. He looked straight ahead towards the source of the strange noise and saw the most peculiar sight he had ever seen, and he had seen some weird things in his time.

Scorpicle looked straight into the eye of the strange abhorrent creature in front of him and gasped. The orange cloud was being emitted from an opening at the top of what could only be described as its head, although it looked more like a misshapen frog. The creature had one bulging eye that protruded outwards and pulsated as it looked around and a large blue bulbous body that was oozing a thick orange liquid through various pores that covered it's body; the sight was quite overwhelming and for Scorpicle the decision was simple, destroy it!

Scorpicle aimed his laser towards the frog shaped head and more specifically the bulgy eye and fired with the highest power setting he had; the destruction was not a simple obliteration of matter but a complete vaporisation of the entity leaving nothing behind but a few wisps of blue and orange vapour that dissipated into the surrounding atmosphere. As soon as the orange cloud diminished in its strength the four young Stonimions began to recover from their dehydrating ordeal; they slowly stood up and their bodies began to absorb the moisture in the air around them. This absorption was enough to give them the strength to walk back to Scorpicle to replenish their dry bodies completely by drinking plenty of fluids summoned from their ever plenty food supplies. Another reason to be grateful to the oracle Farmoeen, who had provided them with an instrument that, could produce emergency sustenance. She had advised for them to use it only when absolutely necessary and when there was no other available food or water source, as its ability to supply these was limited; but now was a good a time as any considering they had been shrivelled into prunes.

"I don't know how much more I can take of this, one place after another, one or all of us are afflicted in some way! Nasami exclaimed totally exasperated by the entire situation. They all looked at him with complete empathy but they also knew that their entire world and the Earth, although unknown to them, were also relying on them to succeed and put everything back as it had been before the selfish and evil Sheram had ruined everything.

"Well don't get disheartened, we're nearly half way there and although we've had some close shaves, we're all still intact" Scorpicle said cheerily but wary of Dilyus and his still strange demeanour.

"Notice how he didn't look at me when he said that!" Dilyus pointed out to the others, "That's coz I have not really come out of this situation fully intact" He exclaimed.

"Ah! Not at the moment but you will heal and be totally intact, well physically anyway, your mental state is a whole different matter!" Simsaa remarked.

Dilyus was too tired to retaliate but realised that this was probably revenge in Simsaa's part for his earlier comment, so he just smiled and acknowledged her, by nodding his head continuously, that she had got her own back.

They sat inside Scorpicle for a while and mulled over their next move; they ate supper and contemplated if there was any way they could be prepared for any surprises that awaited them in the next location, but they soon realised that even if any of them had minds as warped as Imfalin's, they still would not have been able to anticipate what other types of attacks she had planned, ready and waiting for anyone trying to find the Initiation Stone. The only conclusion that they all came to was a unanimous one, in terms of keeping their chances of survival high, and that was to make sure that they had their artefacts, from the Great Stone, ready as soon as they arrived at the next location, especially Amafiz's glass globe which could be used in conjunction with Scorpicle's defence mechanism, seeing as Amafiz had not acquired his own powers yet. The day's events had left them more fatigued than when they had started so they settled down for the night.

The next morning, Scorpicle had just presented the map for them to examine and see the next hot spot to go to, when Farmoeen's face appeared out of nowhere. They all jumped and gasped at the vision, their reaction spooked Scorpicle as well. "Sorry children, I didn't mean to frighten you!" Farmoeen's ethereal vision said. "I just wanted to find out how you've been getting on; I can't keep this link with you for too long as it can be dangerous for you."

"We're okay apart from Dilyus who has suffered from a possession, but he's okay now, aren't you?" Amafiz questioned Dilyus, who nodded humbly.

"Farmoeen, we're being directed by your map to possible locations but the energy pulses are mainly because of some affliction or incantation being left by Imfalin." Simsaa explained.

"I'm sorry children, but with all the evil magical obstacles put into place by Imfalin this was the best I could do, please just be careful and may you be successful in your mission." Farmoeen sounded upset that she had been unable to help them and sensing this sadness Scorpicle spoke up.

"Don't worry Farmoeen, we will be successful and careful." As soon as Scorpicle spoke these words the link was broken and Farmoeen's beautiful face disappeared as suddenly as it had appeared.

"I don't feel alone anymore!" Nasami said to everyone's surprise. They then realised why they had been feeling so heavy hearted, it was the thought of being alone, away from friends and family that had made them so pessimistic, the sight of Farmoeen had lifted their spirits and invigorated their desire to defeat the wicked Imfalin and ultimately Sheram.

They left for the next destination without a single word, each quietly trying to reach deep within themselves for that extra bit of energy and courage to complete the mission they had been given. A short while later they arrived at a mountainous area of Stonidium that reminded them a bit of the area where the Great Stone was situated; not just because of the mountains but also the fact there was some sign of life. They could hear birds and other similar flying animals singing, they heard the rustling of animals moving through the nearby forest, it felt good to be so close to other forms of life again.

The Stonimions stealthily exited Scorpicle ready for the potential danger that could confront them. Wary of their surroundings they headed towards the area that the map indicated as the location of a large surge of energy. Inwardly each of them wished deeply that this would be the place where the Initiation Stone had been hidden by Imfalin, however, with every step they took towards the source of energy they lost a bit of their hope as it became apparent that this place did not conceal the Initiation Stone.

"This place is too peaceful and serene; it doesn't seem to have an air of malevolence like the other places did." Amafiz commented.

"And we haven't been attacked yet, usually by now something would have happened." Dilyus added, still looking slightly dishevelled as his fur was growing back here and there. The medicine that Amafiz had applied was good but Dilyus' injuries were so severe that it was taking a while for him to recover.

"The question is if there aren't any of Imfalin's nasty surprises here and the Initiation Stone isn't here either, then what's giving off the energy surge?" Simsaa questioned.

Simsaa's question was soon answered as they stepped further into the forest ahead of them. As they walked through the medley of trees they came across a perfectly round patch of grass. It was a bright purple in colour and dotted with small orange, red and blue coloured flowers whose petals were rhombus like in shape. In the middle of the patch of grass sat a group of small yellow coloured feathery creatures and it was these that were singing like birds. Although they had feathers and sang like birds they looked nothing like other birds that they had seen in Stonidium before; they had plump round bodies and small limbs with hands and feet, their heads were square in shape with big round blue eyes, round red button noses and a large smiley mouth.

"What an odd looking creature!" Scorpicle remarked.

"That's an interesting comment coming from you!" Nasami said as he gave Scorpicle a sideways glance and a look that said 'you know I'm only joking'.

They all walked closer to the creatures and saw that they were all sitting around a small pool of water; they were all swaying from side to side as they sang. Suddenly they stopped and turned in unison to look at the party of strangers that approached them. One of the yellow creatures stood up and looked at them intently and as it stared at them its eyes grew wider and wider until they looked as if they would pop out of its head. The creature turned around to its companions and said "The Four Guardians of Stonidium have arrived!" on hearing this news the remainder of the creatures stood up and cheered wildly.

The Stonimions and Scorpicle all stared at each other not quite sure what to make of this strange sight and indeed, reaction from these strange looking creatures. The one who had stood up before noticed the puzzled expressions of the party that had arrived and so proceeded to explain to them what was going on. "My name is Otlan, and I am the leader of the Yatlows. We have been expecting you for a long time and you have arrived as it was written."

"Why were you expecting us?" Amafiz questioned Otlan

"We have been told by our forefathers that in a time after a time the Four Guardians of Stonidium will come to the Yatlows and we will show you the way!" Otlan said in an excited voice.

"Come, come this way and see." Otlan held aloft his hand and gestured to them all to follow him. He led them to the pool of water and pointed at it. "Look into the Waters of wisdom and see what you seek." As they all looked into the water they saw a copy of the map that Farmoeen had given them and it clearly showed the possible locations of the Initiation Stone. "Ask the waters to show you what you seek!" Otlan instructed them.

"Waters of wisdom we seek the Initiation Stone of the Ston-imions." Amafiz looked into the pool of water as he spoke. There was a rippling within the waters and as they all stared at the map in the water one of the locations let out a light which projected an image of the Initiation Stone in mid air right in front of their eyes. "That's the sixth location on the map; at least we've been saved some time and probably pain!" Dilyus said smiling with relief.

The search party thanked the Yatlows and set off for the sixth location, hopeful that they would now be successful, but mindful that if this is where the Initiation Stone was, Imfalin would not have left it unguarded. They knew that they would need to be fully prepared with all the physical strength and powerful weapons that they had. Scorpicle used his speedy teleporting device to stop anymore time from being wasted; the faster they could retrieve the Stone, the faster they could restore power to the Stonimions.

They soon arrived at the sixth location on the map; it was unlike any of the previous locations or anywhere else on Stoni-dium. "I suspect that this place is so strange in appearance because it's protected by some heinous magic." Scorpicle said as he scanned the desolate looking area. The four young Ston-imions stared at the place where the Stone was located; it had no colour, all they could see were varying shades of grey. There were large rocks and boulders scattered around the area as if they had been thrown there by giant hands, in the distance they could see some odd looking plants, trees that had roots waving in the air, flowers that were growing hori-zontally and amidst all of these absurd looking objects they saw a giant rectangular black box.

"I wonder where the Stone could be?" Dilyus remarked, as he pulled a face indicating that he was not the cleverest Stonimion around. The others laughed at Dilyus' face and also the fact that he was right, it was extremely obvious as to where the Stone was hidden, but that made the situation more dangerous as it meant that Imfalin was so confident that the Stone could not be retrieved that she had not even bothered to disguise its location.

Dilyus took out the monocle and placed it on his left eye; he looked around and spotted a strange looking animal scurrying amongst the rocks and boulders. Dilyus stared at the animal and, with the help of the monocle, caused it to steer from its path and towards the black box. The small creature was within ten feet of the black box when it was blown into smithereens and simultaneously vaporised by the unseen force field that was obviously surrounding the black box.

"Oh dear! I wasn't expecting that to happen, otherwise I wouldn't have sent that poor creature towards the box." Dilyus exclaimed looking really upset.

Scorpicle asked "What did you expect to happen then?"

"Well I thought it might have triggered some sort of alarm system that might have manifested another strange creature that could have attacked us!" Dilyus replied rather bewildered.

"Never mind Dilyus you meant well, and in times of war there will be sacrifices I'm afraid." Simsaa said reassuringly.

The others all patted him on the shoulder to tell him that he had done the right thing. The question was, however, how to get to the Initiation Stone? There was a long silence as they all pondered about the next move, when Scorpicle gave an excited cry that made them all jump. "I think I know a way we could get the Stone without being annihilated!" he said as he turned to Nasami, who looked decidedly nervous about what might come next. "Nasami, where's your telescope?"

"Here." Nasami replied as he removed it from the pouch that was tied around his waist.

"I know you don't have any powers, but this telescope itself is quite powerful and if we all concentrate we could use it to lift the black box out through the force field." Scorpicle explained.

"Sounds like a plan." Simsaa nodded in agreement with Scorpicle's idea.

"I'm sorry to spoil your idea Scorpicle but if we do manage to lift the box, we don't know the height of the force field and if the box is destroyed then the Stone could be destroyed too!" Amafiz said.

The cheery mood suddenly dissipated as they all realised that Amafiz was right. Once again they were silent as they all tried to think of a solution to their problem. This time Amafiz had an idea. "Scorpicle you have a pretty good defence system, can we use the globe I got from the Great Stone to enhance your cloak around us so that we might be able to get near the box?" Amafiz questioned Scorpicle.

"I think it could work, but we need to be prepared for what might happen once we get near the box, I still don't think getting past the force field will be our only problem, but one step at a time!" Scorpicle replied.

With that comment he proceeded to display, in mid air, some

powerful incantations for the Stonimions to use against any undesirables they could come across and increased the power of his weapons. Scorpicle gingerly crawled towards the black box, with the Stonimions safely sitting inside him; he felt that their forces would be more intensified this way. He reached the outskirts of the black box, being mindful of the scarred area where the creature had been obliterated. Scorpicle turned on his defence shield and Amafiz produced the globe; he held it aloft and said out aloud "Globe do your thing!" The others looked at him as if to say "Are you serious?" Amafiz shrugged his shoulders, "I don't know, what am I supposed to say then?" Whatever Amafiz said did not seem to matter because the globe started to emit a bright light as he held it up high. The light penetrated throughout Scorpicle, seeping into every atom of the vehicle and amalgamated its power with Scorpicle's defence shield.

Once they were surrounded by the shield, Scorpicle slowly entered into the danger area and at that moment sparks flew, whilst simultaneously they all heard a massive explosion, but felt nothing. They passed over the threshold and were just a few feet away from the black box; they had succeeded, but it was not over, they saw through the windscreen that at the moment they crossed the safety threshold a giant figure emerged from the ground. It stomped towards them and its intentions were quite obvious - their destruction. Scorpicle moved out from its path in lightning speed and as he turned around to face the creature they saw it in its entirety; it was like a giant eel but with huge feet and paddles for arms, it was half orange and half blue like a mutated lobster. For a lumbering giant the creature was able to move quite quickly and it started to move towards them at a faster pace than any of them had anticipated. However, Scorpicle was faster and within an instant he had aimed his laser, powered it to its fullest potential and fired at the horrendous creature.

There was an almighty explosion and a light so bright that it blinded them, for a moment they were stunned and dazed; slowly the light faded and there in front of them stood the Initiation Stone. It was beautiful and radiant. "Magnificent!" Simsaa said in total awe of the Stone.

"Okay let's go home!" Dilyus as always was straight to the point.

"There's one thing I don't understand, what happened to the black box?" Nasami questioned.

"I reckon that the black box was connected to that creature and when Scorpicle destroyed it the box was destroyed as well" Amafiz answered.

"I thought it may have been more difficult to get, I mean I was expecting more powerful guarding of the Stone." Simsaa said.

"Maybe Imfalin thought that what she had left was enough, but she didn't count on our hero Scorpicle!" Dilyus said with a huge grin on his face. They all looked at Dilyus and burst into laughter; with that they left for the Great Stone and home to their loved ones.

14
THE RE - INITIATION

The four guardians of Stonidium and Scorpicle returned to their familiar haven with the Initiation Stone, safely carried in the force field that surrounded Scorpicle. To stop any more time from being wasted Scorpicle used his fast teleportation system to take them back. Their arrival was welcomed by eagerly awaiting parents, Elders and the Stonimion race. Before they had left for home Scorpicle had made a telepathic link to Farmoeen and informed her of their success and pending return home. The news had spread like wild fire amongst the Stonimions; of course, great secrecy was still adhered to as they could not afford for Imfalin and her hoards to get any hint of what had happened, they needed to make sure that they returned the Initiation Stone to the Great Stone without being intercepted.

As they appeared inside the Great Stone, there was an almighty cheer from those present and a sigh of relief from the parents was like voile falling gently on the Stonimions and encasing them in a shimmering happiness that could never be expressed in words. The four young Stonimions ran into the arms of their eagerly awaiting parents; who hugged them so tightly that it seemed they would never let them go.

After all the greetings and welcomes came to an end, Scorpicle presented the Initiation Stone to Samaan. Samaan gently placed the stone on the hovering platform placing his hands on one side of the stone and loudly spoke out to the Stone and all those present. "Oh Great Initiation Stone of our forefathers, you have been parted from the Stonimions by the evil present in our precious land, you have returned to us, show us your power!"

It was as if Samaan's words were the switch that turned on the power for the Initiation Stone, it juddered slightly as if the power surging through it was making it shiver with cold. Then they all heard it, a beautiful voice so eloquent and calming that it brought a smile to all their faces. "It is good to be back amongst you all, it has been too long and I think it's about time that the real Stonimions were returned to the land of Stonidium, let us begin the initiation ceremony immediately!"

Samaan proceeded to prepare for the initiation of the Stonimions present at the Great Stone, and then the plan he had was to slowly bring small groups of the rest of them to be initiated.

"Who will go first?" he turned to the crowd of Stonimions as he spoke, they all looked around at each other, eager to access the powers that was their right, but too polite to admit that they wanted to go first.

"I think it only fitting that the Four Guardians of Stonidium go first." All eyes turned towards the voice of the Oracle, Farmoeen,

"I think I know why you're called the Oracle, you're smart!" Scorpicle grinned as he looked at Farmoeen. She in turn just smiled serenely and simply said "I know!"

One by one each of the Guardians stepped into the stone, first was Amafiz, the others witnessed the spoken words of the Stone, the coloured smoke that was emitted, the glowing lighting and the emergence of Amafiz with all his powers. "Ooohhhh! Look at his stone" remarked Simsaa. All eyes instantly turned towards Amafiz's belt around his waist and they saw that the plain opaque stone was now a beautiful amethyst stone that glowed and emanated radiance that was second only to the inside of the Great Stone. Once the four Guardians had been initiated and had received their battle armoury, the rest of the Stonimions present were initiated as well.

It was a long process that took all night, but no-one complained; the Stonimions had waited far too long to be bothered by a further small delay of a night. By morning the group of Stonimions at the Great Stone had gained the power that was their birth right. They were a new born invigorated race that finally fully understood who they were and realised exactly what they had been robbed of all these years. Their disgust, anger and hatred of Imfalin had increased tenfold; they were ready for revenge and to return Earth and Stonidium back as it should have been.

Over the following few weeks trickle by trickle the remainder of the Stonimions were initiated, but all had to take great care not to reveal their stones or powers to any of Imfalin's hoards, for surprise was their biggest weapon. It had been agreed by the Elders that they would not plan any form of attack until they were all prepared in every single way and the most important and urgent factor was to get the Book of Quantime and return the two worlds back to their original historical Sheram free form.

Once news had got around that all the Stonimions had been initiated there was a silent celebration amongst them all and an eager anticipation of what was to happen next. For the four Guardians the wait did not last much longer, Luman had been sent by Samaan to each of them. As Luman sat in Amafiz's home nursing a cup of drimble tea that Salani had made from the drimble flowers she had been growing, Amafiz sat in front of him staring at him as if he had never seen him before in his life. Luman started to feel a bit uneasy and ended up smiling nervously. "Sorry to stare Luman" Amafiz said as he realised how rude he was being "I was admiring your stone, it's a very unusual colour"

"Er! Yes it is, it's a cross between purple and orange, but that's not the real reason as to why you're staring at me is it?" Luman said.

Amafiz grinned and shook his head "No, sorry I was just trying to make conversation, I wasn't really staring at you Luman, but I was just thinking about what news you may have for me?"

"Well let's wait till your father returns home and we will discuss it fully then. Luman smiled. Salani returned from the kitchen laden with snacks and nibbles she had been preparing for the guest. Luman stood up to help her with the heavy tray she was carrying. "My word Salani, there really was no need for all of this, I cannot stay for too long anyway!" Luman expressed looking concerned at the amount food she had just presented him with.

"Nonsense, it's only a few snacks!" Salani replied.

Amafiz laughed "Sorry Luman mum's idea of a few snacks is the equivalent to a feast for anyone else!"

"Cheeky!" Salani said as she grinned at her son knowing he was absolutely right.

As they tucked into the snacks Salani had made, Akjam eventually returned home, entering his house wearing an extremely cheery demeanour until he saw Luman. "This is getting to become a habit!" he commented rather sarcastically."

"What is?" Salani asked looking confused

"These visits from the Elders" Akjam replied in a rather hostile voice.

Luman looked very embarrassed, but said nothing, for he knew Akjam very well and knew him to be a very polite, gentle and strong Stonimion, however, he also knew that Akjam loved his son dearly and the thought of putting him in danger time and time again was getting beyond bearable. Indeed, that would be the case for any parent.

The silence over the next few minutes was overwhelming and extremely awkward but thankfully it came to an end when Akjam sat down with a thud and like a sulky child who had not got his own way said "Ok Luman what's the plan?"

Luman explained that he was only there to pass on the message to them that their presence was required at the Great Stone in two days. Amafiz was to make sure he had all of his battle armoury and additional artefacts that he had acquired from the Great Stone. "This sounds ominous!" stated Salani, "Does this mean that Amafiz will be going on his mission from there then?" she asked nervously, knowing what the answer was but still in the hope of hearing something different, her hopes were dashed when Luman nodded to indicate that she was correct.

Two days later they were all present at the Great Stone, including the other Guardians and their parents, Samaan, the Elders and Farmoeen. Samaan stood in front of some of the people present and began his explanation of the Elders decision as to the next step in the restoration of peace and the riddance of Sheram.

"Well, my dear friends; the time has come, hah! If you pardon the pun!" no one batted an eyelid, Samaan coughed and spluttered as he continued "Anyway, as I was saying, the time has come to retrieve the keys and use the Book of Quantime to release Earth and Stonidium from Sheram." Suddenly there was a giggling and sniggering coming from the party of people gathered there. Everyone turned towards the sound and looked intently at Dilyus. "Sorry, I just got the pun about time & the Book of Quantime!" he explained looking rather sheepish. There was a mass rolling of the eyes towards the sky and shaking of heads.

Samaan continued quite unperturbed by the interruption. "As I was saying, the next step for us is to get the keys, or should I say the next step for the four Guardians is to get them". With that he turned towards them and gestured for them to come forward. The four friends gingerly stepped forwards until they were distinguishable from the crowd of people. Samaan looked at them with great affection and admiration, he knew that what they were about to embark upon was far riskier than anything that they had been through so far. Samaan addressed the Stonimions stood before him. "I would be grateful if you could all say your farewells to the Guardians because before the night is done I need to prepare and instruct them for the quest ahead of them".

On his instruction the Stonimions stepped forward and started saying farewell to the four friends and one by one departed from the Great stone as they did so, their minds full of trepidation and hope for a return of the world they had but could not remember. Each of the Guardians looked at their parents as they slowly approached them, they could feel the anxiety of their parents, their concern, but most of all the deep love they had for their children. Not a single word was uttered, as it was not needed; they simply took their children into their arms and held them as tightly as they could and for as long as they could. Eventually Samaan interrupted them by saying "I'm sorry everyone but it's time for you to go and for me to brief the Guardians on their mission.

With heavy hearts the parents slowly parted from their children, each one deep in thought as to whether they were doing the right thing. However, they knew that they had no choice because life could not carry on as it had been since Sheram had abused the Book of Quantime.

Samaan smiled at the four young Stonimions and asked them to sit down at the stone table, Farmoeen was also present.

Amafiz stared at Samaan and asked point blank "Are we going to get back alive from this quest?" The others were slightly taken aback by this blatant form of questioning, but Samaan did not flinch, instead he replied quite simply "My dear boy I truly hope so because if you don't then we're all doomed".

Samaan sat down with the youngsters and began telling them about the four keys needed to open the Book of Quantime; Farmoeen sat and listened patiently, thinking about when she had explained it to them the first time, before everything had changed. When Samaan finished he stood up and looked at Farmoeen for approval, which she awarded in the form of nod. "Wow!" was all that Nasami could respond with. "So, these keys are all over Earth and we've got to find them?" Simsaa confirmed in the form of a question. "Really! Searching for something- that's new!" Amafiz exclaimed sarcastically. "Sometimes I wonder if we're going to do anything else apart from look for things." Dilyus added.

"What else were you expecting to do?" Farmoeen questioned gently.

"I think my dear you'll find that when there are occasions when you may have to do something 'different' you may wish for the mundane searches!" she stated.

"I didn't mean it badly, Farmoeen, of course I don't want any of us to be in danger, but I'm just aggravated about getting to Sheram and putting a stop to his evil ways." Dilyus explained. The rest of the young Stonimions nodded their agreement, and the two adults could understand their frustration. "This is why you need to keep your wits about you as there is no room for error, once you're on Earth any mistakes will become known to Sheram and he will not show any mercy on any of you!" Samaan sounded dramatic but they all knew he was telling it as it was. "Anyway, I've full briefed Scorpicle, so he will be taking you to Earth using his accelerated transportation system and Akjam has installed a fully informed map of the Earth, which of course, Farmoeen has weaved her power into; it should be able to give you some clue as to where possible locations for the keys will be." Samaan explained.

"I was wondering Samaan, I've read books about Earth and I know that we don't look like them, so will we not stand out on Earth and end up alerting Sheram to our presence?" Simsaa queried.

Samaan smiled as if there was something he knew that they did not. "Well, Simsaa, I'm glad you asked that because I wouldn't want you to get scared at what will happen to you once you get there, because you will not remain as you are, but will be able to take on the form of the people that are native to the part of Earth where you are present. You will also have the ability to understand and communicate in their language."

Nasami looked stunned and said "How will we recognise each other?" Amafiz looked amazed at his question, "Really Nasami, we'll be together when we change form so we will see our new forms!"

"I meant if for example we're separated and can't remember what we looked like!" Nasami exclaimed looking quite indignant.

"I doubt you should have any trouble but you will all have your bracelets and more importantly still maintain your stones of power." Samaan replied.

"Aah yes but! People in civilisation wear outer garments called clothes, similar to our cloaks and tunics but the area of the torso are usually hidden so if we are in the situation that Nasami mentioned we'd have to ask to see people's stomachs or show them ours!" Dilyus said looking very serious as he did so.

However, as usual even though he was being serious the others could not help but laugh at his comments.

"Don't worry Dilyus I'm sure we'll work something out." Farmoeen reassured him and left the conversation because they had to continue with the remainder of the brief.

Samaan picked up where he had previously stopped the brief; he went on to explain that they would be arriving on Earth at the location that gave off the initial signature of energy from Sheram's arrival, the energy that would have remained as background energy from its use. From there they would begin their mission to seek the four keys of light and activate the Book of Quantime. "You need to realise that this may take some time, however, you need to remember two things; one, you don't have a lot of time and two, you cannot fail!"

"Oh is that all, we just can't fail, that's okay then I thought this might be a very difficult mission!" Simsaa exclaimed, her unusual out of character sarcasm amused Farmoeen who commented "Have you been taking lessons from Dilyus, Simsaa?"

Samaan looked at Farmoeen quite surprised, as he had never witnessed such humour from her; the usually wise, serene and serious oracle. He understood, however, that she was trying to make light of a serious situation to try and alleviate some of the worry that had encased all of them. "Okay children you need to get some rest, Scorpicle has already been fine tuned and checked by Akjam and is resting so you should do the same." "What get fine tuned?" Dilyus asked.

"Never an opportunity missed Dilyus!" Nasami laughed.

That night they rested albeit none of them actually managed to get any proper sleep. Each of them was going through their own turmoil, worries and anxieties; Scorpicle was anxious but deep down he was excited as well, mostly at the idea of 'returning' to Earth; his world.

15

THE JOURNEY TO EARTH

Early that morning at the Great Stone there was a subdued atmosphere, as even the Great Mountain was apprehensive about the quest facing the young Stonimions. Samaan, Farmoeen, Scorpicle and the four guardians stood inside the Great Stone, silent in their own thoughts and getting themselves mentally ready for the next step. Farmoeen stood holding the precious Book of Quantime that Nasami had managed to grab from Sheram's clutches; it had been kept safe inside the Great Stone for all these years. Samaan looked fondly at the nervous young Stonimions and then addressed Farmoeen. "Well I think we cannot avoid the inevitable, the children are ready, and Scorpicle is waiting outside so it's time for them to be on their way." Farmoeen gently nodded in agreement.

"Okay children let's go." Farmoeen said as she ushered the children towards the entrance of the Great Stone. Farmoeen was still holding the very precious item in her hands; it was wrapped in a plain looking cloth, so as to not attract any attention to it. As they were exiting the Great Stone she carefully handed it to Amafiz and simply said "I have protected it so that its power cannot be detected, otherwise Sheram will find you in an instant." Amafiz thanked her and carefully took the Book of Quantime and placed it inside his satchel.

Outside Scorpicle stood alone and proud, the Stonimions as a people had agreed that the young Stonimions would leave quietly as a large gathering outside the Great Stone would attract unnecessary attention from Imfalin and her nasty hoard. Samaan and Farmoeen hugged the children and bid them farewell, as they sat down inside Scorpicle they buckled up and reluctantly waved at the two adults who stood watching them. Scorpicle lowered his door and they were shut off from Stonidium and, for all they knew, it could be forever.

Scorpicle started his engine and activated the teleporter system; the first step in the journey would be to exit Stonidium without Imfalin becoming aware, so it had to be done at the speed of light; literally! Scorpicle's entire body began to pulsate and the Stonimions heard a low humming noise as his engine was creating the energy needed for the teleporter system. They began to feel a strange sensation as if every molecule in their bodies was beginning to vibrate faster and as they looked around at each other and the inside of Scorpicle they were physically looking different; they looked as if they had been stretched and distorted into long thin strips. "Whaaaat's haaa-ppp-eee-nnning?" Amafiz asked, but his voice had also become distorted, it was very low and slow. Scorpicle's answer did not make sense at the time, it was only when he later explained did they realise what he meant by the term 'spaghettification'.

As the strange sensation continued Scorpicle and the Stonimions saw Stonidium melt away in front of their eyes and in a matter of seconds the scenery outside was the complete opposite of their beautiful, luscious green Stonidium, instead it was pitch black, a complete void, a vacuum from which there was no escape. The Stonimions stared at each other and as they did so the rate of their breathing intensified as the panic they were feeling as a group began to crescendo out of control.

Sensing their panic Scorpicle quickly intervened. "Hey, outer space isn't as bad as I thought, a bit quiet and dark but quite peaceful!" Scorpicle's nonchalant manner as if he was commenting on some outing destination did the trick, the four friends snapped out of their panic mode.

"Wow that was weird, I could feel everyone's panic as if it was my own!" Nasami said sounding quite breathless.

"I know it made my stress worse! What happened to us Scorpicle?" Simsaa asked the vehicle.

"I'm not sure, but it must have been because of the sudden speed that we left Stonidium with, we're not used to travelling at near speed of light, but we're going to have to get used to it as time travel means overcoming time and the realms of reality." Scorpicle replied.

"Oh Great another science lesson!" Dilyus complained.

"Don't be so ignorant Dilyus we need to understand what's happening to us" Simsaa glared at him as she spoke.

"Sorry" Dilyus said once again. It was becoming a habit, Dilyus saying something inappropriate and then apologising, but his friends did not think anything of it as they knew he never meant any malice; he was too nice a Stonimion to do that.

Scorpicle was moving through space like a packet of photon energy, moving closer to his destination; Earth. Unknown to his passengers Scorpicle had other reasons for going to Earth, for Scorpicle was returning home, after a long time.

Before long Scorpicle was at a high enough speed to break through into Earth's dimension, and as he did the solar system, in which Earth was present, came into view.

They just all stared; the beauty of what they could see was beyond words, as Scorpicle flew past the planets of the Solar system his excitement grew and he started humming and as his humming became louder he suddenly burst out with words that took the others by surprise "This is planet Earth....., you're looking at planet Earth, pah pah rah pah pah pah rah rah"

"Are you feeling alright Scorpicle?" Amafiz asked looking really concerned.

"Er yeah sorry I, well er never mind- Oh look! We're here Earth."

The Stonimions had been told about Earth, but its beauty was such that it had to be seen to be believed. "There it is the third planet from the Sun, home sweet home." Scorpicle said with such passion and adoration for the world in front of him.

"What did you say- home?" Nasami quizzed.

"Well I meant it's like Stonidium so it's like our second home!"

"That's not what he said" Simsaa whispered to Dilyus who

nodded in agreement, but the young Stonimions did not pursue the matter, as they had more important things to think about at that moment in time.

"The Earth's atmosphere is hard to penetrate so I'm going to turn on my heat resistant shield and put it to full power, as we're going to enter at a very high speed so that we're not picked up by satellites or radars and most importantly Sheram.

Within a matter of seconds they had reached the Earth's atmosphere and had ripped through it in a blink of an eye. The young Stonimions had a vague idea where they were going to land but Scorpicle knew exactly where for two reasons; firstly because of the energy left behind by the Book of Quantime being used, which they were also briefly aware of and secondly the point of landing was in his home country.

Scorpicle stopped and as the young Stonimions peered out of the door's windows they saw a bleak, dark and dingy looking place. "This does not look like the Earth I have read about." Simsaa said looking quite shocked at the sight in front of her.

"That's because humans have, in their wisdom, managed to build areas that look like this; this is an alley way, a sort of passage to reach homes, but this looks much worse than anything I have seen before, something is wrong." Scorpicle sounded worried and when Scorpicle was worried it usually meant that the matter was quite serious.

"Let me check something." He continued and began checking his instruments to find out exactly where they had landed, for he suspected that they may be in the wrong place. However, when he checked the co-ordinates they were in exactly the right spot, there was another reason for the dramatic change in the location and the atmosphere that was seeping in through into the vehicle and he suspected it was due to the interference of the evil one Sheram.

"Is everything okay Scorpicle?" Simsaa asked the very quiet Scorpicle.

"Yes and no, the reason why this place looks so different is because of the mischief Sheram has done since he came to Earth using the Book of Quantime." Scorpicle explained miserably. "This means that what we knew about Earth may not be the same, I don't think many countries will geographically be very different but there may be major changes in other ways."

"What kind of ways do you mean Scorpicle?" Nasami asked looking worried.

"I'm not sure; all I know is that we're going to have to be more careful and vigilant."

Scorpicle drove slowly down the alley way unnoticed by the few people that walked past as he no longer looked like Scorpicle but instead he had taken on the form of one the many vehicles that were on Earth, Scorpicle also scanned the number plates of the surrounding vehicles and made up one that was similar in fashion to the others. As he drove on he came close to where Sheram had first entered Earth, he came to the house of the old man, whom Sheram had so cruelly eliminated.

"Scorpicle, I think you should conduct a search through your databank to find out who lived here and what happened to them." Dilyus suggested.

"Absolutely, there must have been a very important link to Sheram's plans for him to come to this house in particular."

"Wow Earth is full of miracles, Dilyus actually made a sensible suggestion!" Simsaa just had to add in.

"Don't hate!" Dilyus grinned.

Scorpicle was searching through his databanks, when there was a knock on his driver door window. They all froze, weary of the stranger knocking on the window; they did not know what to do next and the following few seconds that passed seemed like hours.

The young Stonimions looked at each other not sure whether they should acknowledge whoever was outside or to just ignore them, the knocking persisted and grew louder, whoever, it was knew that there was somebody inside the vehicle, despite the windows being slightly tinted. "Transform children, I will show you images of British people in this day and age, just focus on an image and will yourself to transform into that person, we will attract less attention if we look like the humans here." Scorpicle said hurriedly. As he spoke he brought the images he was talking about and displayed them on the screen on his dashboard. The four of them all picked an image and stared at it, within seconds they had changed; Amafiz who was sitting in the driver's seat had changed into a young Caucasian male in his late teens, Dilyus had picked a male around the same age of Middle eastern descent, Nasami a male of Afro-Caribbean descent and Simsaa a young Caucasian female of a similar age to the boys.

When Scorpicle saw that they had transformed, he quickly

processed false identities for them, driver's license and passports were the documents that he deemed the most relevant at the time; the documents came out from a slot just underneath the dashboard. "Here take these; if it's the authorities then they may ask for ID."

"What's ID?" Simsaa asked

"Identification documents!" Scorpicle replied as if she should have known this bit of Earth information.

Scorpicle slowly wound down the driver's window and Amafiz beamed nervously at the stranger. Scorpicle's guess had been correct for it could only have been someone in authority of some form to have persistently and so brazenly knocked at the car window.

The person at the window was a law officer, in Scorpicle's previous encounter with Earth they were known as police officers and in Britain they had a very distinct and noble looking uniform that commanded respect and also deployed a form of approachability at the same time. However, this law officer did neither; he inserted a form of fear unlike any law enforcement personnel that Scorpicle had seen himself; however, he did remind him of a very nasty regime he had read about in the history books. He was wearing a dark grey uniform that had the letter 'S' embellished on the collar, cuffs and front pocket.

Amafiz's beam soon turned into a look of fear as the lawman stared viciously at Amafiz; there was not a slight bit of friendliness anywhere on his pointed gaunt looking face. He peered into Scorpicle and scrutinised the others that he saw, he stared at the dashboard, which looked like any other, but he seemed to linger his gaze on it, as if he knew there was something suspicious about it. Once he had satisfied his curiosity he simply barked "papers" at Amafiz and held out his hand. Thankfully the papers that Scorpicle had produced were synonymous with the papers of this current time and place; Amafiz did not know how he had done it but was very grateful that he had. The lawman stared at the driver's license, looked back at Amafiz then at the license then at Amafiz, as if he was not sure if this was the same person. Amafiz tried to lighten the mood by saying "I know it's hard to believe that anyone could be so good looking in real life and in an image." The lawman simply stared and repeated "Image?"

"I mean er photo!" Amafiz almost screamed the word as Dilyus told him telepathically. The lawman was slightly taken aback at Amafiz's outburst but luckily it did not encourage him to pursue the matter any further. He simply said "You can go" and gestured for them to move on.

"Phew! That was close, thanks for the word photo, I didn't know what the word was and I started to panic." Dilyus just smiled at Amafiz, appreciating his gratitude.

"That was not the uniform belonging to HMC, which would have been the law enforcement body in Britain." Scorpicle said solemnly.

"Did you see the 'S'?" Nasami questioned them all.

"Yeah, I wonder what that stands for?" Amafiz said sarcastically.

Scorpicle was unusually quiet again, and Simsaa noticed that he had nothing more to say about the situation they had just encountered. She wondered to herself what could be troubling him, but thought better of asking him.

As they moved closer to the location where Sheram had origi-nally arrived, the Book of Quantime began to emanate a strange hue that filled up Scorpicle; it trembled slightly inside Amafiz's bag. Nasami seemed to go into a trance, and he was soon followed by the rest of the Stonimions. They were telepathically connected and it was as if the Book of Quantime was letting them in on a secret. Slowly in their minds they could see what had happened at this location almost a century ago.

They saw it all; Sheram entering Earth, the near death of an innocent in their home and most brutal of all, the murder of the elderly man. Scorpicle was also a part of this mutual vision and was the first to break the silence once they had witnessed the abhorrent behaviour of Sheram.

"I knew he was vile but even he has surpassed himself. It's obvious that he will stop at nothing to achieve whatever he wants to."

"The question is why here and why him?" Nasami asked no-one in particular.

"I'm already on it." Scorpicle replied as he started searching through his databanks.

A few minutes later he spoke, "Oh dear, it's not good news I'm afraid."

"I didn't think it would be." Dilyus commented.

Scorpicle had discovered part of the reason behind the killing of the elderly man, Frederick Stephens, and as he explained this to the Stonimions they sat horrified at Sheram's actions. "I can't believe he went back and killed the old man." Simsaa said despairingly.

"Well unfortunately some do not understand that to take one life is just as bad as killing all life." Nasami added.

"I can't get over how he went back so far, as if he wasn't going to take any risks and make absolutely sure that he'd succeed!" Amafiz said shocked by what the Book of Quantime had revealed to them.

They now knew and to some degree understood what happened here and why, however, they now needed to rectify everything that had happened. The real problem lay in the fact that because everything had changed Scorpicle's previous knowledge about Earth would not be as useful as they had initially hoped, but they knew that there would still be some similarities and they also knew which places in the world could be more troublesome to them in comparison to others.

It was time to move on and find the Keys of Light; Scorpicle checked the map on his sat nav system, as he scanned the map of the world and arrived closer to one of the possible locations for the Keys, the Book of Quantime vibrated slightly, as though hinting that this could be the correct location. "Wow the Book of Quantime is like a homing device" Simsaa said looking at it admiringly.

Indeed it was, but known to the Stonimions and Scorpicle, they were not looking for one location alone to find the Keys. The ancestral Elder Stonimions had, quite wisely, distributed each of the four Keys in different parts of Earth. They could not afford to make it too easy for anyone to find them and use the Book of Quantime.

"Okay kids we know where we're going!" Scorpicle said excitedly.

"And where's that then!" Amafiz asked.

"Balochistan!"

They all looked at each other and shrugged their shoulders in unison, as if to say, that does not tell us a lot.

THE KEYS OF LIGHT

16
THE SEARCH BEGINS

Scorpicle had activated his shrouding system to make sure that they did not leave any energy surges as they transported to Balochistan, but for added security he asked Amafiz to create his protective defence shield around him. Amafiz placed one hand on his amethyst stone and his other hand on his bracelet; he then closed his eyes and focused on producing the protective shield. The purplish cloud that oozed from his stone penetrated out through Scorpicle's molecules and surrounded him, forming a much needed additional protection from Sheram.

In an instant the dark grey sky of England had disappeared, the street disappeared from under them and they found themselves in an eerily quiet mountainous and arid looking place. Scorpicle's exterior had changed again and was as the other cars that were driven by the people of Balochistan, although he wisely did not go for some of the more traditional style of vehicle; the auto rickshaws but instead the four by fours that most people drove around the mountainous terrains. It was not just Scorpicle who had changed, for he had shown the Stonimions the native people of Balochistan and they too had taken guise on reaching their destination. The four of them decided to step out of Scorpicle to allow them to stretch before they encountered any more problems.

They stared at their surroundings the beauty of what they could see was beyond comprehension; in front of them a road stretched out that seemed to reach the horizon and on either side they could see nothing but a beautiful wilderness of rocks, stones, shrubs and trees, but most wondrous of all were the mountains, some so far away and so high that their tops were lost in clouds, others where the tops were covered in snow, however, the most astonishing of those were the ones that seemed to radiate different colours. Some were copper like, some purplish, others green and some were white. Their beauty was truly remarkable.

"Wow! This place must have an interesting history." Simsaa said looking around in awe of her surroundings.

"It had a very rich history; it had been ruled by many different cultures ranging from Persians, Arabs to the British when they ruled the Indian subcontinent, but looking at my databanks it's also a place where Sheram is now in control, because of its natural resources and wealth." Scorpicle explained.

"Well there's a surprise!" Dilyus remarked. "That man really knows how to go about world domination, doesn't he?" He added; the others nodded in agreement.

"Well at least it seems to have retained its beauty, going by the images you have of Balochistan before Sheram's domination."

Scorpicle looked at Simsaa and understood her passion for the landscape and her relief that at least Sheram had spared the Earth any more grief by not ruining its natural beauty. Whilst the others had been busy admiring the mountains and vegetation of Balochistan, Nasami had stepped back inside Scorpicle and had been busy looking at the map to try and locate the position of the Keys. He spotted a point near a large area called the 'Sulaiman Range' that indicated an energy surge.

The others stepped back into Scorpicle and looked at Nasami to see what he was up to; as he looked up he started telling them about the 'Sulaiman Range' and its significance in their search. Nasami explained that the range of mountains was named after a prophet called Sulaiman. "When you say prophet do you mean someone important?" Simsaa questioned.

Scorpicle interjected "Prophets are holy wise men."

Simsaa nodded and simply said "You mean religious."

Scorpicle sounded surprised when he acknowledged her comment for he did not think that the Stonimions understood the concept of religion, but it was probably similar to their beliefs of power.

Nasami continued with his explanation that there were several peaks in this range of which the twin peaks that showed power surges were Kaisagarth and Takhte Sulaiman which meant 'throne of Sulaiman' and were located at the northern most end of the range. These peaks were known to be the highest; however, Nasami informed them that he noticed a power surge at another high peak which was near a major city called Quetta.

195

"I think our best move will be to go to Quetta and get some more information from locals or maybe a library, they don't just have books but also tourist information as well." Scorpicle suggested.

"Er, how are we going to communicate with the people here?" Dilyus asked Amafiz.

"What do you mean? The same as we did with the law enforcer in England." Amafiz replied looking astonished by Dilyus' question.

"I was surprised when the law enforcer in England could speak as we do but they may not be able to here." Dilyus said.

"Oh, Dilyus did you forget that when we change our appearance, our powers also give us the ability to communicate with the humans in their different languages; all of which are different to our language of Stonidium." Scorpicle told the confused Stonimion.

Scorpicle set off for Quetta, which luckily was not too far from their current location. They soon arrived into the city after a rather treacherous trek through a poignantly named road, called 'Luck pass', which wound down from the mountain that led to the city of Quetta.

Scorpicle carefully drove through the main road that was the complete opposite to the quiet, dark and desolate streets of London. There were people everywhere in every corner, there were people going about their business; shoppers bargaining, children playing, old men sitting drinking green tea and the manual and clerical workers, all busy but with no real sense of urgency in what they were doing.

Scorpicle pulled up next to a group of elderly gentlemen who were sitting on a large rectangular bench made of wooden slats and criss crossed ropes. "These gentlemen look like they may have a fountain of knowledge on the history of Quetta, which may give us some clues as to where to head to exactly as those power surges on the map seem to cover quite a large area." Scorpicle said as he stopped a few feet away from them. "Okay kids, it's your turn, find out as much history as you can and also find out where the local library is." He instructed them as they were getting ready to step out of Scorpicle. They turned and nodded their understanding of the instruction.

They tentatively stepped out of the car and headed towards the group of men. They greeted them in the native language brahui, which was one of the few languages spoken in this area of the world. They asked if they could sit with them and when invited to do so they pulled up some old plastic chairs that were arranged around a single table near at a nearby stall selling snacks and tea; that the old men pointed towards indicating to them to bring them closer.

"How can we help you children?" asked one of the men wearing a traditional headdress called a dastaar.

Amafiz spoke up "We're doing some research for a school project." The others turned to look at him; they had never heard Amafiz speak anything but the truth and his current tactic at extracting information was rather surprising. He ignored their reaction and continued "We er, know about the Zarghun range east of here and a bit about the Sulaiman range and the Chiltan Mountain and the legend of the forty children but we were wondering about the 'Takhte Sulaiman' peak and what exactly is the legend behind it.

197

The elderly gentleman looked really pleased and had a twinkle in his eye as he began talking. "You've come to the right person, for the legend of the Prophet Sulaiman and the highest peak of the Sulaiman range, 'Takhte Sulaiman' is shrouded in great myth and mystery." As he spoke his voice became more intense in its intonation and excitement.

"It has been said that the Prophet Sulaiman had great powers and was able to control the mischievous jinns and confine them to the peak, and that they are unleashed at a certain time in the year. The people here believe that, when the shadows of the range looms over the vast plains of Damaan during this time then it's best to keep children indoors to protect them from these evil spirits. The legend has it that Sulaiman would stay on top of the Takht whilst floating on his carpet, it's also believed he would bless women with fertility." He added as a matter of fact."

One of the other elderly men in the group wearing a traditional cap from their neighbouring province, called a Sindhi cap, spoke this time. "My friend here knows a lot of legends and tales but for more facts you could try your school library but if that's not helpful then the Provincial Library in Spinney road would be an excellent source of information.

The Stonimions stood up and thanked the group of elderly men, for their information and hospitality; for during their conversation the elderly group had made sure that the youngsters had been given plenty of food and drink, the people of Balochistan were a nation of hospitable people who thought of guests as a blessing; the Stonimions experienced this first hand.

They headed off to the library not worried about getting there too late as they had their own means of getting in; their ability to bend light with their stones and become invisible. When they entered the library they went to the Earth sciences section to try and find some more information on the area that they needed to go to. They each grabbed a couple of reference books and started looking through them; it was not long before the presence of Sheram on Earth became apparent again to them, for as they were researching a whistle blew in the library. They looked up from their research books puzzled at what was going on as libraries were usually quiet and a place of serenity. The Stonimions were on the first floor of the library and the commotion had come from the ground floor, Amafiz slowly walked over to the balcony and peered over the edge to see what was going on.

He gasped and within seconds had scuttled back to the others. "We need to hide; there are law enforcers similar to the one in London, but these look really mean and they seem to be questioning random people." Without a word they ran, books in hand, to a hidden corner, which was surrounded by shelving, and touched their stones to become invisible. Amafiz also produced his defence shield to ensure added protection. No sooner had they huddled in the corner than the law enforcers could be heard coming up the stairs.

They stood huddled together, trying hard not to breathe too deeply or too loudly. As the law enforcers walked past them one of them stopped in his tracks and as he did so the Stonimions all held their breaths in fear of being discovered. One of the law enforcers in front of the one who had stopped turned around and asked "What's wrong?"

"I'm not sure, I feel like there's a presence but I'm not sure what it is exactly, I don't like it, it seems very powerful." The law enforcer who had initially stopped replied.

"Do you think we should inform the master?" the first one questioned.

"I don't think so, do you remember a while back someone had reported something similar to the master and it turned out to be a false alarm, he had him vaporised on the spot for wasting his time!" The second law enforcer nodded and gestured for the first one to move on. There were a couple more law enforcers that followed but they soon left without any serious incidents occurring, much to the delight of the Stonimions, who were beginning to feel really cramped, huddled in a corner trying not to move or breathe.

Once they had left, Amafiz turned off his defence shield; they all removed the invisibility shields and cautiously stepped out of the corner. They headed back to the tables and continued their research as quickly as possible before there were any more serious interruptions. This little episode made it apparent to them that whilst they were on an Earth ruled by Sheram then danger lurked in every nook and cranny. They had soon collected sufficient information to help them understand and get to the power source where they were hoping to find the Keys of Light.

They returned to Scorpicle who had been waiting amongst a row of other similar looking vehicles, so as not to attract attention. He had seen the law enforcers enter the University and was going to send a telepathic message to Dilyus but thought better of it as he did not want to risk them detecting any form of energy surges in the area; alerting them to the fact that there were beings of power in the area. Scorpicle knew that anyone connected to Sheram would either have the ability of detecting power or would have been given instruments, created by Sheram, to detect it and as usual Scorpicle was correct. To his relief the law enforcers came back out of the university library quite quickly, there was no commotion and no-one else in tow, so he knew that the youngsters were safe.

17

THE SULAIMAN RANGE

They climbed into Scorpicle loaded with the information from
the library and were ready to go. Simsaa uploaded the information they had found onto Scorpicle's databank; *The
Suleiman range is a mountain mass in central Pakistan extending
southward from Gumal pass to just north of Jacobabad separating
Khyber Pakhtunkhwa and Punjab from Balochistan. The height of
the highest peak called 'Takhte Sulaiman' is three thousand three
hundred and eighty two metres above sea level. A legend, recorded by
the medieval Maghrebi explorer Ibn Battuta, stated that Prophet
Sulaiman climbed this mountain and looked out over the land of
South Asia, which was then covered with darkness, but he turned
back without descending into this new land, and the fact that he had
visited this land resulted in the mountains being named after him.
The Sulaiman Mountains extend four hundred kilometres from
North to South along the western edge of the Indus River valley in
East Balochistan. The vegetation is scarce in the southern slopes, but
in the central part, wild olives are abundant, and especially in river
valleys, there is a high diversity of flora, including ephedra, pista-*

chios and orchards of apples and cherries, as well as wild almonds and junipers. The Ziarat District is a tourist destination, famous for its large forests of the juniper species of juniperus macropoda (or "Pashtun Juniper"). Further to the northwest near the Koh-i-Baba mountain range, the higher altitudes of the Sulaimans are in alpine meadow ecoregion, characterized by meadows and willows, as well as blue pines which cover the summits. Interestingly there was also a mythical story about a magical sword that was said to have belonged to the Prophet Sulaiman, which is said to protect one of the hoards of treasures that belonged to him. As legend states there is a section of mountain near the peak Takhte Sulaiman that is invisible as it is protected by magic, and if anyone is able to overcome the magic then they would still not be able to get to the treasure as it is protected by the magical sword.

When Simsaa had finished entering the information she sat back looking pleased with her work. She turned around and looked at Amafiz, "It seems that we need to head towards the Sulaiman Mountains and in particular the Takhte Sulaiman!" He smiled as he settled in the driver's seat. "Scorpicle, let's go!" Scorpicle did not need to be told twice. They drove out of Quetta at normal speed but once they had reached a more secluded area of the arid terrain Scorpicle became invisible and moved at top speed. Within a matter of seconds they had arrived at the foot of the Sulaiman Range. The Stonimions peered out from Scorpicle and looked up the mountain range. It was vast; they had seen some large mountains in Stonidium but the splendour of these was beyond compare. "I think it's safe to teleport to the peak from here, the energy surge shouldn't be noticeable as we're so near." Scorpicle said as he began to rev up his engine to provide him the energy to teleport.

When they appeared at the Takhte Sulaiman they stood for a few minutes staring at the scenery in front of them. They could feel the ancient powers that encased the mountains and sensed the presence of the jinns beneath their feet; they could feel their mischievousness and evil intent and it did not comfort them or ease their anxiousness in coming to face to face with the jinns.

The Stonimions stepped out of Scorpicle and immediately realized that they were not alone; they could feel a multitude of eyes staring at them full of pure hatred. Before they had time to react they were surrounded by the jinns; demons of all shape and sizes, some tall and muscular looking, some almost wisps of faded spirits, some who looked angelic in their features while others were menacing in appearance, all were slowly advancing upon them. Instinct kicked in and before they knew what they were doing, the Stonimions were ready for battle. Dilyus and Nasami had already tried to penetrate the minds of the jinns, but there were two problems with this tactic; their minds were very unstable and full of abhorrent thoughts, so they had no choice but to retreat from this manoeuvre and looked at Amafiz, all Dilyus then said was "Shield all of us." Amafiz produced his shield to protect them from Dilyus' time slowing move. It worked on the more solid looking jinns but the more ethereal ones without a lot of substance to them seemed unaffected by this power. Nasami stepped in at this point and manipulated these particular jinns to turn them into solid objects; anything that came into his mind. This led to strange bits of furniture, and odd objects sprouting up along the peak of the mountain. Strange as the sight may have been it reduced the threat as these objects could not harm them in anyway.

Scorpicle turned to Simsaa and said "I want you to target that jinn standing towards the back of the group, I have a feeling that he is the leader, we need to know why they were so ready to attack us? Are they working for Sheram or are they just protecting the treasures of Sulaiman? Without any further instruction Simsaa placed her hand on her garnet stone and was soon surrounded by a misty red vapour which slowly made its way to the large mean looking jinn standing at the back of the group. He looked as though he was telepathically sending signals to the other jinns and instructing them where to go and what to do. The mist hit him like a punch and he flinched and immediately looked straight at Simsaa; he snarled and lifted his hand sending a power surge of energy straight at her. Luckily Dilyus' time control and Amafiz's defence shield slowed down the attack from the jinn and deflected. In fact it deflected off the shield and hit a few of the inanimate objects that had been jinns. Simsaa stood still as she stared at the jinn and absorbed information from him. She shuddered as she saw all that he had seen and done in his time and she saw that all he was concerned about was protecting the treasure of Sulaiman; he had no connection to Sheram. As soon as she found this out she relayed this to Scorpicle.

"Dilyus, freeze time" Scorpicle yelled at him.

"I don't think I can!" Dilyus replied.

"Try!" Scorpicle screamed at him, this last instruction sounded really urgent so Dilyus did as he was told. The green colour around him intensified as he put all his energy into freezing time. It took a few minutes but he succeeded, the Stonimions and Scorpicle were still protected by Amafiz's shield so were not affected by time standing still. They did not have too long as Dilyus was weakening and also he knew that to hold time for too long could have serious repercussions in this world and parallel dimensions as well. Scorpicle quickly spoke to the Stonimions. "It seems that the only thing these jinns are concerned about is the treasure, I'm thinking that we will need to defeat them as the Keys could be in amongst the treasure."

"Even if they're not we will still need to defeat them in order to get away from them I'd say!" Nasami added.

They knew that they would need to combine their different powers to defeat the jinns as there were so many of them meaning that their combined magical powers were also strong. From what they had read they knew that the jinns could not be destroyed; they were going to have to copy the prophet who had controlled them and do likewise. The question really was how?

They had to act fast as Dilyus' power was waning and soon the jinns would be back to their normal speed and free again. As Dilyus' hold on time began to waver the frozen jinns started to move albeit slowly, at that point Amafiz knew that they somehow had to be contained before the effect completely wore off; he stood quite still and stretched out both arms, as he did so his amethyst stone pulsated and an energy surge passed from the stone through his body and out of his outstretched arms. As the energy left the tips of his fingers the Stonimions saw a shiny metallic looking purple rope drift towards the jinns. When Nasami saw what Amafiz was doing he quickly moved some of the jinns, which he had transformed, with his mind. The rope slowly descended around the gathered slow jinns and as it did so it began tightening so as to bring the group closer together.

"Nice work!" Scorpicle commented as he looked at the sluggish struggling jinns confined by Amafiz's purple sparkly rope.

"I think it's my turn!" Simsaa said as she stepped forward and began to increase in size and transform into a very large and scary looking jinn.

"Wow a big improvement!" Dilyus said laughing but the instant the words left his mouth then regret took over as Simsaa the jinn turned around and looked at him as if she was going to crush him. Dilyus yelped and ran behind Nasami for protection. Amafiz laughed but with a serious look on his face said to Simsaa "Ignore him and concentrate Simsaa, you know what we need to find out."

Simsaa stood in front of the captured crowd of jinns and telepathically began to communicate with the jinns; she was more successful than Nasami and Dilyus as they were only able to link with them as Stonimions and the thoughts and memories of the jinns were unbearable. Simsaa also knew that she could not stay in this form for too long as it could cause irreversible damage to her own persona. Simsaa decided to communicate with the largest of the jinns. "We are the 'Four Guardians of Stonidium' and we do not wish you any harm, we only seek the Keys of Light that belong to our people the Stonimions."

"Then why do you come here to our mountain and near the treasure of the Prophet of Sulaiman if not for some greedy reason of empowerment; just like the humans that occupy this world?"

"We only seek what is rightfully ours." Simsaa repeated.

"We will comply only because you have shown yourselves to be more powerful than the humans and have managed to capture us."

"We would like to release you from this bond but can we trust you?" Simsaa questioned the jinn.

"You have our word as jinns of honour." The jinn replied.

Simsaa gestured to Amafiz to release the jinns from his purple constraint. Scorpicle was ready with his lasers on stun in case any of the jinns had any other ideas. As the jinns became free from Amafiz's rope they stepped towards the Stonimions but unlike before their demeanour was not threatening but humbled. The jinns had succumbed to the Stonimion's will because they respected anyone or anything that demonstrated enough intelligence and power to overcome them.

The jinns walked towards the Stonimions and suddenly stopped dead in their tracks. The jinn that Simsaa had been communicating with looked concerned; there was something wrong. "We need to disappear now as the evil human on Earth has sent his law enforcers in this direction, they may have picked up your energy surge!" the jinn pointed towards the centre part of the peak Takhte Sulaiman; the Stonimions could not see anything but solid rock, however, as they stared at the area the jinn had pointed to they noticed a shimmering wave above the spot; as if the air above it was becoming hotter and the molecules of gases were vibrating faster and moving around at a greater speed than before.

As they watched they saw the rocks move aside and a hole appear, they drew closer towards the hole at the suggestion of the jinns, and as they got closer they saw that the hole was an entrance to an inner cave. There was a vibrant looking stone slope that wound downwards into the dark depths of the mountain. Scorpicle and the Stonimions carefully went down the slope with some of the jinns taking the lead and the remainder following suit. Once they had descended into the mountain they realized that they were surrounded by radiant, sparkling and colourful jewels and bizarre objects made of numerous different precious metals.

The jinn, who had been communicating with Simsaa telepathically, now spoke out loud to all of them; they understood every single word he spoke. "Here is a small portion of the treasure of Prophet Sulaiman you may seek here for your Keys of Light." The jinn said as he pointed around the cave. Scorpicle, who had miniaturized himself so that he could go down into the cave, had restored to his normal size, opened his door and said "Amafiz take out the Book of Quantime and try to find the Keys of Light." Amafiz obliged and removed the Book of Quantime from Scorpicle's glove compartment. Once the book was present in the cave a very strange thing happened. The Book of Quantime was a rather plain looking book; it was almost stone like in appearance, it was greyish-brown in colour, thick in volume, but unlike other books it was seized shut, impenetrable and only the Keys of Light could open it correctly; thankfully the book had not changed after the violation that Sheram had committed on it. As Amafiz held the book in his hand the stony looking front cover began to shimmer and wave in front of their eyes. The jinns backed away from the book, as they were beings of power they understood that this object was one of great power. The shimmering led to a section of the front cover changing shape and colour.

The stony grey-brown colour on the section that was changing became a vibrant red with the centre of the section turning into a square shape that had regular equilateral triangles on each edge of the square. "Ooh mathematics! That's the open net shape of a base pyramid." Everyone present in the cave turned around to look towards Scorpicle. Scorpicle realized what he had said and smiled sheepishly and said "I was just saying it looks like that."

The red shape emanated a reddish vapour that spread around the cave and as its trails of colour touched the treasure in the cave an old crown that was dented and almost bent out of shape rose out up above the remainder of the treasure. At first glance the crown looked rather dull although it was distinguishable that it was made of gold, but that was the only thing about it that was noticeable; the inner part only became noticeable as the crown rose higher and began to glow red. They all stared at the rising crown and realized that where it had begun to glow red was where a section of the crown was also beginning to separate.

Simsaa turned to the large jinn and said "Catch it before it gets out of reach." The jinn immediately reacted and grabbed at the crown. He carefully lowered the crown and handed it over to Simsaa as if he was handing over a baby. Simsaa smiled and thanked the jinn as she took hold of the crown and walked over to Amafiz and the book he was holding. Simsaa held aloft the crown and looked at Dilyus and Nasami "Could one of you remove the key please?" they looked at each other and Dilyus realized that she was actually referring to the strange red glow on the inner side of the crown. Dilyus walked over to her and cautiously reached inside the crown and placed his hand over the red glowing section. He did this carefully as he was wary of touching unknown objects from prior experiences; the object almost jumped into his hand, which made him flinch slightly, as if it was happy to go to him.

Dilyus raised the object, which was as they had all suspected the same shape as the red indentation that had appeared on the Book of Quantime. "Is this easy or what?" Nasami questioned no-one in particular. Simsaa looked at him and asked "What do you mean?"

"I mean knowing that this is the key that fits into this lock on the book."

"For someone of your intelligence, you show no common sense!" Amafiz exclaimed. It's obvious it's going to fit because the book sensed which key was here and made apparent the correct lock on itself!"

"Oh Yeah!" Nasami said looking a bit embarrassed.

"It's okay Nasami it must be the lack of oxygen, Quetta is quite a way above sea level and this mountain is extremely high as well." Dilyus' humour may not have been appreciated too much by Nasami, but it made the jinns laugh.

"I like your sense of humour, Stonimion, your world must be a jovial place to be." The large jinn said to Dilyus.

"It was, until Sheram used this Book to come to Earth, changed things here and ruined our world as well, but don't worry, we will restore everything back to how it was, even if our lives depend on it!" Dilyus spoke with such passion that it brought a tear to Simsaa's eye, who, put her arm around him as a way of comfort and confirmation that they were all with him on this.

The large jinn looked at Dilyus and the other Stonimions with admiration, and to get a response like that from a jinn was no mean feat. The jinns respected those with honour and strength and these Stonimions had shown that and more. Dilyus was still holding the red key, which he then placed into the indentation on the Book of Quantime; no sooner had he placed the key into its lock the key disappeared into the lock which then also faded from sight. Scorpicle looked astounded and said "Okay what now?"

"I don't know, the locks for the other keys haven't appeared so what does that mean?" Amafiz asked looking a bit puzzled.

"Is there more than one key for your book?" the large jinn asked Simsaa, who nodded yes to him. "Then it seems that the rest of the keys are not here amongst these particular treasures of Prophet Sulaiman."

Scorpicle projected the digital map of the world onto one of the walls of the cave. "You're absolutely right; the map is now showing an energy surge elsewhere." They all looked at the map and saw exactly what Scorpicle was referring to. "Is it highly likely that this is the green key location?" Dilyus asked Scorpicle.

"Yep, it wasn't coincidence that the first energy surge led us to the red key, I think the Book of Quantime is guiding us to obtain the keys in the correct order." Scorpicle said as he stared at the map he had projected onto the wall of the cave. The jinns all stood and watched, in awe, at the digital map that was showing on the cave wall. They saw a small energy pulse in the region of China. "I don't think that the next key is there." Nasami said as he stared at the spot of pulsating light.

"Why do you say that?" Dilyus asked.

"Because when we saw the energy pulse showing this location it was much larger, the question is what is this spot showing us?" Amafiz said.

"Well whatever is there we're going to have to go there and find out what it is!" Simsaa exclaimed. She turned to the large jinn with whom she had been communicating with and said simply "Thank you for your help." All the jinns looked at Scorpicle and the Stonimions and bowed to demonstrate the respect they had for these strangers to Earth.

The peak of the mountain opened up and the jinns led the party back up out of the mountain just as they had led them down into the cave before. As they all stood on the Takhte Sulaiman the large jinn looked at them and said "I wish you luck in your quest, for this Sheram has disrupted many things on Earth and we too want rid of him." They said their goodbyes and the Stonimions went and sat inside Scorpicle. Scorpicle set the co-ordinates for the spot on the map and in an instant had left the Takhte Sulaiman.

18

THE GREAT WALL

They landed with a thud; a strange sensation fell over them as if they were being watched. The Stonimions stepped out of Scorpicle and stood on what turned out to be some ancient stone slabs. "Where are we?" Simsaa asked turning around to look at Scorpicle. Scorpicle checked the co-ordinates and replied "The Great Wall of China!"

"I've read about this, it's one of the Seven Wonders of the World and..." Nasami was interrupted by Dilyus.

"Oh great another history lesson, I haven't got the energy for this, I'm sorry but I'd like to learn more about Earth when I'm not stressed about a creep who's taken over it and my ruined my world at the same time!" Dilyus sounded extremely exasperated when he blurted out his feelings on the matter. Nasami stayed calm and just to add to Dilyus' annoyance continued with what he was saying. "The building of it began around 770 BC and this Great Wall that we're standing on was rebuilt and completed mainly during the Ming Dynasty in

1368-1644." Nasami looked around smugly as he finished his sentence and then grinned at Dilyus, who rolled his eyes.

"That's all well and good but we really need to locate this small energy surge before…" Scorpicle did not get the chance to finish his sentence; there was an almighty uproar from behind them and as they turned towards the noise they were startled to see a mass of black robed bodies descending upon them from the sky. Within a split second Amafiz impulsively produced his defence shield, but he was not quick enough for these robed strangers were as fast as the speed of light and Amafiz's shield just emanated far enough to protect him and Scorpicle, whom he was standing next to but not the others. Before he or Scorpicle had a chance to react, Amafiz saw the rest of them being swiftly swooped up and whisked away into the distance. There was an eerie silence as he and Scorpicle stood staring at each other trying to get to grips with what just happened.

Amafiz spoke in a startled voice as if he had just been woken up from a deep sleep. "Scorpicle what happened? What or who were those things? And where have they taken the rest of them? Scorpicle looked at the young Stonimion not knowing quite what to say to him for he did not have the answers to any of Amafiz's question, in fact, these were his questions as well. Scorpicle was extremely upset and guilty because he was supposed to have been guarding the young Stonimions and he knew he had let their parents down. Scorpicle's lack of response frightened Amafiz but he realized that Scorpicle's silence was greater than just his concern for the missing Stonimions; he knew Scorpicle too well and understood his despair at what had happened. Amafiz drew closer to Scorpicle and placed his hand on his wing. "Scorpicle it wasn't your fault, it happened so quickly that we didn't get the chance to react. What we need to do now is find them!"

Scorpicle knew Amafiz was right and immediately turned on his map to try and locate the Stonimions. "How are you going to use the map to find them I thought it only located the power surges of the keys."

"This map has been programmed to pick up your stones as well, so if there isn't a lot of interference from other power sources we should be able to get some idea as to where they have been taken." Scorpicle explained.

"That's excellent but the real question is how we are going to get them back from those things? They were far too fast, very skilled and a lot of them."

"Aah but we're smarter!" Scorpicle grinned. Scorpicle projected the map onto the Great Wall of China and adjusted his settings so that the map homed in on the stones of the Stonimions. "Ooohhhh! There's a pulse very near here, in fact it's right here!" Amafiz said excitedly. Scorpicle looked at him and said "Are you missing Dilyus?"

"What do you mean?" Amafiz looked mystified.

"That pulse is you!" Scorpicle said totally exasperated. Amafiz grinned sheepishly and shook his head at his own silliness, maybe he was missing Dilyus.

Amafiz sat down inside Scorpicle and they immediately arrived at the location, which was still on the Great Wall, but much further along than their current location, where they were hoping to would find the rest of them. "We need to be careful with using my teleportation system too often as I'm worried about Sheram picking up the energy from it." Scorpicle remarked.

"I know but this is one occasion where we can't afford to waste any time." Amafiz sounded very concerned about his missing friends.

"Amafiz, you need to keep alert when you step outside because those things could already be aware that we're here and may be ready for us!" Scorpicle sounded rather frightened and this did not do anything for Amafiz's confidence. Amafiz turned on his shield and stepped out of Scorpicle, who in turn activated his own defence shield.

No sooner had he stepped out of Scorpicle than the group who had abducted the Stonimions was standing in front of him. Face to face they were more terrifying than Amafiz had originally thought; their faces were completely covered but he could see their eyes through the narrow slits on their masks. Eyes that did not exhume any friendship but a whole load of animosity towards him and, by the way they stared at him, Scorpicle too.

Amafiz stood his ground ready for a fight, when it occurred to him to try and reason with these fighters. "I mean you no harm, I only want my friends back." He spoke in Chinese so fluently it was as if he had been speaking it his entire life. One of the captors stepped forwards and spoke. "We know you are not human, but we have also now come to realize that you are not followers of the evil that has taken over the world, an evil form who has managed to worm his way into power and world domination."

Amafiz stood transfixed on the spot; he was shocked to hear

that these 'people' knew that they were not human and more so that they were aware of Sheram, although they did not know him by name. This meant that they were powerful enough to be aware of the real Earth, before it had been interfered with by Sheram's meddling using the Book of Quantime. "Who are you and what have you done with my friends?" Amafiz questioned the one who had spoken to him, hoping that the question would not annoy him.

The man covered in black from head to toe stepped towards Amafiz and as he did so he drew something quickly from his side, the sudden movement made Amafiz flinch and take a step backwards. Amafiz intensified his shield and braced himself ready to defend or attack; nothing happened. The hooded man had not reached for a weapon, as Amafiz had originally thought; instead he had reached for a scroll much to both Amafiz's and Scorpicle's surprise. He slowly opened the scroll and gestured to Amafiz to take the scroll, Amafiz lowered his defence shield and Scorpicle readied himself with his lasers on standby in case there was a sudden attack, but it never came. Amafiz took the scroll and slowly opened it, as he did there was a bright orange light that blazed out of the scroll; it surrounded the entire group and as Scorpicle and Amafiz stood in awe of this beautiful display they found the ground underneath started to move and slowly sink. They found themselves being gently lowered into the ground and as they landed on the soft ground Scorpicle and Amafiz saw their friends standing in front of them safe and well.

Amafiz and Scorpicle's delight was immeasurable; Amafiz ran towards his friends and gave them all a large group bear hug.

"Are you guys okay?" Amafiz asked totally astounded that

they were standing in front of him safe and sound. "I was so scared when these people whisked you away!" he exclaimed gesturing towards the group of darkly dressed strangers. "These are the defenders of the Stone" Simsaa explained to Amafiz, "They have protected the Stone of Wisdom of Stonidium for many generations."

"From Stonidium?" Amafiz said shocked "What is a stone from Stonidium doing here and how come I've never heard of this stone before?" Amafiz turned to look at Scorpicle as if he would have the answer. In fact he did.

"Well the reason is simple, it was placed here by the ancient Stonimions many millennia ago and as time went on it was forgotten about, but if you were good children and read the old scriptures you would have come across the Stone of Wisdom." Scorpicle retorted smugly. The Stonimions looked at him indignantly. One of the Defenders of the Stone said, "Is he always such a know it all?"

Dilyus laughed much to Scorpicle's chagrin, who grunted his displeasure at being made fun of. Scorpicle was not going to let them get away with that comment and simply said "Don't hate just because I have knowledge." The Stonimions laughed, however, the Defenders of the Stone did not get the joke.

Simsaa had been listening intently to Scorpicle's little history lesson and was intrigued by the Stone of Wisdom. "Scorpicle is the Stone of Wisdom similar to Farmoeen's Crystal of Knowledge?"

"Not quite, the Stone of Wisdom doesn't communicate like the Crystal does, it works by simply holding it and thinking about the knowledge you seek and it will tell you what you want to know!" Scorpicle replied.

"Okay that's all well and good but what does that have to do with the Keys and why did this lot kidnap us?" Dilyus asked gesturing towards the Defenders.

One of the Defenders spoke, "It's written in ancient scriptures that there are beings from another world that have been known to enter our Earth, but not as foes but as friends, they are described as creatures who are of human size, covered in fur and with stones embedded in their stomachs, it is also written that they can take on human form when on Earth, but will remain powerful. We were always aware of you and when our sensors detected powerful beings on the Great Wall of China, we knew who you were. We only took you so that we could protect you from the evil that is present on Earth at this time and help you by taking you to your Stone of Wisdom. We couldn't take all of you as you had enveloped yourself in your defence shield."

Amafiz looked a bit embarrassed about this but the Defender continued. "Your defence shield and quick reaction reassured us that we had the right beings and when we got here we explained to your friends who we were; we were going to come to you when you found us!" Scorpicle stared at the Defender suspiciously, "Sooooo, exactly how are you aware of the 'evil' that is on Earth?" The others looked at Scorpicle wondering why he sounded so suspicious of these humans who were trying to help.

The Defenders realized that Scorpicle had his doubts about them and so decided to reveal another secret to the Stonimions and their vehicle. They gestured to the group to follow them and took them into a secret alcove that was incorporated into the depths of the Great Wall; it was as if they had moved into an alternate dimension that was attached to the Great Wall. The lead Defender walked over to a podium made of stone, but unlike a podium the upper part that was resting on a giant stone pedestal, was not a solid base to lean on when giving a speech; it was hollow. The lead Defender reached into the podium platform and removed an ancient book and handed it over to Simsaa, who was standing nearby. She took hold of the book so carefully as if it was so fragile it would shatter at her touch. She looked at the book then at the Defender with a quizzical expression. "Open it in the middle and read it please". Simsaa did as she was instructed she opened the book to its middle page and began to read out aloud.

"There will come a time when the history of the Earth will be changed. The source of the change will be of this Earth but will be the most evil being that ever existed. He will alter life on Earth to suit his own means, however, there will come those who will fight against him and win for they are the power of good, they are the ones with stones of power." As she finished her sentence she looked up and stared intently around at the others. "There's only one problem with what this book states." She said.

"What's that?" Dilyus asked as he walked over to Simsaa to take a closer look at the book himself.

"Well it refers to the evil as a being of Earth, but Sheram is from Stonidium, isn't he? She questioned them.

Scorpicle tried to look as shocked as the others on hearing what was written in the book about the 'Evil One' as it did not make sense to the young Stonimions, however, he knew differently. The thing with Scorpicle was that he may have been a super car and weapon with a good sense of humour but he was a terrible liar and even worse actor. "Oh that doesn't make sense does it?" He questioned no one in particular. Nasami looked at the others and then slowly walked over to Scorpicle and stared at him. "Okay Scorpicle what do you know?" Nasami quizzed Scorpicle.

Scorpicle hummed and hawed and tried to avoid the issue, but there was nowhere for him to hide. He had no choice but to reveal what he knew about Sheram. "Well, the truth is the book is correct, Sheram is actually from Earth, and all I know is that Imfalin travelled to Earth especially to find Sheram. He was born to a young couple, but had been abandoned and Imfalin found Sheram and took him to Stonidium."

This revelation had stunned them all into silence; never had even one of them suspected that Sheram was not from Stonidium.

Suddenly Dilyus said in an extremely loud voice "Well you think you know someone and they do this to you!"

"I'm sorry Dilyus but I didn't think that this piece of information was important and Samaan and all of your parents told me it was not necessary to burden all of you with too much information all in one go!" Scorpicle explained looking really perplexed at Dilyus' reaction. Dilyus turned to look at Scorpicle and simply replied. "I'm not talking about you, I meant Sheram! You think you know a guy and he turns out to be something quite else." The defenders looked puzzled on hearing these comments and especially when Scorpicle and the Stonimions burst into laughter. Simsaa explained to them

"This is a Dilyus moment! Making a comment that really is irrelevant." She smirked.

"Hey! What do you mean irrelevant? I have made a very valid point." Dilyus said sounding rather indignant.

"Yeah in your strange little world maybe!" Amafiz retorted.

Dilyus looked rather upset at being ridiculed by his friends when he thought he had made a perfectly legitimate comment about the deceit in terms of what or who Sheram was.

"Well no matter, the fact is that your book seems to have the correct information. It mentions Sheram and us, but does it say anything about how we might defeat him or is that too much to hope for?" Simsaa the voice of reason spoke up. The Defender holding the book looked back at it and said, "It simply states that they will defeat the evil being with the book of time."

The visitors knew that this was their destiny and there was no turning away from it, but they also knew that they had a battle on their hands, however, for the sake of two worlds, defeat was not a choice. The question now was where next? Simsaa looked at the defender holding the book and asked "You spoke of the Stone of Wisdom, we would like to go to it as it may have the information we need."

The Defenders gestured to the group to follow them and took them deeper into the alcove. Within a few minutes they had arrived at a brightly lit cavern that branched off of the main alcove. Unlike the alcove this cavern was not as brightly lit because it did not have any fiery lanterns; it did not need them as it actually glowed itself. The walls were lustrous in their appearance and reflected the light from a single source of

light, a tiny flame in the centre of the cavern. The flame flick-
ered as it stood proudly on a small stone round saucer; its tiny
light was sufficient to illuminate the entire cavern. They all
stood in awe and it was then that Scorpicle realised what
phenomenon he was witnessing. "So, this is what it's like to be
inside an optical fibre!" They others looked at him quizzically.
He simply replied "Total internal reflection!" he beamed and
thought to himself 'If only my science teacher could see
me now!'

They had all been so busy looking at the flame in the centre of
the cavern that they had not noticed that there was something
of interest to them towards one side against the east facing
wall. Nasami turned to face the wall and pointed towards it;
the others turned and saw what he was pointing at. The
Defenders acknowledged that Nasami had found the Stone of
Wisdom and they slowly walked towards it. Although they
knew now that the Stone of Wisdom communicated differently
to the Crystal of Knowledge, they were still unsure as to what
to expect. The Crystal of Knowledge in Stonidium was able to
communicate with them telepathically but the Stone of
Wisdom had its own way; as they approached the stone they
saw a slight shimmering of the light that was reflecting off of
the stone and as they drew closer they witnessed firsthand the
stone's method of communication. They stood in front of the
Stone and placed their hands on it. As they watched the
writing appeared on the stone and it was simple and to the
point, no mystic conundrum, no ancient language that no-one
could understand, it was a language that anyone could understand as it had the power to appear to whoever was reading it
in a language that was familiar to them. Simsaa looked
intently at the words and repeated what was written. "Wel-

come Stonimions! You will find the next key at Hokkaido Island."

"Well we don't need to be told twice!" Dilyus reacted, showing an eagerness and energy to move onto the next place which was unlike his usual lethargic nature.

"I think he's right if we have the location we should move fast, the more time we waste the more chance there is that Sheram and his cronies might find us!" the ever sensible Nasami agreed.

The decision was made and the group knew that they needed to depart; they thanked the Defenders and the Stone of Wisdom and within an instant had left the cavern deep within the Great Wall of China.

19

THE HOKKAIDO ISLAND

The sight that awaited them at Hokkaido Island was something that had to be seen to be believed. The Stonimions stepped out of Scorpicle and stood in silence, there were no words that could express their wonderment at the sight that greeted them. Scorpicle had seen some places on Earth that were beautiful, but he had never witnessed anything like this. The air was quite chilly as the autumnal season was just beginning to present itself to the Island; however, the last remnants of summer were still fighting for their right to be there. From where they stood the Stonimions and Scorpicle could see the beginnings of the changes to the foliage; they saw a myriad of greens, oranges, reds and yellows that were intermingling amongst the different shaped and sized leaves of the trees and bushes that stretched out as far as the eyes could see; it was indeed a spectacular view and equal in its beauty to the man made fields of flowers, these were rectangular rows of flowers that from afar looked like a rainbow carpet that had been laid onto the ground. It was certainly breathtaking and hard for anyone to turn their gaze away from the scenery that was displayed in front of them.

A few minutes of silence had passed as the party of visitors absorbed the scenery, a few moments of serenity which were abruptly broken by an uninvited and unpleasant sound. "The master thinks they may come here so we need to look no matter how long it takes we look in every corner!" The voices were drifting in the wind from below where the party of friends were standing. They all turned to look at each other and with military precision they had nimbly entered Scorpicle and were now invisible. "Do you think we should leave this particular area of the island?" Simsaa asked Scorpicle.

"I don't think we should do anything that may draw attention to us; Sheram's military police may have devices to pick up energy surges, it may be best to stay put." Scorpicle explained and so they did. Despite the déjà vu of this situation of being the same as in Quetta, there their fear had not been as great maybe because they were in a public place or maybe because the reality of Sheram was not as apparent, but here things were different. There was a sense of impending doom, a feeling that was unanimous amongst them all.

Their wait seemed as long as a life time and just as they thought they were safe it happened. One of the law enforcers who had ventured further away from the main group stepped closer to where Scorpicle was standing and as he got closer the Stonimions, who were watching from inside, gasped and flinched as the law enforcer walked into Scorpicle. For a few moments he was stunned as he bumped into nothing, he stretched out his hands in front of him and started to feel his way around Scorpicle. As he reached half way around his breathing became heavier as he realised that this was what they were looking for, he screamed out to his fellow guards and the commotion he created made the Stonimions jump; the noise from the guard also disturbed the wildlife on the island adding to the bedlam that was the shouts and screams from the other law enforcers, as they raced over to the one who had called them.

"Scorpicle it's now or never, if they capture us it's all over, we need to make our move!" Amafiz literally screamed at the car. Scorpicle knew that he was right and that there was no time to waste, there was no need to worry about any surge detection now. Within a split second they were gone, leaving behind a confused man who had felt a rush of hot air for a minor moment in time and had then fallen forwards as there was no longer anything in front of him. By the time his fellow law enforcers had reached him he stood looking sheepish, as if he was a child who had just been caught being naughty. The guards all looked at each other and one of them spoke "What happened?" the one who had called them looked really confused. "I'm not sure! I thought I felt something I couldn't see but then in a split second it wasn't there." The other law enforcers stood quietly for a few minutes then one of them said "I think we should still inform the master, this may be of significance." The others nodded their agreement.

Scorpicle and the Stonimions were still on the island but much further away from where they had originally arrived. Scorpicle checked the map and realised that the energy pulse was nearby, "That was lucky, the energy surge is just beyond that mountain." Scorpicle said as he pointed his headlights in the direction of a beautiful enormous mountain whose peak was covered in snow. The Stonimion party headed off towards the mountain, silently as they were still in shock from the close encounter with Sheram's police. Finally Nasami spoke up and stated what they had all been thinking. "Sheram is going to find out about this and soon this place will be swarming with his minions, the longer we're here the more danger we're in!" he sounded melodramatic but they all knew he was right.

"Which means we need to move and act fast, we need to get the key and go before Sheram turns up for the party" Dilyus added.

Scorpicle set his co-ordinates to the location of the power surge on his map and using minimum power transported them to the other side of the mountain; this took a few minutes longer but Scorpicle decided that adding on a few minutes was better than attracting Sheram to their location immediately.

They were at the foot of the mountain and the Stonimions had exited Scorpicle. They looked up towards the peak but could not see it clearly because of the clouds that covered it; it was a long way up and they had no idea as to whether they would need to scale its entire height. In fact they were not even sure if they needed to go inside the mountain for the next key. "Scorpicle is there anything on your map showing the precise location now that we're here?" Simsaa asked as she sat back inside Scorpicle.

"No I'm afraid not but I was thinking you could take a look at the map from Farmoeen and.." before Scorpicle could finish his sentence Simsaa was already taking out the old parchment from her bag as well as the map that Farmoeen had given them.

"I'm already on it" Simsaa smiled.

She laid the map on a small table and carefully laid the old parchment on top of it; the layout was wrong so she lifted up the old parchment and changed its orientation until she could see that the two pieces of paper matched in size and shape. The moment the two papers were in the correct orientation then the old parchment and the map instantly fused together emitting a bright light as they did so. The map and parchment glowed for a few seconds and without any warning they rose from the table where Simsaa had laid them down, Simsaa tried to catch hold of the now fused paper before it went up any higher but she should not have bothered because as soon as she stood up to try and catch hold of it, it spun around in midair and then fell back onto the table. Simsaa looked at the map parchment combination quizzically "Weird!" she thought. She leaned closer to the map and stared down at it, the parchment had done its job; she could now clearly see the location of the key as it pulsated on the map. Simsaa stumbled out of Scorpicle and in her hurry to show the location to the others she fell into them, sending them hurtling to the ground.

"Whoa Simsaa what's the hurry?" Dilyus asked rubbing his back as he got up.

"Sorry guys I didn't mean to hurt you but it's just that I've found the location of the key!" Simsaa explained breathlessly.

Without another word they quickly followed Simsaa back into Scorpicle. They closely observed the energy surge showing on the map. "It looks like the key is about a third of the way up this mountain!" Amafiz said scrutinising the map. The others moved closer to see what he was pointing at and realised that they were all staring at a very small image of a key. "That's very clever!" Nasami commented.

"You're easily impressed!" Simsaa retorted. This comment caused the others to stare at her intently "What?" she demanded. "After everything we've seen I wouldn't expect anything less from the parchment but to show us exactly what we're looking for!"

"That's a fair point you know." Scorpicle added trying to inter-ject before a quarrel broke out.

"Okay let's have a look then exactly where we need to go and more importantly how are we going to get to the key?" he added.

Amafiz set about scanning the area for any potential dangers using his powers of defence and just to be on the safe side, he also used the globe to enhance his own ability. As he held up the globe he touched his stone and instantly a purple light emanated from his stone through his arm and hand, it trav-elled through his torso and into the globe held aloft in his left hand. When his light of power entered into the globe it too turned purple in colour, which radiated out into the environ-ment. The purple light scanned the area and fed back the information into Amafiz's mind; he could see that there was no immediate danger from anything lurking inside or near the mountain and neither from surrounding forest. However, Amafiz did notice that there was an intense amount of some kind of life form in the nearby trees.

Whilst Amafiz was carrying out his scan the others waited patiently, once he had finished he told them what he had found. "Scorpicle do you think these life forms could be dangerous?" Dilyus asked Scorpicle nervously.

"To be honest with you I don't know, I mean even if it's an animal it may be ferocious!" Scorpicle replied.

"Well there's only one way to find out, we'll have to go and see. I'd rather face any dangers now while I'm on the ground than get attacked as we're going up the mountain!" Nasami said as he looked at the others for approval.

"We could teleport, using our bracelets meaning that we don't expose ourselves to any animals here!" Simsaa said.

"I don't think we can because there may not be any appropriate landing spot a third of the way up the mountain." Dilyus added.

"Okay then let's go and find out what could potentially attack us then!" Scorpicle said, although he was serious about his comment he did sound rather sarcastic.

"Before we go there's one thing." Simsaa caused them all to halt in their tracks. "We look like the people of the country we're in so why do we need to hide when Sheram's men are around?"

"You're right we don't really need to hide but I can't risk us being identified even though we are disguised, they obviously have some sort of device that picks up our powers but it could also reveal our true identities as well!" Scorpicle replied.

"Good thinking Scorpicle you never know!" Amafiz said as he patted Scorpicle's bonnet as a gesture of his approval.

"Thanks as long as you're happy!" the sarcasm had returned in full force this time making Amafiz flinch slightly as he realised his gesture may have been slightly condescending.

"I think we should get going" Nasami interjected before any more unnecessary comments could be made by anyone else.

They headed towards a spot on the map that showed life forms as infrared thermo-gram images. As they got nearer to the life forms they were ready for a confrontation; Scorpicle's lasers were poised as were the Stonimions with their bracelets, stones aglow and all defence systems braced and ready for action. They were almost upon the life forms when Scorpicle stopped suddenly, the others, who were already on edge, launched into full defence mode. It turned out to be totally unnecessary as when they approached the trees that contained the life forms, they found native animals only found on Hokkaido Island.

"Awwww look at those beautiful creatures!" Simsaa cooed as she carefully stepped towards the animals that were hiding in their homes. "I've never seen anything like them on Earth before" Scorpicle remarked, Dilyus looked at him suspiciously, but before he got the chance to ask Scorpicle how he would know such a thing Scorpicle saved him the trouble and explained. "Well you all know how much I enjoy studying and learning about Earth, I've not seen animals like these in the countries I've studied."

"That was weak Scorpicle but if you insist then okay we'll accept your explanation." Simsaa said shaking her head in disapproval.

"Whaaaaat?" Scorpicle protested.

"Are they actual animals from Earth or is this some sort of invasion by Sheram?" Nasami asked Scorpicle.

"I'm sure they are, let me search my database."

Within a few seconds Scorpicle had projected pictures and information about the creatures that were hiding amongst the trees, and daring to take sneaky peeks at the strangers. The Stonimions stared at the images of the unusual creatures, Simsaa stared at an owl that was staring at her from one of the branches of a nearby tree, and she looked at the image that Scorpicle was projecting. Simsaa stepped closer to the image and asked Scorpicle to translate the name. "This is the **Ezo Fukurō**, it's an owl and..." Scorpicle was cut short by Nasami "Wow look at that strange looking flying squirrel, what's that called?" Nasami questioned as he stared up towards the trees. They all followed the path he was tracing in mid air and saw a cute fuzzy looking creature jump from one tree top to the next. "That's the **Ezo momonga!**" Dilyus shouted excitedly.

Amafiz stood and looked at the others as if they had all lost their minds, he could not believe that with all they had to do the rest of them were getting excited over these native Japanese animals, yes they were cute but something did not feel right to him and he wondered why they were all so besotted with the animals around them, even Scorpicle, but he was immune to the euphoria the others seemed to be experiencing at the sight of these animals. Amafiz looked at the animals the others were cooing over and realised that the state of the others were because of the animals, the more he stared at them the more he realised the animals were emitting a strange humming sound but it was not the sound that was the only problem, for that it seems was only part of what he was witnessing, it was their eyes; the animals were mesmerising the others with their eyes. Amafiz wondered why he had not been affected like the rest of them; he soon got his answer; Amafiz realised that the globe he had in his bag was glowing and gently ebbing, without Amafiz realising the globe and his inner defence power had initiated an aura that very slowly manifested itself and surrounded him, once again protecting him from the danger around them.

Amafiz knew he had to act fast as every moment that passed meant that whatever danger these animals, or whatever was controlling them, presented would soon show and could put their entire mission into jeopardy. The only way to break the hypnotic effect of these animals would be to extend his defence shield towards the others, but he was not sure if it would have any effect now; he had to try!

Amafiz touched his bracelet and concentrated, his thoughts were imagining his defence shield as a large all encompassing entity that would surround him and his friends. The more he concentrated the more his shield grew in size and began to envelope Scorpicle, Nasami, Dilyus and Simsaa, but as it penetrated the air around them Amafiz could feel an external power pushing his shield back.

Amafiz opened his eyes to see what was pushing back his defence shield and was horrified to see an energy vortex swirling like a mini tornado slowly making its way towards them all; it was this energy vortex that was pushing back his shield. Amafiz knew he had to act fast as to his horror the vortex was pulling objects, living and inanimate into it, and if he did not bring his friends out of this hypnotic trance then they too would be sucked into the vortex and transported to some other dimension or world or worse! He did not know what the consequence of this vortex would be and this added to his panic. Amafiz froze in his panicked state, feeling helpless and almost coming to tears; when an image of his father

Akjam came to him, Amafiz was not sure if his father was really standing in front of him or was just a figment of his imagination, as the entire situation seemed quite surreal and he felt as if he was having an out of body experience.

Although deep down, he knew that his father was not standing in front of him, just his imaginary presence was enough of a comfort to Amafiz to give him the energy and confidence to save his friends. With one hand extended and emanating his purple defence shield, Amafiz carefully took the crystal globe from his bag and held it against the stone in his belt. Immediately the purple hue of his shield intensified and pulsated with the additional energy it was being supplied with from the crystal globe.

It was enough, enough to push back the vortex and enable his friends to become encompassed in his purple defence shield, all of them except for one. By the time the rest of them came to and shook of the hypnotic trance they had been under from the animals, and the realisation that one of them was on the edge of the protective shield, Amafiz saw his friend Nasami pulled into the vortex and disappear from sight.

There was a momentary silence as the shock of what they had witnessed was slowly seeping through every cell in their bodies. There was an almighty scream as the realisation of Nasami's disappearance hit Simsaa. The scream brought them all to their senses. Scorpicle tried to track Nasami using the energy pulse that would be emitted from his stone, he managed to pick up a signal; it was extremely weak but it was present. "He's alive but I'm not quite sure where he is?"

"What do you mean?" asked a sobbing Simsaa.

"Well, I mean that I'm picking up a faint signal, which can mean one of two things; that Nasami has been injured in some way and his stone is emitting a pulse but a weak one, or he is in between two dimensions!" Scorpicle explained.

"How do you know that he's in between two dimensions, what I mean is that he could be in another dimension in another universe?" Dilyus asked.

"If he had passed into another dimension completely then I don't think we'd be able to pick up any signal, isn't that right Scorpicle?" questioned Simsaa.

Scorpicle agreed with Simsaa, however, the question still remained 'how were they going to get him back?'

The vortex was still open and that was the only chance of getting Nasami back but they needed to do this without getting trapped themselves. Whilst they were thinking of strategies to rescue Nasami they did not notice the man standing next to the tree near the vortex. Suddenly he stepped out in front of them and without a word jumped into the vortex.

"What the....?" Amafiz gasped at the sight of the man disappearing into the vortex.

They all stood still for what seemed like an eternity waiting to see what was going to happen next. Just when they thought that they would never see Nasami nor, the stranger again, there was an enormous explosion; the sound was deafening and the smoke blinding. As the smoke subsided they saw a lone figure standing where the vortex had been, for a moment they could not tell who it was, but soon they realised it was

Nasami. They ran towards him and embraced him in a giant group hug.

"What happened?" Scorpicle asked him, Nasami was quiet and stared at them all as if he had not seen them for a lifetime. Eventually he spoke.

"I don't understand what happened, I've been away for days but you guys are still here and it feels like time hasn't moved on here!" Nasami explained shocked and bewildered.

"It has only been a few minutes!" said Simsaa soothingly as she gently placed her hand on his upper arm and patted it reassuringly.

"It can't be!" Nasami protested.

"What makes you say that?" asked Scorpicle.

"Well...." Nasami proceeded to tell them everything that had happened inside the vortex.

When Nasami was inside the vortex and in between dimensions it had been as if he was inside a vacuum; there was no sound, he could not even hear his own breathing, not until the old Japanese warrior entered the vortex. Somehow he could hear again and the vacuum like quality of the vortex disappeared. Nasami told his friends how the old Japanese man had introduced himself as one of the greatest Kyujutsu warriors of Japan but would not reveal who he was; however, Nasami did hear him muttering to himself about his legendary ancestor. It seems the Japanese warrior was aware of Stonidium because he told Nasami that he had only risked his life by entering Sheram's vortex so that he could help the Stonimions take back power from Sheram and rid the Earth of him once and for all. Nasami told them how the old warrior had given him a talisman of great power that would enable him to cross the vortex's threshold without coming to any harm, but it could only be used by one person, ultimately the warrior sacrificed himself to save Nasami.

"And so here I am!" he ended his short tale as he gestured his presence by outstretching his arms.

Simsaa walked over to him and gave him a hug and said "Well it's good to see you safe and sound!"

"May I look at the talisman?" Dilyus asked as he stared at the ornament around Nasami's neck.

"Sure" said Nasami as he removed it and handed it over to Dilyus.

Dilyus took the talisman and sat down inside Scorpicle. "Scorpicle, can you bring up the map of Hokkaido Island please?" Scorpicle projected the map on his mini screen. "Can you pinpoint our exact location at the moment?" Scorpicle did as he was asked. Dilyus looked closely at the area and called to the others "Look!" he said as he pointed to their exact location. "I knew that the design of this talisman looked familiar; look at that tree where the vortex appeared and where those hypnotic animals disappeared."

Amafiz looked at the talisman and realised what Dilyus was talking about; the talisman was a kite shape with thin wire like projections arranged around its edge and as he stared at the map it dawned on him that it looked similar in shape to the mountain and the location of the trees around it, although on the map it looked more like a triangle with projections of trees around. Amafiz understood at that point exactly what Dilyus was trying to tell them. "Dilyus, you're right it's the same, which means that the bottom part of the talisman could be indicative of something underground."

"Exactly!" Dilyus said pleased that Amafiz had understood the importance of what they had just figured out.

They all stood at the foot of the mountain looking for a clue connecting the talisman to the mountain. "Look there!" Nasami shouted with excitement. They all looked towards where he was pointing and sure enough they saw a small boulder at the foot of the mountain that was almost triangular looking in shape. They ran over to it and Dilyus placed the talisman on top of the boulder; nothing happened, as they all stood in anticipation of some kind of sign for what, none of them really knew.

"Oh that's a bit disappointing, do you think there may be a special shaped slot on this boulder that the talisman fits into?" Scorpicle asked them.

As they were all pondering on this thought they did not realised that the talisman had become absorbed into the boulder but when they heard it moving from its place they saw they had not been wrong.

As the boulder moved it revealed and entrance into an underground cavern. Cautiously they stepped into it and luckily for Scorpicle he too was able to slowly roll down the incline. Initially it was quite dark, being underground, but as they walked they noticed how the 'cavern' became brighter as if lit by a multitude of lamps. It was not long before they understood that they had not just entered into a cavern within the mountain but in fact had found a portal to another place altogether. The talisman, it seems, had not only been the safe passage out of the vortex but was also the key to a portal leading to a long lost city.

As they walked Scorpicle suddenly said loudly, "I think we've found the next key, the energy surge is pulsating quite violently on the map." They headed in the direction of the energy surge, led by Scorpicle, and before long they were standing in front of a magnificent palace made of glass.

"Wow it's beautiful, is the key inside?" Simsaa asked Scorpicle. He checked the map again and replied. "No, it seems to be coming from behind the palace.

They hastily ran behind the palace, staring in awe at its beauty and each of them wishing they had the time to go and explore inside this splendid building. As they all turned the corner they came across a beautiful garden, full of the most amazing plants; shrubs, trees and flowers, even more amazing than the ones they had seen on the surface of the island.

Amongst the plants they noticed a tall monument, as they got closer they realised that it was a replica of the Great Mountain in Stonidium; however, this was not a mountain but a fountain. The closer they got to the fountain the more the energy surge pulsated. Nasami went over to the edge of the fountain and looked into the waters; he removed his miniature telescope from his bag, he held the telescope over the water and concentrated on an image of the key. The waters started to bubble creating ripples that extended from the epicentre of where the telescope was being held to around the whole of the fountain. With a sudden loud sound as if something was being pulled from a glutinous jelly, the key emerged from the waters and became attached to the telescope.

They took the green key and placed it carefully onto the lock of the green key on the Book of Quantime and, as with the red key; it became absorbed into the book. Simsaa noticed that there was something else floating on the surface of the water, she picked it up a found it was a shiny round pebble. She turned it over and found a word engraved on the underside which simply read 'Nevada'. Simsaa showed it to the others and Scorpicle replied in answer to the word on the stone, whilst simultaneously checking on the map. "Looks like we're gonna have to get the sun hats on because we are off to the desert.

20
THE NEVADA DESERT

The trip to the Nevada desert was fast, initially, but once they arrived at the desert Scorpicle decided to drive, like a normal car, and enjoy the breathtaking scenery. The Stonimions were riveted to the door windows, trying to take in every molecule of the scenery that was passing by. They watched as giant mountains stood proudly amongst the arid dry sands, as if they were watching the small boulders, shrubs and cacti peasants from their regal positions. What was so amazing about this place was the way the scenery changed as they travelled through it. Mountains and dry ground were soon replaced by a stretch of open ground that seemed to go on forever, with no sign of the majestic mountains they had witnessed before. Throughout their journey Scorpicle was giving them a running commentary of the landscape they were passing through.

"If you look over there can you see some mountains to your right?" the Stonimions looked to their right and saw some very strange looking mountains. "There aren't any like those in Stonidium at all!" remarked Nasami.

"No, because if you look at those lines, that is not igneous rock which would be magma that has been expelled from volcanoes as lava, but is in fact sedimentary rock because this was once under water millions of years ago."

Scorpicle seemed to be enjoying showing off his knowledge about Earth's geology.

"It looks spectacular!" Simsaa said as she stared in total awe of the sight before her.

"Oh look! There's a small petrol station, we'll stop there for a while and get something to eat." Scorpicle said as he pulled into towards the petrol station. As he approached closer to the shop and small café he started to feel slightly unnerved.

The Stonimions sensed Scorpicle's uneasiness and felt the evil that was outside seep into every pore of their being. "Scorpicle don't stop, just keep moving." Amafiz warned. Scorpicle did not need to be told twice, he swiftly changed gears and without even a notion to anyone who could have been watching he smoothly drove past the petrol pumps, passed the shop and café. As he moved further away he sped up to ensure there was no chance of being caught by whatever was at that place. Once there was enough of a safe distance between them and whatever had been there Scorpicle pulled over to the side and turned his engine off.

They all sat in silence; this was the weirdest thing that had happened to them by far and the most frightening, even though nothing had actually happened. They were all shaken to their core; they could still sense the malevolence of the presence that had been at the petrol station. There was only one explanation for this – Sheram!

"What happened back there?" Dilyus asked directing the question to anyone of his friends who was willing to answer. No-one replied, not because they were ignoring him but because they themselves had no idea exactly what they could have possibly encountered at the petrol station. All they knew was that whatever it was, it had the sense of such abhorrence that they could not even imagine meeting it. Scorpicle sped off still wanting to place as much distance between them and the petrol station as he physically could.

She stood behind the glass door, staring out at the world beyond. The heavy panting of her breathing was raspy and reeked of death. She was not of this earth, for she had been placed here by her creator – Imfalin. Imfalin in one of her more creative evil moments had made this creature that was the reflection of every evil being, thought, act or deed.

Ragirly was watching as the car came towards the petrol station, she sensed their power and this excited her. Her breathing rate increased as every cell in her evilly created body was respiring more and more to produce the energy she needed to carry out her evil desires. She smiled to herself at the thought of what she would do to these strangers with powers. Her smile soon turned into a grimace of anguish and frustration as instead of heading towards her and the shop the car calmly cruised by the petrol pumps as if it had changed its mind. Ragirly could not understand why they had not stopped and the rage inside her escaped as a gurgled scream full of spittle and slime that drooled from her thin lips. In her rage she swung her arms around causing the items on the shelves to crash violently to the ground. Ragirly lumbered into the back of the shop and stopped dead in her tracks as she caught a glimpse of herself in the mirror. She walked over to the mirror and gently stroked the image of her face, almost in admiration of the hideous reflection that was looking back at her. Ragirly did not find her wild grey hair strange, nor did she recoil at her little button eyes, large bulbous nose and pointed face. The enlarged veins on her face added to the evil that was within her, but despite her hideous looks her true nature was the thing that the Stonimions and Scorpicle had all sensed, for it was so powerful it permeated through the air and into their very being. As Ragirly stared at herself she began to whine like a small child or lost pet; she was yearning for her creator, she wanted to be near the source of evil that would allow her to flourish.

At that moment she made contact with the next best thing, her creator's adopted child, the being that had taken over this putrid world – Sheram.

The board meeting, as with every board meeting ever held, was pointless, arduous and never ending. Sheram sat watching the other board directors, whilst they were arguing over the latest figures and reduced mining of their natural resources from around the world, Sheram mulled over the thought that with one gesture of his hand he could eliminate them all before they could even take another breath. This thought brought a crooked smile to his slender gaunt face; which, instead of making him look more human, made him look even more hideous than his internal evil soul did.

"Well what do you think?"

"Mmmmm?" Sheram asked, suddenly aware that the attention of those present was now upon him. Despite the fact that Sheram had not been listening to the conversation that had been occurring for the last hour, his wits were always about him and he answered without even flinching.

"I think we should sell the copper mines and cut our losses." He answered in such a matter of fact way that the directors did not know how to respond. One of them finally came to his senses.

"Samuel, copper is one of our biggest assets; we rule the world because of the power we have accumulated starting with the acquisition of copper, how can you say that so calmly?"

"David! Really... We? I think you're confused old boy WE didn't do anything it was all ME!" Sheram's voice rose into a delirious scream. The other directors stared in silence; it was Samuel's anger that had always scared them into submission and allowed him to slowly but surely take over the company as CEO and spread his special law enforcers around the world. They were not ashamed to admit he scared them, they did not understand why? If they knew what he was then they would truly understand what it was to fear him.

Sheram stood up with a jolt and said "I need to go" and without further explanation left the boardroom. The company directors were not shocked by this sudden exit, in fact, this was quite usual, they were used to his abrupt and rude behaviour. Many of them feared him because they had witnessed his wrath; others were secretly in awe of the power he portrayed. Either way Sheram, or as they knew him, Samuel was allowed to do whatever he liked.

In the privacy of his office he sat at his desk and allowed the telepathic communication, with Imfalin's creation, to go ahead.

"Sheram, they were here, your enemies from Stonidium."

"Are you sure?"

"I smelt their power, it was beautiful, so much to devour and feast upon!"

"So, did you get them?" Sheram asked eagerly.

There was silence, no telepathic voice telling him something good for a change; his anger began to bubble up inside like carbon dioxide being shaken inside a can of fizzy drink.

"If you did not have anything good to tell me then why did you contact me you foul beast? Sheram's words were like poisoned darts being thrown at Ragirly. Although Ragirly was indeed a beast without any feelings, she felt something close to 'upset' as Sheram's words hissed at her.

"I thought you'd be happy to know that they are on Earth!" she cried in protest at his vehemence.

"I know they are you useless wretch! I've not been able to track them because of their protective powers; that's all. They have been sighted but escaped my men."

"Well they're here in the Nevada desert. Shall I kill them for you Master?" she asked eagerly, wanting to please him like a puppy would want to please its owner. The truth was she was hoping that pleasing him would please her creator, for Imfalin was everything to her, she made her, she commanded her every move. It was because of Imfalin that she had come to this vile world, she could not refuse Imfalin.

"No!" he mentally screamed at her.

"Find them, capture them BUT they are mine!"

Ragirly was beginning to realise why she did not take to Sheram. She was evil and gross, but he was different. She realised what it was about him that was truly frightening, even to SOMETHING like her. He was mad.

The forces around Scorpicle were all balanced; he was travelling at constant speed now that there was sufficient distance between them and the thing back at the petrol station. For a while none of them spoke; they were almost too frightened of saying anything, as if mentioning what they had all felt and experienced would bring forth the being that they had almost encountered. Finally Amafiz spoke up. "We know now that if one of Sheram's hoards is here in the Nevada desert then it won't be long before he will find us, this means time for us here is limited, we need to find the third key quickly and get out of here!"

No one replied, there was no point, they knew Amafiz was absolutely right. The urgency of their mission had just increased tenfold, they had had some near misses with Sheram's police force earlier but the threat was greater now as he would know for definite that they were here. "Scorpicle, could you display the energy map please?" Simsaa asked. Scorpicle complied without a single word being uttered. Nasami noticed the unusual silent behaviour that Scorpicle was currently displaying.

"Scorpicle, what's wrong?" Nasami asked the normally jovial vehicle.

"I think since we encountered that entity it's really hit home how much is riding on us being successful in this mission. I'm scared about what will happen if we can't defeat Sheram."

Scorpicle's negativity was rather a shock to the young Stonimions as well as a wakeup call to the fact that they had no choice but to succeed in this mission. They could not afford the same mistake as before, losing possession of the Initiation Stone was a gross mistake but not to get back the Book of Quantime would mean irrevocable damage to both worlds.

The next hour was spent in silence, which was broken by a rumbling sound. "Is that thunder?" Simsaa asked her friends as she peered out of the car door window.

"I don't think so I can't see any clouds." Nasami answered her.

Dilyus was very quiet and seemed to be ignoring the current conversation a bit too purposefully.

Scorpicle started to giggle like a school girl; this confused the others more as they still had not ascertained what the noise was.

"It's you isn't it Dilyus?" he scoffed.

The others suddenly realised what had happened and Simsaa asked Dilyus "hungry?" to which Dilyus simply nodded whilst looking rather embarrassed at the loud sound made by his stomach.

They soon came across a diner that was not menacing, but just an ordinary good old greasy cafe, and stopped to eat. They also stocked up on food as there was no way of knowing when they might come across another eatery. Before they set off Scorpicle examined the map again just to make sure that they were heading in the right direction. "Can you see that immense energy pulse" he asked the others. They nodded to affirm their observation of the energy pulse. "Well that's the next key, but I think there's something else as well."

Scorpicle's comment took the others by surprise. "What do you mean something else? And more importantly something good or bad?" Dilyus asked looking rather worried about this unexpected bit of information.

"I don't know and I don't know!" Scorpicle replied. The answers did not do anything to ease his anxiety on this matter.

"Well whatever it is we still need to get there!" Nasami commented.

As they were about to drive off there was a knock on the driver's window. Amafiz who was sitting in the driver's seat wound down the electric window. They were all poised ready for the attack, hands ready on their stones, bracing themselves for whatever was out there.

What was out there took them by surprise; as the window descended they saw a young teenager peering curiously into Scorpicle. "Hi, I'm Aaron." He smiled looking extremely happy that he had not been ignored.

"Err, hello" Amafiz replied uncertain as to why this human was trying to talk to them.

"I'm sorry to trouble you but my friends and I are really into cars and your car is fantastic, but we've been arguing as to what make and model it is. Could you settle our argument and tell us?" said the young man.

Amafiz was stunned; he did not know what to say. He turned to look at the others for help but help came from the dashboard, as Scorpicle displayed on his digital screen the words 'this is a unique one off design made by a mechanical engineer from England and his Japanese university friend. Amafiz repeated what he saw on the screen. There was a momentary silence as Amafiz stared at the teenager and his friends, wondering if they had understood him.

"Wow I knew it, I told you Amy, it's not any common model but something unique." Aaron said as he turned to the girl standing next to him.

"It's really cool, you're so lucky to have a car like this, was it expensive?" asked another girl who was with the group.

"What do you think Sarah? Of course it must have been expensive if it's a one off design!"

"Okay I was just asking!" retorted the disgruntled Sarah.

As the group of friends were admiring Scorpicle there was a sudden and raucous noise coming from the diner. They all looked towards the noise and saw another two teenagers running towards them. It turned out they were friends of the three talking to the Stonimions.

"We need to get out of here now!" said the boy as he ran towards them; he was closely followed by the girl who looked as if she was going to burst into tears any moment.

The Stonimions did not get the chance to protest their disagreement towards the human teenagers entering Scorpicle; as they all clambered in and the boy who had been running from the diner simply shouted "DRIVE!!!!"

From the panic that had taken hold of the teenagers, Scorpicle knew that there was not any time to argue or ask what was going on, that would come later, now he just had to drive out from their present location. As they were driving away from the diner, Amafiz saw two of Sheram's special police force running out of the diner. This was not good. Unfortunately for Scorpicle and the Stonimions the two police officers had their own vehicle nearby; they got into it and pursued Scorpicle.

"Oh no! This is not good- why are you all here? Because of you we have those dangerous police following us! Sheram will find us now!" Dilyus yelled at the human passengers who had crammed themselves into Scorpicle.

Nasami glared at Dilyus as a warning not to say anything else. But despite their panic and fear the human teenagers picked up on the word Sheram.

The girl who had come running out of the diner spoke up. "Er! Sorry did you say Sheram?"

"Eloise, it doesn't matter what he said! Now is not the time." The boy who had been running with the girl scolded her. He looked at the Stonimions apologetically, as the oldest in the group of friends he understood that you should not start questioning those helping you.

"My name is Liam and I just want to thank you all on behalf of me and my friends for helping us."

"That's okay but we're not out of the woods yet, the two police officers are still chasing us." Simsaa replied.

"Liam where are Conor and Lacey? Amy asked.

They've already gone home, they had a call from their parents to go home as their cousins had arrived from out of town and they left in the car." Liam explained.

"Nice, so how were we supposed to get home?" Aaron questioned.

"Hitch a ride in a cool car I guess!" Eloise grinned.

The friends all laughed, but the others in the car; namely the Stonimions were silent as they were focused on those chasing them.

They were driving at top speed but the officers were still on their tail; Scorpicle made a decision that changed the course of their mission and took it to a new level. Without any warning he turned on his invisibility device and teleported away from the chasing police.

"What happened?" Sarah asked, holding onto the sides of the seat.

Amafiz knew that they would have to reveal to these human youngsters who they were, as they would need their help and cooperation because there was no doubting that Sheram was after them. Amafiz realised why these teenagers were being chased by Sheram's police; they had mistakenly thought these human teenagers were them!

"It's time we showed ourselves to these humans, maybe they could help us find the next key." Dilyus said almost reluctantly, knowing that this mode of action could end in disaster; however, they had no other option that would lead to a rosier outcome.

When Scorpicle deemed that they were at a safe enough distance, he stopped. At that moment the Stonimions changed their human appearance form back to their original Stonimion form. The sudden change of form had a rather bizarre effect on the humans, instead of screams of shock or horror they sat in absolute silence, simply staring at the Stonimions. What did bring them to their senses was the voice of Scorpicle.

"Hey human kids what's wrong, never seen a Stonimion before?" Scorpicle laughed at his own so called joke.

"Who said that?" Aaron asked, looking around at the others trying to work out who had spoken.

"That was me Scorpicle, car extraordinaire!" Scorpicle; once again, enjoying the shock he had caused.

"I want to get out, I don't like this!" Amy said in a startled voice. She was pulling at the door handle as she spoke. Scorpicle obliged, he did not want the young human to become startled if the door was locked. She tumbled out of the car in her haste and fell flat on her face. Nasami quickly went after her to help her up, but she flinched as he put out his hand towards her.

This was too much for Simsaa. "Look, we didn't ask you to come with us- you all wanted help to escape and we obliged and this is the thanks we get!" the other Stonimions were a bit taken aback at this new Simsaa, who had found her voice. The human teenagers looked rather embarrassed but this time Sarah spoke up. "Look, you really can't blame us, one minute you're normal looking humans the next you're..." she did not know how to finish her sentence.

"Stonimions, we are Stonimions!" Dilyus retorted with a touch of animosity in his usually friendly voice.

"I've never heard of any such thing before, why's that then? Where are you from?" Liam asked.

It was with this comment in mind that Amafiz gathered the human teenagers, sat them down on a large rock and began to tell them everything; from the history of Stonidium, the Stonimions and Sheram. When he had finished the humans stood up and looked at Scorpicle and the Stonimions, Aaron spoke "We will help you find the last primary key, if it's here in the Nevada desert then we'll find it!"

Aaron's energy and positive attitude spurred them all into action. Eloise asked Scorpicle to show her the map. "I'm really interested in geography and I'm quite good at map reading as well." She said trying not to sound too boastful. Scorpicle displayed the map that showed the energy pulse indicating the final primary key. Eloise looked at the map for a few minutes and then said "I think that is the 'Valley of fire' but just to make sure could you superimpose your map on a map of the Nevada desert so I can see exactly the spot that's showing the energy pulse?" Eloise's request was simple and proved to be very helpful. As soon as she saw the two maps superimposed she knew exactly where they needed to go.

The Stonimions found the company of these human teenagers refreshing and comforting; they had not really realised why they all had a feeling of emptiness ever since they came to Earth, it was because they were alone. They were missing their parents, family and friends and it was not until now when these young humans were accompanying them, had they felt the impact of their loneliness.

Scorpicle locked in the co-ordinates for the exact spot in the Valley of Fire, where the key was highly likely to be, if the energy pulse was anything to go by. Scorpicle got them to their destination in super speed and just to show off in front of the humans, he added a bit of whizz bang in the form of coloured smoke from his exhaust system.

"Honestly Scorpicle!" Nasami exclaimed "I didn't take you for the show off type"

"Well when you've got it flaunt it!" Scorpicle laughed. Amy giggled and as she stepped out Scorpicle she stroked his bonnet. "Absolutely Scorpicle, why not?"

The Valley of Fire was a magnificent place, found in the oldest state park in the state of Nevada. It covered more than forty two thousand acres of sandstone formations made from giant sand dunes which had become solid nearly one hundred and fifty million years ago. The Valley of Fire was aptly named as temperatures in the summer were known to climb to about forty nine degrees Celsius.

The beauty of Earth did not cease to amaze and leave the Stonimions in awe, each new place left them breathless and the Valley of Fire was no exception. They found themselves surrounded by a multitude of strangely shaped rock formations as far as the eye could see. Rocks that were a vibrant terracotta colour, some with the stripes of time, laid one on top of the other, others in strange shapes that looked like twisted and tormented souls solidified in a moment of the rock cycle.

Amafiz checked the map again. "We need to head north from

here; I'd say about four miles." Within seconds they were at the site of the energy surge, but the Stonimions were met by some unwanted hosts waiting to greet their unsuspecting guests.

The sudden disappearance of the unusual looking car with its occupants reinforced the officer's suspicion that they had found the teenagers that Mr. Watson had told them to find. The two officers stopped their vehicle and phoned Mr. Watson on his direct line.

"Hello Mr. Watson we've spotted the teenagers, they were in a diner near Lake Tahoe, so they're still in the Nevada." one of the officers said.

"All four of them?" Sheram asked

"I'm sorry Sir, don't you mean five?"

"Are you telling me I don't know what I'm talking about!" Sheram's voice raised into a high pitched crescendo at the impertinence of the meagre human that worked for him.

"Of course not Sir, it's just there were five of them."

"Then you were chasing the wrong people you absurd, pathetic waste of space!" Sheram was beyond angry at this point, he was tempted to strangulate this annoyance but decided better of it, too many bodies would attract his enemies.

"But Sir what about the vehicle?" the officer protested.

"Vehicle?" Sheram questioned.

"Yes Sir, it was rather a spectacular looking car, and it had some other kids already inside it."

"You imbecile, that's THEM!"

"How are we going to find them Sir?" the nervous sounding officer asked the ever angry Sheram.

"Leave that to me, just wait for further instructions." They did as they were told and waited. Very soon their instructions arrived and dutifully they obeyed. The two officers summoned back up and turned from two into fifty, fifty armed officers who answered only to Sheram. Sheram had homed in on Scorpicle's energy release essence when he had teleported to the Valley of Fire. The remnants of the energy were enough for Sheram to send his troop to the correct location, along with a little satellite investigation he had managed to pick up on another energy pulse in the area. He did not know what they were up to but realised that if they were in that vicinity then it would be connected to the other energy surge he had picked. This is why his evil officers were waiting.

The attack was sudden and ferocious and without mercy. As soon as Scorpicle arrived at the energy surge spot, before the occupants inside had even the chance to take a breath the onslaught of gun fire commenced. Scorpicle did not even get the chance to take immediate action and put up the defence shield, but he did not have to. A purple hue began to emanate in the car and a shield emerged around Scorpicle; at that point an immense bright light also began to manifest. The humans looked on horrified at the scene in front of them. There was a purplish coloured dome around them and outside of the dome they saw the brightly lit wispy trails wrapping themselves around the guns of the officers. For one horrific moment it looked as if the officers were turning the guns on each other and about to shoot each other. Eloise screamed at the thought

of what would come next but she did not know that the Stonimions priority was self defence and would only attack as a
last resort.

Instead the guns lifted into the air and flew away into the
distance and to everyone's amazement as the guns were
moving away they turned into strange looking flowers whose
leaves were transparent. "Look, plants that don't photosynthe-
sise!" the others looked at Amy with a puzzled expression.
"No chlorophyll, that's why they're not green in colour, no
chlorophyll, so no photosynthesis."

"Well actually they do, but on Stonidium they use a part of the
light spectrum that's outside of the visible light range." Simsaa
explained.

"Wow that would blow my biology teachers mind!" Amy
remarked amazed by Simsaa's explanation.

They were all so busy thinking about the guns turning into
flowers that they had not noticed the green colour
surrounding the officers. Dilyus had taken control of Sheram's
men and so off they went into the desert.

"Where are they going?" Aaron asked.

"I told them to go back to their master, simple."

The next task, before the key, was to tend to Scorpicle.

They all stood around him staring at the damage that had
been caused by the enormous amount of bullets that riddled
Scorpicle's bodywork. "I don't know how we're going to sort
this out, we can't take him to a mechanic, he's not an ordinary
car and we'll bring more attention to ourselves." Liam
explained to the concerned group.

"Wait a moment guys!" Scorpicle interrupted their thoughts and discussion as to what to do to help him. "Are you worried about me? Don't be, my interior is fine, my circuits are protected and my brain, I mean computer system is still working and..."

"Yes but what about your bodywork? You could get rust and then..." Aaron said worriedly.

"Step back all of you." Scorpicle instructed them, they did as asked and in front of their very eyes they saw the outer metallic bodywork drop off of Scorpicle like a snake shedding its old skin. "See, I'm not just a pretty face you know!" Scorpicle laughed. "Amafiz your father is a genius mechanic in more ways than one, he made sure that I have been made pretty invincible."

Scorpicle's speedy recovery spurred them onto finding the last primary key. The Stonimions looked at the map and realised that the strange looking rock formation in front of them was the site of the last key. The human teenagers and the Stonimions moved closer to the strange looking rock; it looked like a thin giant elephant with an extraordinarily long trunk that extended from a giant roundish head all the way to the ground. When they reached the rock formation Simsaa noticed that the energy pulse on the map had increased in intensity. She pointed towards the rock at the end of the 'trunk' of the elephant. "There." She simply said.

Dilyus went over to the rock and placed his hand on it, the rock started to vibrate, one by one each of the Stonimions placed a hand on the rock; the humans watched in silence alongside Scorpicle. Within a matter of minutes the top of the boulder like rock that was attached to the 'trunk' began to crack open. It looked as if the top of the rock had broken off like the top of a soft boiled egg. Amafiz reached inside the rock and slowly picked up something that the others could as yet not see, as he pulled out his hand they saw a vibrant bright cobalt blue object that glowed in his hand.

At that moment there was a humming noise from Simsaa's bag; this was her signal to produce the Book of Quantime. This was quite a poignant moment that was being witnessed by the human teenagers, they saw something that they never even knew existed in this world or in any other world; the Book of Quantime. They watched as Dilyus passed the blue key to Simsaa, who then carefully placed the final primary key into the blue lock. As the blue key became absorbed into the lock, the lock for the secondary key appeared and intermittently glowed cyan, magenta and then yellow.

The human teenagers knew that the Stonimions were moving onto their next destination. This made the sensitive Amy slightly tearful, but Simsaa stroked her arm in a comforting manner. "Don't worry, everything will be okay." She told her.

"It's not that, when you guys restore everything back to as it should have been- whatever that is, we may not exist or even if we do, we may not remember you all." Amy sobbed.

She had a point, but there was nothing any of them could do, and no way of knowing either. Amafiz decided to give them something for them to remember them by, even if it may not be permanent. He produced five stones using the power of his bracelet; stones that were from Stonidium that were nothing like any stone found on Earth. He handed them each a stone and told them to hold the stone in their hand and think of them. They did and from each of the stones they saw an image of the Stonimions and of course Scorpicle, appear in front of them.

It was time to go and so to limit the pain of goodbyes, they all bid their goodbyes quickly, the Stonimions sat inside Scorpicle and, in front of their very eyes, the humans saw them disappear as they teleported at the speed of light.

21

THE PYRAMIDS

"Not that it's important, but exactly, where are we going?" Dilyus asked his sarcasm returning in full force.

Scorpicle laughed, he could relate to Dilyus very well, as he had a similar sense of humour. "We are off to the pyramids!" he revealed.

"The what?" Dilyus asked looking confused.

"Really Dilyus, if you had paid attention to Earth's history lessons, you'd know." Nasami looked at his friend and smiled. Dilyus was always away in his own little world during lessons, but amazingly he always did well in tests.

Scorpicle displayed the map showing the African continent and at the top right was Egypt. The Stonimions learnt a lot about Earth's history as it was one of the most intensely studied in Stonidium and one that the Stonimions enjoyed especially as Egyptology was synonymous to the history of

Stonidium. They were both filled with mystery and power as well as the ever conflict and battle of who would rule over all.

Amafiz looked at the map as they were on their way to Egypt; he looked closely to establish exactly where the energy pulse was. "It looks like the energy pulse is coming from outside of the capital, near the pyramids." Scorpicle stopped outside of the capital but the Stonimions soon realised that getting to the area they needed to get to would not be as easy as they had thought. The popularity of the Pyramids as tourist attractions meant it would be very busy, getting there would not be such an issue, but they had to re-think of another way of accessing the pyramids as tourists were allowed in but only as part of controlled group visits.

Simsaa looked up the local tourist information spots on Scorpicle's database and found one that seemed to have the information they needed on how to get to their destination. They arrived at the tourist information site, Simsaa and Dilyus went in, at this moment in time they thought it best to take on the guise of humans who would be foreigners to Egypt, so they had kept their identity from Nevada. Although they understood everything the tourist guide was saying to them when he spoke in Arabic, they pretended not to understand and so began a game of charades, which lasted about ten minutes. However, the effort was worth it, they left with the necessary information they needed. Simsaa produced a map of the major pyramid fields and as before superimposed this onto their map to try and locate the secondary key.

They studied the map and realised that the energy surge was coming from a particular area; the *Saqqara*. Dilyus produced a leaflet about the area that they needed to get to. He read:

'The Great Step Pyramid Complex at Saqqara, known to the ancient Egyptians as kbhw-ntrw (libation of the deities), is one of those superstars of Egyptian monuments that is almost always on the itinerary of antiquity tours to Egypt. Few monuments hold a place in human history as significant as that of this Pyramid. It can be said that the Step Pyramid complex is a milestone in the evolution of monumental stone architecture, both in Egypt and in the world as a whole. It is the beginning of an evolutionary period that would see the polished, smooth faced true pyramids of the 4th Dynasty master-builders.'

"Well, Saqqara it is then." Scorpicle said. He was about to start his engine when Nasami interjected and stopped him. "We need to make sure that we don't bring attention to ourselves when we get there."

"So what should we do then?" Amafiz asked him. "We need to go there whether it's busy or not!" he pointed out.

"Let's go as near as we can without being too noticeable, Scorpicle looks like one of those big cars that are good for driving on sand, so we shouldn't stand out." Dilyus piped up eagerly. They all agreed with Dilyus, which took him a bit by surprise, no come back or disagreement left him feeling very pleased.

Unfortunately Scorpicle and the Stonimions had no idea that remaining hidden from human tourists was the least of their worries; they had no idea that a more sinister welcoming party awaited them at the Djoser pyramid at Saqqara.

Sheram sat at the head of the board room table waiting and wondering about any news about the wretched Stonimions. He did not have to wait too much longer as there was a hard and fast knocking at the board room door.

"Enter." He commanded.

"Mr Watson, I'm very sorry to trouble you like this but there is an incident happening in reception." Sheram's secretary said in a hurried and panicky voice.

"Then get security to deal with it, do I look like a heavy to you?" Sheram screamed at the already frightened secretary.

"Yes Sir, I mean No Sir, the thing is they're asking for you." She replied.

"Who?" Sheram asked intrigued by what may be going on downstairs.

"About fifty armed men." She timidly replied.

Sheram reluctantly got into the lift and went down to the ground floor. As he stepped out of the lift he was overwhelmed by a smell of body odour, blood and confusion. In front of Sheram was a small army of very bewildered looking law enforcement officers, who on seeing Sheram seemed to come out of a hypnotic trance.

Sheram stepped towards one of the men who was at the forefront of the group, he looked at him closely and said "The Stonimions?", even though he had no idea who the Stonimions were, the mental link he had formed with Sheram filled him with enough knowledge to understand what was being said to him. Sheram gauged from the man's memory that the Stonimions had actually been at the diner, and they had helped the human teenagers to escape. Sheram also found out that the vehicle they were in had escaped at the speed of light. He knew this was Scorpicle, when he had been in Stonidium he had heard about this vehicle, he also knew that Akjam had made him and most importantly he also knew that this was no ordinary vehicle, but one with a secret.

Sheram dealt with the law enforcers by taking them out of the reception area and into the large conference room, often used for international company presentations and meetings. There he removed the mind command that had been placed on them, his power had become slightly diminished and was not the strength it had been in Stonidium but was sufficient to have an effect on the puny humans.

Once the law enforcers had been dispersed and had gone back to their duties Sheram set about determined to find out where the Stonimions were going to go next and this time, stop them once and for all. Sheram knew it was time to take a risk; exposure of his true identity could occur but now was not the time to worry about that because if the Stonimions were to succeed then there would be nothing left for him anyway.

Sheram retired to his office and commanded to his secretary that he was not to be disturbed at any cost. She knew not to go against his wishes. Sheram sat at his desk for a few minutes thinking; suddenly he got up and moved over to the wall on his right. He stood in front of the giant bookcase and scanned the array of books, when he got to the one he needed he picked it out and opened it carefully. The instance he did the room was filled with a red light that penetrated into every corner of the room. Sheram cleared his mind in order to open a telepathic link with his carer – Imfalin.

Sheram sat at his desk for what seemed like an eternity, he was tiring but was not going to give up. Finally, just as he thought that he was not going to succeed; it happened.

"Is that really you Sheram?" Imfalin's voice in his mind was still as grating and annoying as he remembered.

"No, it's the milkman!" he replied sarcastically.

"The what?" Imfalin asked confused.

"Never mind." Sheram answered, he forgot that Imfalin was neither of Earth, nor England at the times of when milkmen existed and he did not have the energy, or more importantly the time, to explain. Imfalin knew better than to pursue this path of their telepathic conversation any further, but she knew that it probably had something to do with his life prior to Stonidium.

"I need the cell destroyer." Sheram was blunt and to the point.

"Sheram no, that is way too dangerous." Imfalin regretted the words as soon as they came out of her mouth, but the shock of what Sheram had asked for did not allow her to think before she opened her mouth.

"Did you really just refuse me?" he asked his anger beginning to percolate through every pore of his body at the thought that she had had the audacity to actually use the word 'no'.

"Er no, I mean I will have to find a way of getting it to you and that won't be easy – but don't worry I will find a way and get it to you somehow and very quickly." She added hastily before Sheram had the chance to retaliate with another cutting remark.

"Be sure that you do, I know why those troublesome Stonimions are here and they are very near to accessing the Book of Quantime." With that last comment he closed the link with Imfalin; he needed her and in his own

269

way liked her but could not stand her. It was a very strange relationship indeed.

Sheram sat back in his chair, thinking about the consequences of making the contact with Stonidium. He did not have to wait long as soon the phone rang; he hesitated slightly before answering it. Sheram was in power but as a human he was simply a powerful business man and this guise suited him until he was totally ready to show his true nature and rule the Earth as he wanted to. This meant that in the process of his rise to power he had to keep those humans in power, on his side. This included those that did not come into the category of politicians, scientists and the rich, but that elite group that were aware of magical powers and knew how to use this power to propel them to a greater status.

"Samuel, the ruler wishes to see you." The message was simple and to the point. Sheram did not contest against the summons but simply complied. He informed his secretary that he was going out and would not be back in the office for the rest of the day.

Sheram arrived at the ruler's lair and used his secret password 'Sheram' to enter. The irony of the fact that the entire circle of power was based upon his legend and that his name was used as the password, still amused him. He so wanted to enter the meeting house and declare that he was the great Sheram the reason that this society of evil had been formed. He did no such thing as there was much more for him to do, before he could as the handful people who were members of the circle of power were not enough to help him rule the Earth. He knew it would not be much longer as he had already gained a lot of power as CEO of one of the world's largest companies and controlled the law enforcement agency that was the ruling law enforcer for many countries; it was just a matter of the right moment for absolute domination.

However, this could be in jeopardy with the contact he had made with Imfalin; the circle of power could have figured out who he was before the correct time.

Sheram entered the ruler's lair and found he was greeted by the chief members of the order. They sat around a large oval table, which because of its colour, looked like a giant black onyx stone. It looked similar to the base of the Initiation Stone, but neither Sheram nor the members of the order knew this, the order was aware of another 'world' and from their society's history they had picked up bits of information about this other world. They were unaware that their table was based on their enemies Initiation Stone.

He walked over to the ruler and was about to bow down before him, as was the tradition to do, when the ruler suddenly stood up from his chair and took a step back away from Sheram as if in shock by the presence in front of him.

"We know who you are - Sheram!" the ruler said with a touch of hurt in his voice.

Sheram did not respond, but just stared at the ruler, who continued. "But what we do not understand is why such a great and powerful being as you has remained hidden like some sort of humble servant of the order?"

Sheram was a bit taken aback by the obvious hurt the ruler was displaying now.

"Did you not think us good enough to be taken into your

confidence, is the society so compromised in its dedication to you that you did not reveal who you are?"

Sheram felt slightly remorseful, albeit for a nanosecond. He regained his composure that had been lost for that split second and replied "I do not need to explain my actions to you; I have my reasons, but now that you know who I am then hear my command. I need you to assist me in ridding the Earth of the Stonimions who have dared to enter and try to stop me in my overall ruling of this world, I need to pinpoint their where-abouts and stop them before they access the Book of Quantime."

On hearing the name of the Book of Quantime there was a gasp and then a ripple of murmurings amongst the other members gathered at the lair. The knowledge the society had accumulated over the years had also informed them of the Book of Quantime, something that Sheram found surprising as Imfalin was the one who had told him about it as he was growing up. It was obvious to him that this society had been established a very long time ago indeed.

The ruler spoke to Sheram again "Sheram... may I call you by your name?" he hesitated when he had realised that he had addressed Sheram by his name. Sheram nodded his approval so he continued. "Sheram these Stonimions that you have mentioned, who are they exactly, what I mean is that we as the society are aware of them but who are the ones who have the audacity to follow you here and think that they can stop you?"

"The Chief Elder of the Stonimions believes that they are the 'Four Guardians of Stonidium'." Sheram simply replied; this comment resulted in the same response as the mentioning of the Book of Quantime.

The ruler dismissed the remainder members of the society who left the room feeling privileged to have been in the company of the great Sheram. Sheram and the ruler moved towards a shrine that was hidden behind a curtain within the lair, there the ruler showed Sheram all the parchments, artefacts and books that had been acquired over many centuries by the forefathers of the society of power. The intention, from the beginning, was to allow evil to rule the Earth, for overall power to be given to one being 'The Evil One'.

Sheram asked to be left alone as he perused through the various resources in front of him. As he was beginning to think that what was in front of him was nothing more than a library of information for humans who were interested in learning about Stonidium, the Stonimions and him, he found what he was looking for.

Sheram spread out the map onto the large oval table in the lair and told the ruler that this was the map of minds and with it he would be able to find out exactly what the Stonimions were going to do next and so stop them. The map was larger than it had originally looked; as he stared down at it he moved his left hand across the map in a sweeping motion, as he did so he was slowly dropping small crystals, which he had found amongst the artefacts, knowing that these were crystals from Stonidium and ones that were attracted to powerful energy, he could not believe his luck. The crystals that had been drizzled over the entire map began to move and slowly gather in a particular spot. Sheram and the ruler of the society looked at the map and then at each other; Sheram revealed his evil smile, which made the ruler flinch slightly, and said "The Pyramids it is!"

273

Sheram once again made contact with Imfalin within the safe confines of the lair, this time being witnessed by the ruler. "I need the cell destroyer you old hag, I told you that before." Sheram was not used to being refused or let down and to say that he was displeased with Imfalin would be a great under-statement. The ruler flinched as Sheram's anger intensified, he was getting worried for his own safety. Sheram broke the link with Imfalin; she was useless to him at this point. "Sheram maybe I can be of help, come with me." Sheram followed the ruler into another room, there the ruler walked towards a large ancient looking chest. He carefully opened the chest, which did so reluctantly, as it was not used to being opened. The ruler pointed towards the chest, inviting Sheram to look into it; Sheram did so and found what he needed. When the ruler realised that he had not received what he wanted and heard Sheram shout out 'cell destroyer' instead of just saying it in his mind, he realised immediately what Sheram was referring to.

The society had acquired the cell destroyer a very long time ago and they knew its power because of the destruction it had caused when it had been used in the past. The inexplicable destruction of tribes of people, small towns and such that were sometimes overlooked in history but still noted and known about by some. "That's why Imfalin could not find it." Sheram commented as a matter of fact. He was ready, Sheram asked the ruler to gather some of the most powerful members of the society to go with him to Saqqara, this time he would not lose.

When the Stonimions arrived at the Djoser pyramid they changed their guise from tourists to locals. Scorpicle now took on the appearance of quite a smart looking four by four.

The incident in the Nevada desert had made them even more

cautious than before, so they made sure that they did not arrive too close to their destination via teleportation. Instead, they drove as the humans did and arrived quite inconspicuously. Their quiet arrival gave them the chance to have a look around. There were some tourists around but it was very early in the morning so it was not as busy; there were more locals around so the Stonimions blended in quite well. The old pyramid was amazing; it was not as large as some of the others as in the pyramids of Giza, but it was enchanting all the same. The Djoser pyramid had an aura of mystery and power that was inexplicable; the backdrop of the desert also provided an eerie feel of complete and utter loneliness that could drive a person insane.

The Stonimions cautiously stepped out of Scorpicle, who had parked a few hundred yards away from the pyramid; he turned on his invisibility device and slowly rolled beside the Stonimions as they walked towards the pyramid. As they neared the pyramid they realised that the other locals and tourists who were in the area had stopped in their tracks and were all staring at them. The Stonimions noticed this and began to feel uneasy, slowing their pace until they came to a halt; something was terribly wrong. The four guardians of Stonidium instantaneously came into action without a single word being uttered to each other; they knew they were in serious danger so their instinct kicked in.

Unfortunately, as fast as the Stonimions were, Sheram and his new found cronies were just slightly faster and before Amafiz had the chance to put up his defence shield they had used the cell destroyer on Simsaa. The cell destroyer had been used in the past to destroy whole tribes or parts of nations but Sheram did not want to attract unnecessary attention so he had adjusted the power of the cell destroyer so that its effects were more localised to a few individuals; enough for him to get rid of his enemies once and for all. By the time Amafiz had produced his defence shield the effect of the cell destroyer was already taking effect on Simsaa.

Sheram had ensured that there were not any humans around at the time of this attack; the society of power had used various tactics to do this, such as, notices being produced that the area had been closed for the day for restoration purposes and the like. This was lucky as the effect of the cell destroyer would have been quite horrific for the humans to see, but unknown to those present there was one human left who was witnessing everything from the safety of his tent; a small inconspicuous tent that was hidden in a corner next to the Djoser pyramid.

Amafiz's shield pulsated with a purplish hue that lit up the entire area, an impenetrable shield that Sheram and the society of power were now trying to infiltrate.

Amafiz found that he was having to multi task, as he needed to keep the shield intact but at the same time tend to Simsaa. Simsaa was not in a good way; when the ray from the cell destroyer first hit her she had become stunned and motionless, almost frozen. Slowly she began to change, first of all the guise of the human changed and she was a Stonimion once more; then the pain started, agonizing pain that started within every cell of her body. One by one each of her cells was undergoing apoptosis; death of the cell brought about by the cell itself, the releasing of destructive enzymes causing each cell to die in a painful way. Amafiz knew he had to move fast as every second meant that Simsaa's life was in greater danger, the more of her that became damaged the harder it would be for him to help her recover. Once Amafiz had established his shield Scorpicle was then able to initiate his own. This then allowed Amafiz to weaken his own shield so that he could tend to the pain-ridden Simsaa.

The process of helping Simsaa would not be easy but he had no choice, he had to succeed. Amafiz asked Simsaa where she felt the most pain as that was the indicator that that was where the most damage was being done. She slowly moved her hand towards her stomach and held onto her stomach, there were tears of pain trickling from her eyes like a stream down a mountain. It was too much for Dilyus to see his friend in such agony and the usually docile and serene Dilyus really lost it. Whilst Amafiz placed his hand over Simsaa's stomach and allowed his powers to surge from his amethyst through his fingers and into Simsaa's body, Dilyus and Nasami began to tackle the enemy that was the root of their friend's anguish.

They worked as a stupendous team, their ability work together without having to give instructions; the reason as to why Samaan had recognised them to be the 'Four Guardians'. Dilyus touched his emerald stone which pulsated as a surge of green light filled up the shield they were in; he concentrated hard pointing his hand towards the enemy outside. Dilyus was attempting multiple mind control, which was not that difficult but was proving to be, as in this case the minds he was trying to control were powerful because of the power they had accumulated over the years. His task was made easier with Nasami's help; as Dilyus was using his power of mind control Nasami was using his telekinetic powers to control the cell destroyer. What happened next was swift and shocking.

Sheram realised within moments of the shield going up that this was not going to go well so had already put into action his escape plan. As the members of the society were operating the cell destroyer and looking pleased with themselves at having targeted one of the Stonimions and causing them great pain, Sheram realised that with the defence shield going up the Stonimions would soon be attacking them. It was every man for him-self which meant that Sheram had no qualms about leaving his cronies to it. Just as Nasami had taken control of the cell destroyer; Dilyus using his power of mind control got the members of the society to line up; Nasami released the power of the cell destroyer upon the members, but as a Stonimion he could not bring him-self to hurt them as they had hurt Simsaa, instead he gave them a small enough dose to initiate a response of pain. However, Nasami did not realise that once the cell destroyer had affected even a single cell, due to cell signalling, the message of self-destruction would spread until all the cells had been destroyed.

At this point in time Sheram had departed; he was not going to hang around to be hurt by the wretched Stonimions. Sheram had teleported from the area just as he saw the green hue being released from Dilyus' stone; he knew he was in danger. Once the threat from the enemy had subsided Scorpicle removed the defence shield. Amafiz had completed the healing of Simsaa, who sat on the ground weakened by the entire experience; her cells needed time to replenish, which thanks to Amafiz, were now replicating by mitosis in record time.

"Amafiz I think those people need your help." Nasami turned to his friend as if ashamed at what he and Dilyus had done.

"Not to worry, I've got this." Amafiz replied. He stretched out his hand towards the humans, who were by now writhing on the floor in absolute agony. Within minutes their pain had subsided and they began to recover from their ordeal. Nasami moved the cell destroyer away from them and the humans who had used it on them. Scorpicle then proceeded to destroy it with his laser and as he did so he said "Good riddance."

The Stonimions and Scorpicle left the humans where they were; they knew that they could not harm them now as they realised that Sheram, whom they had all seen before, was no longer present. Like the coward that he was he had gone.

With the danger over they turned their attention to their mission; the secondary key. They looked again at the map and saw that the energy surge was coming from the Djoser pyramid. The next couple of hours were spent by them searching it from top to bottom; they left no corner unsearched, no stone or artefact unturned. They were now beginning to worry, so far the map had not let them down and now just as they were close to completing their mission things were going against them. They stopped for while to eat and to re-strategise their tactics. As they sat in silence each deep in their own thoughts they were unaware of the old man watching them; the same man who had witnessed the defeat of the humans by these incredible creatures, who had shown more 'human' compassion than the humans had done towards them.

He cautiously entered the pyramid and cleared his throat by way of an introduction. "Ahem, I am sorry to interrupt you, I am Abdul Wahid and I...." the old man was interrupted by Amafiz.

"How did you get in? Where is Scorpicle? He was supposed to be keeping guard." Amafiz was looking very concerned.

"If you are talking about your vehicle then he is fine and dutifully standing at his post, I came in another way." The old man explained. "I think I can help you Stonimions." He continued.

The Stonimions were stunned by this last comment, stunned that he was aware of them and seemed to think that he could help them; the question was how?

Abdul Wahid sat down beside the Stonimions and produced an old tattered book; he waved the book at them as he explained how he knew so much about them. "This book has been passed down from generation to generation in my family for the past one thousand years. In it there is the story about these strange beings from another world; good beings that are on our side, beings that will come to the aid of Earth when a really evil man shall try to take over the world. Beings that created an extremely strong and invincible fortress made from stones and crystals from their world." He emphasised the last sentence with eyes widened and turned the book around to show them a drawing of a Stonimion inside a giant pyramid holding a key.

The Stonimions could not believe their eyes; their ancestors had built a pyramid like the Egyptians, but the question was where?

"So our ancestors made a pyramid like the Egyptians then?" Nasami asked the old man.

"No, the Egyptians made pyramids like your ancestors." The old man replied looking so proud as if his ancestors had made the first pyramid.

"Wow, that's impressive." Simsaa said, looking surprised by this revelation as in history classes nothing of this sort had been revealed. She explained this to the old man who simply replied. "Your ancestors did not revel in glory; their job was to simply protect our two worlds and they did so valiantly, so the fact that their production of the first pyramid is even unknown in your history is no real surprise." He told them. "I believe that the key that you are looking for is not in this pyramid but in the one built by your ancestors."

"Then why is our map showing the energy pulse here?" Dilyus asked.

"I believe that the pyramid is down here." The old man pointed down towards the ground as he said this. The Stonimions looked puzzled for a moment they then realised what Abdul Wahid was trying to tell them.

"How do we get down there?" Dilyus asked mimicking the old man by pointing downwards.

"This book tells about a secret passage to the original pyramid." Abdul Wahid explained.

"Why has it not been discovered by humans?" Amafiz asked,

"Because the pyramid is not visible to them, as I said it's made of the stones and crystals from your world and it has the power to cloak the pyramid, not only can it not be seen but it can alter its existence in this dimension if there is any danger of people approaching it.

This was really no surprise to the Stonimions as their ancestors were well known for their thoroughness, so it was just a case of working out from the book that Abdul Wahid possessed how they were going to get to the pyramid. They also had at the back of their minds the fact that Sheram could be returning with reinforcements.

Abdul Wahid gave Amafiz the book as they all gathered around it; Scorpicle had by this point reduced his size and entered the pyramid as well. Scorpicle stared at the writing and simply said "What is that?" looking extremely puzzled.

"For a vehicle who claims to know every language, are you telling me that you don't know what it says?" Dilyus said in a teasing voice.

"I still know more than you." Scorpicle retorted.

"It is not just an ancient language it is also in code." Abdul Wahid explained.

"Great, we don't have time for this." Nasami looked panicked as he started to pace up and down wondering how they were going to solve this problem.

"I have an idea." Simsaa said as she took out the old parchment she had picked up from the Great Mountain in Stonidium. She carefully placed the parchment of knowledge over the cryptic words in the book and closed her eyes. Simsaa began to see an image of the writing appear in her mind in a familiar language. "Write this down." She said to no-one in particular. Nasami was ready and said "Okay go ahead."

"Through the apex of the Djoser, you will find me, directly beneath the palm tree." Simsaa stopped.

"Is that it? Wow that's really helpful." This time it was Amafiz whose sarcastic side had come through, due to the frustration of the situation. It was a case of so near yet so far that gave the Stonimions such a feeling of despair.

"Yes it is very helpful." Abdul Wahid said as he rushed over to the far side of the pyramid. He carefully moved his hand over the wall in front of him and stared at the hieroglyphics in front of him. He stopped abruptly and he began to tremble with excitement. "There" he said "look." He pointed towards one of the symbols on the wall. The others gathered around and saw a large pyramid and underneath it was a drawing of a palm tree, as they followed an imaginary line straight down from the tree towards the ground they found another symbol etched very discreetly into the wall of the pyramid. The drawing was of another pyramid but this time inside the pyramid was the drawing of a key, a key which was pointing straight down.

They realised that the access point to the pyramid built by the ancestors was in that position, so they began shovelling and removing the sand from the ground. They had removed quite a bit of sand and seemed to have dug quite a big hole when Amafiz hit something solid. They quickly brushed away the sand and there it was a spiral shaped stone that looked like the gateway to somewhere else. Nasami took his miniature telescope from Simsaa's bag and looked at the spiral access through his telescope; he saw that the spiral needed to be turned anti-clockwise, he did this carefully and for a moment nothing happened. They all looked at each with anticipation, not daring to breathe in case they caused something to go wrong.

There was a loud groan as if the ground was in pain, and then the trembling began. Abdul Wahid, Scorpicle and Stonimions all toppled over as the ground beneath them jolted and opened up as if it was being pulled apart, then without warning they fell downwards.

After the dust had settled they found themselves inside a pyramid, however, there was no doubting that this was not the Djoser pyramid. They were inside a beautiful sparkling clean pyramid that displayed a myriad of colours and light. Abdul Wahid looked around in awe, then at the Stonimions. "Is this what your world is like?" he asked.

"Yes this looks very similar to our Great Mountain." Dilyus told him. Scorpicle shone his headlights around the pyramid to try and locate the key. Futile maybe, but it actually worked; at the apex of the pyramid his light beam reflected off an object that was embedded in the apex and as they all saw it reflected three very important colours; cyan, yellow and magenta. It was the secondary key. The problem was how they were going to retrieve it.

Amafiz had an idea, with Scorpicle providing the light, Simsaa changed her form into a large round pebble, which Amafiz stood on and Nasami moved with his telekinetic powers towards the apex of the pyramid and to the secondary key. Once near enough Amafiz carefully reached for the key and to their surprise retrieved it without any further problems. "Finally; we've managed to do something without any added issues." Dilyus declared as Amafiz descended holding the secondary key.

They had to leave the pyramid but luckily this was not an issue for Scorpicle; he teleported them back to their original coordinates and they soon found themselves back in the Djoser pyramid as if nothing had happened there at all; it was all intact, there was no hole from which they had fallen into the hidden pyramid, it was as if nothing had been disturbed at all.

The Stonimions thanked the old man for his help for without him they would not have succeeded in their mission.

"It was an honour and a privilege to have helped you all. I wish you good luck and peace." He replied to their thanks.

Abdul Wahid watched with excitement as they placed the secondary key into the Book of Quantime, a bright white light emanated from the book and in front of his very eyes they disappeared.

THE VICTORY

22

THE DELIVERANCE

Abdul Wahid stood alone in the Djoser pyramid not quite sure if everything that had happened had been real or his imagination. His question was answered by the stone left in his hand; a stone that had been given to him by Amafiz before they disappeared. He left the pyramid wondering where the Stonimions had gone, and whether they had truly been successful in their mission; he would soon find out.

As soon as Amafiz had placed the secondary key into the Book of Quantime, the power of the primary and secondary keys had combined and produced the white light of time. The instant the white light had appeared, Amafiz uttered the word "Stonidium." Within an instant they felt as if they were being sucked into a vacuum. "Good grief, we've just experienced spaghettification." Scorpicle grinned as if he had just been on a park ride that no-one had ever experienced before.

"What's that then?" Nasami asked.

"Well it's what we're supposed to experience if we were on the edge of a black hole, which is a large concentrated area of gravity, before we'd get sucked into it." Scorpicle explained.

"Amafiz, when are we?" Simsaa asked as they landed with a thud.

"Didn't you hear what I said, as the light opened the book, I said Stonidium." Amafiz said perplexed that she had not heard him.

"And you didn't hear what I just asked, I asked WHEN are we?" Simsaa repeated.

"Oh sorry Simsaa, to be honest I'm not sure, I think I assumed that if no time was mentioned it would automatically take us to the present time." Amafiz explained looking rather sheepish.

Scorpicle tried to ascertain what time they were in but was unable to pick up anything on his databank. This rather worried them all. The Stonimions stepped out of Scorpicle and looked around; this was not Stonidium or rather not the Stonidium that they were familiar with. They looked around and saw nothing but barren land as far as the eye could see.

Scorpicle checked his databank once again. He realised what the problem was. "Kids I don't mean to panic you but I think we should get out from here as quickly as possible." Scorpicle's panicked voice did not help their already raised stress levels.

"Why? What's wrong?" Dilyus the not so brave asked.

"When Amafiz told the Book of Quantime, Stonidium, it did as it was told. It's brought us to the point when Stonidium was first formed, the beginning of time for this world." It took the Stonimions a few minutes to get to grip with this information.

"So what does this mean for us? Why do we need to get out of here?" Dilyus asked.

"The Stonimions don't exist and I'm worried that if we are here for too long we could affect the future in some way or be affected by being in this time." Scorpicle explained.

"What you mean like I could grow an extra leg." Dilyus scoffed.

"Or even a miracle could happen and you might grow a brain." Simsaa's remark received hysterical laughter from them all except for Dilyus of course.

Without any further delay they opened the Book of Quantime, nothing happened, no white light appeared to allow them to go back to the future, time did not exist and so the book was not working. The panic amongst the group became heightened as they realised this phenomenon, the thought of being stuck here and not be able to help their people or Earth after every-thing they had been through was unbearable, so much so that the usually brave Simsaa burst into tears. Nasami tried to console her but she was getting worse.

"Simsaa please get a hold of yourself, we'll figure something out don't worry!" Scorpicle sounded like an adult for the first time ever instead of his usual happy go lucky adolescent persona.

Amafiz turned to Simsaa and said "I have a way for us to get back don't worry." She looked at him and smiled, more from embarrassment at her breakdown than the thought of Amafiz thinking he had a way to save them.

They had no choice but to try Amafiz's suggestion; it was a case of trying it or being stuck in that time forever.

Amafiz's suggestion was for him to produce his defence shield, for Scorpicle to then create a space within the shield that was independent of the external surrounding. The idea was that this space within the shield would then allow the Book of Quantime to work as time had been created within the shield itself. In theory it was brilliant but putting it into practice would be another thing. Firstly Amafiz had to create a defence shield large enough for Scorpicle to create gravitational waves; which he had to do so by distorting the space in one area of the shield and moving it fast enough to create a ripple movement of that distortion. When Amafiz explained this to the others Nasami looked confused.

"There are two questions in my mind; the first how is Scorpicle going to create this distortion and secondly how fast is he going to have to go for the gravitational waves to be created?"

"Aha!" Scorpicle exclaimed "I know my science and thanks to good old Einstein I know what to do." He then continued to explain. "I am going to create the distortion by vibrating, that will create waves, like sound waves, and then I am going to move with the speed of light which will eventually create these travelling distortions which are gravitational fields."

"Okay, two things." Simsaa said.

"Why is it always two?" Dilyus questioned, everyone just ignored him this time as they had more urgent things to worry about than Dilyus' absurd questions.

"Where are we going to be when you are moving at the speed of light? And also how are the gravitational waves going to help?

"Well, you guys are going to sit inside me otherwise you'll probably be obliterated in such a small space with me travelling at the speed of light and as for the gravitational waves, Amafiz had the right idea because once we create gravity within the shield, space and time are linked so we should be able to create a space for the Book of Quantime to work." Scorpicle explained.

There were a lot of ifs and maybes in this idea but it was the only one they had.

"I don't mean to be negative but will our powers still work?" Nasami asked. This was a factor that none of them brought into the equation and really one that none of them wanted to consider. There was only one way to find out. Amafiz placed his hand onto his belt and concentrated, initially nothing happened and the others began to panic, but then slowly a purplish hue began to radiate from his stone, albeit it slowly. The effort he had to put into producing his shield was far greater than he had ever had to muster up before, but he did it.

As soon as the shield was produced they all sat inside Scorpicle, Amafiz still concentrating hard to make sure his shield remained intact. Scorpicle began to vibrate and they could all see as he started this the air inside the shield was moving like ripples in water. Scorpicle then began to move he did so slowly at first and then began to increase his speed. The initial vibration motion and then the speed increasing caused the Stonimions to feel nauseated. The nausea was a controlled symptom because if it had not been for Scorpicle's interior build and defence mechanisms the phenomena they were experiencing would have had more dire effects on their bodies. As Scorpicle reached light speed they noticed that the inside of the shield changed; they peered out of the windows and saw mists that swirled around Scorpicle who was now stationary.

On closer examination the mists seemed to take shape, it was then that they noticed the mists were Stonimions, some familiar and some unfamiliar. It was as if the future of Stonidium was being established within the shield. It was now or never; Amafiz opened the Book of Quantime and the white light filled Scorpicle, this time Amafiz knew what to say "Stonidium present day, The Great Stone." He even remembered to mention the exact location.

Within a matter of seconds they were standing inside the Great Stone, their sudden appearance turned the occupants of the Great Stone into frozen statues. Samaan and the Elders had been holding a meeting about how to contact the Four Guardians of Stonidium, as it had been quite a while since they had left for their mission. The meeting came to an abrupt end with some good news for a change.

Samaan's delight at seeing Scorpicle and the young Stonimions was so overwhelming that he could not contain his emotions and he burst into tears. "Oh! My dear children you cannot even begin to understand how happy I am to see you all. Are you all okay, you're not hurt or anything are you?"

All Samaan could do was to give the children a big group bear hug, he held them so tightly and for so long they thought that they were going to be stuck like that forever. Eventually

Samaan let go of them and took a step back. "You four have a lot to tell me..." Samaan started to say.

"Ahem!" Scorpicle interjected.

"Sorry, I meant you five." Samaan grinned and winked at Scorpicle. "But before that we need to get your parents here straightway."

Samaan sent two messengers; one to the Stonimions' parents the other to Farmoeen. He did not want to risk any attention brought towards them or the Great Stone because of any power surges as a result of telepathic links. Within the hour the parents and Farmoeen arrived, their joy at seeing the young Stonimions knew no bounds. The relief of the parents at seeing their young children safe and sound was evident on their faces; however, as parents of the Four Guardians they knew that their children's duties were not yet over. Over the next couple of hours the young Stonimions sat and told the others what had happened to them on Earth, whilst filling their quite empty stomachs with their favourite food and drink; which was in plenty of supply thanks to their parents.

"Children I think it's time you went home, tomorrow we shall all meet again to decide the next move, we need to think carefully as the taking back of Stonidium will be a struggle as Imfalin will not want to give it up so easily.

In the dark of the night the Stonimions all left the Great Stone, deep in their thoughts about what was to come. The young Stonimions slept in their own beds after what seemed like an eternity to them; safe in their homes with their parents the mission they had completed seemed like a dream now. Scorpicle sat talking to Akjam for a while, reminiscing and a bit upset that he did not spend more time in England, Akjam promised him he would help him once all of this was over.

The next day the news of the return of the Four Guardians spread through the Stonimion community like wild fire, however, this was done with a lot of discretion as they all knew that if Imfalin got even a whiff of their return then she would not hold back in trying to destroy them all. She still had no idea that they had found the Initiation Stone and that slowly one to two people at a time were being initiated in the Great Stone.

The meeting at the Great Stone had commenced with Samaan heading it as usual. He first welcomed everyone present and then proceeded without wasting any time to the most important point on the agenda; the removal of Imfalin from power.

"I think we should use the Book of Quantime to go back to the point where Sheram had got hold of the book." Amaran suggested as a starting idea.

"Unfortunately, although that sounds like the ideal thing to do it would be very risky. If the Book of Quantime in the past was to come into contact with this one of the future it would create a paradox that would essentially destroy everything." Farmoeen explained.

"Well we'll have to do it the good old fashioned way then, Stonimion power." Akjam declared, standing as if ready for the battle now.

"I agree with Akjam, we have the Book of Quantime, the Four Guardians can use that to stop Sheram, but here we have now all been initiated and with the help of the Guardians we are ready to take down Imfalin." Samaan said to all those present.

The decision had been made but now the plan had to be put into action to remove Imfalin from power.

The next day the Stonimions had put their plan into action. In the Stonimion village everything seemed as before, the shops opened, the children were heading into school, there seemed to be nothing to suggest to Imfalin's hoards that something was wrong, that a plot had been brewed to topple their leader.

Unknown to the hoards the Four Guardians, Akjam and Samaan were all sitting inside Scorpicle, who was invisible. After their usual bullying, scaring and looting of the village they headed back to their lair, and so were followed by Scorpicle and the Stonimions. The strange creatures arrived at the lair, they entered through the magical portal, which was protected by Imfalin' evil sorcery. Scorpicle kept as close as was physically possible to the end of the group and slipped in with the strange creatures into Imfalin' s lair.

Once inside they slowed down and separated from the strange creatures; so far so good, Scorpicle's defence shield had also cloaked them so that they would not be detected by any magical incantations that Imfalin may have installed at the entrance. They roamed through the maze of passages getting closer to where she was; finally they arrived at a large central atrium. They looked towards the far wall and saw the old wretched woman sitting on a large chair admiring her hoards. The very sight of her repulsed them all, so much so that they almost forgot why they were there for all they could think about was getting away from the evil being in front of them.

Before they had time to make their next move, Imfalin turned and looked towards the spot where they were and cackled "Welcome Stonimions, can I get you anything to drink?"

At that precise moment her entire hoard turned to face the spot where they were standing. There was no time to waste. The Stonimions exited Scorpicle and were ready for battle. The attack was launched with such ferocity that Scorpicle and the Stonimions were stunned and unable to react, but when the first blow hit Samaan the others woke up from their trance and reacted to this. Scorpicle aimed his charged laser at the creature that had attacked Samaan and blasted him; the creature toppled backwards from the impact but slowly got up. Samaan reacted as well by touching his turquoise stone; instantly a pale blue light surrounded him which he then concentrated into a single beam that obliterated the creature completely.

"Nice!" Scorpicle said as he looked at Samaan admiringly. Samaan simply smiled back at him.

Imfalin had gotten up from her chair by this point and was hobbling over towards Akjam. "You and your family, past and present have always been a thorn in my side." She hissed as she got closer. "Killing you will be the most pleasurable thing I have ever done."

Amafiz was horrified as the hideous being came closer to his father. "But first I will kill your son in front of your eyes, watch your anguish then I shall kill you as well." She was so close now that Akjam could smell her putrid breath.

"You are heartless." Akjam replied.

"How do you know about my anatomy?" She squealed with delight at her own joke.

They were surrounded, with Imfalin facing them all, she was

ready to attack and take them down. They too were ready, ready to keep hold of their tradition, way of life and survival.

Imfalin's hoards attacked with such vehemence that for a moment they all thought that they were going to lose this battle far more quickly than they had anticipated, if they were going to lose. The strange creatures did not need additional weapons as their own bodies had been constructed to be weapons; knives, swords, chain saws and guns were extra limbs on the abhorrent beings, which were used with ease. They started attacking at will, not caring who or how they hurt and maimed; all they understood was destruction of the enemy.

Nasami screamed in pain as a sword whooshed past his face, he held his face and when he withdrew his hand he saw blood. Luckily the sword had just grazed his face and not cut it too seriously. "Children please be careful, these creatures are relentless and will stop at nothing, we need to get this over with quickly and effectively; you know what to do!" Samaan shouted at them as the noise of the whooping and cheering from Imfalin and her hoards rose. This was part of their tactic to make noise and unnerve their enemy.

Akjam immediately produced his long silvery orange rope using his stone; the rope vanished for a moment and then appeared over Imfalin's head and dropped over her shoulders. When it landed on her it tightened so that she could not move. Akjam looked at Dilyus and said "Dilyus you're going to have to control her mind, I have physically held her down but she could still use her evil magic so you will have to stop her." Dilyus nodded his understanding of what he must do. It was not an easy or pleasant task but he knew he was a much stronger Stonimion now than he had been when he had started out on this journey and he knew what his capabilities were. The green hue that began to surround him and Imfalin was intense; she began to struggle as she knew what Dilyus' intentions were. Dilyus opened his mind and entered Imfalin's mind; she was waiting for him. "Did you think I was going to let this be easy for you, you silly child, watch and learn what I am, what I have seen and what I am all about." The creature Imfalin knew no mercy, she exposed to Dilyus all the hideous things she knew; torture, killing, evil magic with no bounds and for a moment it looked as if she had corrupted his mind so that he would never be able to function as a normal Stonimion again. Dilyus groaned with the agony of what he was witnessing, however, she had underestimated the Guardian of Stonidium and as painful as it was Dilyus mentally stood his ground and forced Imfalin into a corner of her own wretched mind and held her captive. "You will not do or say anything." His mind told hers and mentally he had gagged and bound her so that she could do no harm.

Meanwhile, whilst Akjam and Dilyus were dealing with Imfalin the rest of them tackled her hoards. Imfalin's creatures had not noticed that their beloved leader had been lassoed and was being kept a prisoner both mentally and physically because Simsaa had changed her form to look like Imfalin. So when she told them to follow Scorpicle, Samaan Amafiz and Nasami to the other side of the chamber on the pretence that they were running away; they did so obediently. As soon as they were far enough away the running group turned around and attacked the hoard. Simsaa had changed from Imfalin into a large wall and Amafiz then produced his defence shield to encapsulate them all. At this point Nasami stepped in and sent his brilliant white light across the creatures and as the light hit them one by one they turned into stone statues. Once they were immobilised Samaan and Scorpicle destroyed them with their lasers; all that was left of them were tiny pieces of stone all over the floor.

They walked back to Akjam, Dilyus and Imfalin; Samaan signalled Dilyus to vacate her mind, which he did so, almost collapsing to the floor with exhaustion. Imfalin struggled in her orange-silver bond and was truly frightened, so much so, that she did not think to use her powers in this small window of opportunity and before she could get to that point Samaan had created the vortex he had used on Nadrog and sent the screaming Imfalin to the same fate.

23
THE RETURN OF SOLACE

There was a peaceful silence inside the lair that had never existed before; the walls seemed to breathe a sigh of relief as if the removal of all the heinous behaviour that had been displayed by Imfalin and her hoard of nasty creatures had cleansed the entire building. Tranquillity had descended within the lair that made it look physically different, before it was dark, dingy and grey looking now it was bright and colourful.

Scorpicle and the Stonimions headed back to the village, unafraid of being attacked, followed or simply bullied. They had taken back their home and it felt good. Samaan had telepathically sent a message to Farmoeen and the other Elders about their victory and had instructed them to spread the word and get the Stonimions to gather at the village square.

By the time they arrived at the village square the celebration had already started. When the Stonimions saw Scorpicle, Samaan, Akjam and the Four Guardians an almighty roar of cheers exploded from them all; their joy was something that only those who have been under siege, tormented and tortured would understand. The celebration continued long into the night but eventually the Stonimions headed back to their homes. For the first time they would be able to sleep without fear of any evil power making their lives miserable. Tonight they will sleep as Stonimions in Stonidium the free land.

The following day Samaan, the Elders, Scorpicle, the Four Guardians and their parents were once again at the Great Stone, this time although the discussion they were having was serious their mood was light. The victory over Imfalin had left them elated as they knew that their home was now safe and they had one less problem to deal with. This left them with the problem of Sheram still on Earth. Every day he was there meant he was closer to overall power and total dictatorship of the Earth; his power on Earth could make him more dangerous than he already was and it could mean devastation of other worlds in other dimensions, including theirs.

The main problem was to figure out when, where and how to deal with Sheram on Earth.

"I think we should go to a time just before he got to Earth." Luman suggested.

"Why do you think that would be a good point then?" Akjam asked him.

"Well it would mean that he would not be able to cause any mischief and get to rule over Earth."

"I don't think that's a good idea." Akjam replied

"Why do you say that Akjam?" Samaan was curious as he had been thinking along similar lines to Luman.

"Well knowing the obstinate and stubborn being that Sheram is he would not give up, even if we got there before him he would try another way of carrying out his intentions. He would not give up." Akjam explained.

"I agree with you both." Farmoeen interjected.

"I think that we should find out exactly when he changes the history of Earth and intervene with what he did." Farmoeen suggested. They all agreed with the oracle as the plan of action that they needed to take would have to be one that would cause limited damage on the time lines of both Earth and Stonidium.

Farmoeen suggested that the best way to find out the exact second that Sheram entered Earth would be through the Crystal of Knowledge and the Book of Quantime.

The Crystal of Knowledge was just as awesome as they remembered it from their previous visit. This time as they stood around the giant rhombus Farmoeen gently placed the Book of Quantime on one of its flat surfaces so that it could make a connection with the book. "Oh Great Crystal of Knowledge the Four Guardians of Stonidium have managed to find the keys on Earth and have returned with the Book of Quantime intact." Farmoeen spoke to the Crystal as if she was speaking to an elderly relative.

"Congratulations to you all." The crystal spoke sounding genuinely pleased for the young Stonimions.

"Thank you very much, it wasn't easy." Scorpicle said who was reduced in size so that he could enter Farmoeen's home.

The crystal continued "I see you have brought the Book of Quantime as well, exactly how can I help you?"

"Well, we need to know from the book the exact point Sheram entered the Earth." Samaan explained.

"Very well, please give a few moments and I will speak to the book." The crystal answered.

Dilyus looked intrigued by this last statement made by the Crystal and was very tempted to make some sort of comment but refrained from doing so, as he thought the Crystal might get annoyed. "You're right Dilyus I would get extremely annoyed." The Crystal said. Everyone looked at Dilyus who looked rather embarrassed by the Crystals comment.

They stood around the Crystal and waited for what seemed like hours, although it was maybe ten minutes or so. Whilst they stood there the large rhombus Crystal pulsated and glowed changing its colour as it communicated with the Book of Quantime. The only response they could see from the book was the indentations where the keys had been placed, glowed their respective colours.

Finally the Crystal communicated with them again. "I have seen from the ancient and wise Book of Quantime that Sheram went back to the twenty third of July in nineteen twenty one to the East End of London, England. He went to, seventy two Orchard Close, where he proceeded to eliminate an elderly man by the name of Frederick Stephens. Although you know that already. The time was five thirty five pm." The crystal paused for a moment. "I understand the Book of Quantime told you why it was Frederick Stephens, children."

"Yes but it seemed so unnecessary" Simsaa remarked

"He was a poor man it seems with no connections to anyone important in history." The Crystal answered.

"But he had some real significance for Sheram to risk killing him." Amafiz commented.

"Well there is something that the humans call the 'Butterfly effect' and it was this that influenced Sheram to do what he did."

"And before anyone asks, the 'Butterfly effect' is a theory that refers to the ripple effect of a factor and the outcome it causes, the example is that the flapping of the wings of a butterfly in one place could lead to a hurricane in another place a few weeks later."

"That's interesting but how does this explain why Sheram killed the old man and not anyone else." Salani asked.

"Well from the history contained within the Book of Quantime and all the alternative paths that a time line could take, it looks as if the simple comment Frederick Stephens made to someone, who then said it to someone else causing someone else to enter British politics and become extremely influential in the world of law and politics was his undoing." The Crystal replied.

"So why not kill the person who was going to be the influential person?" Akjam asked looking puzzled by the long winded way that Sheram had gone about this.

This time Samaan answered on behalf of the Crystal. "I think it may have been either too difficult, troublesome or attention attracting to kill this person directly." Samaan's answer seemed to make sense and even the Crystal did not say anything to the contrary, so everyone accepted this reasoning.

"So we need to get to Mr. Stephens before Sheram, but to stop him trying to kill without him knowing it is going to be difficult." Scorpicle said.

"What do you mean?" Nasami asked.

"Well if we try to hide Mr. Stephens or stop Sheram he will try again later, he obviously doesn't have the Book of Quantime so would not be able to go back in time but he might try to kill him again later." Scorpicle explained.

"We're going to have to think carefully about how to go about this." Amafiz added, going deep into his own thoughts on how to overcome this problem.

They thanked the Crystal and left for the Great Stone with Farmoeen in attendance. At the Great Stone Samaan had informed the other Elders about the information that the Crystal had relayed to them and also about the problem that Scorpicle had identified about how to save Frederick Stephens and cause Sheram to fail in his attempt to rule the world.

"This certainly is a dilemma." Amaran said, thinking hard if there was anything that he could do.

Samaan looked at him wondering what his old friend might have up his sleeve. He knew him to be a great inventor, in fact very innovative. Thanks to Amaran they had accumulated a vast array of weird and wonderful gadgets, where some of his earlier inventions were now part of the artefacts collection, Samaan always teased him that he was so old he should also be part of the ancestral relics.

"Leave it with me Samaan, I'll see what I can do." Amaran said.

"Please my dear friend just be wary of time. The longer we wait the more damage Sheram will do on Earth. I don't want Earth's time line to be tainted so much that his effect lingers and influences its normal time line." Samaan said to his friend.

"Don't worry, I will not sleep tonight." Amaran left the Great stone and went straight to his workshop. It was going to be a long night.

At the Great Stone Samaan told the others to return to their homes and rest, especially the Four Guardians. They had one final mission that on the face of it seemed less dangerous and hazardous than their mission searching for the keys on an Earth where Sheram was present, but it was a mission where failing was not an option; Sheram had to be removed from Earth and should not be allowed to be a threat in the future either.

Whilst the Stonimions and other Elders returned home, Samaan and Farmoeen stayed. There was another matter that Samaan wanted to discuss with Farmoeen that nobody had thought of yet. He had telepathically told her to stay but not let on that he had asked her to stay.

"What's the matter Samaan?" Farmoeen looked concerned she could tell it was a serious matter because of his agitated manner.

"Everyone is so concerned about saving Frederick Stephens and quite rightly so, that no-one has stopped to think about Sheram. What are we going to do we cannot leave him on Earth because as soon as he realises that his plan is not going according to his predictions he's going to know something went wrong." When Samaan finished he looked at his friend and waited for a response.

"I think I know of a way out of this, you're right if we leave Sheram loose on Earth the problem will still be in existence and we need to remove him once and for all."

"Talking of problems I hope he hasn't caused too much mischief." Samaan said knowing full well this was probably wishful thinking.

Indeed it was, back on Earth the moment Sheram realised that he was in danger he escaped and left the members of the society in the hands of the Stonimions. He never looked back, something that really worked in his favour; his true selfish nature had been revealed and instead of despising him the members of the society became in awe of him and instantly accepted him as the Sheram their society had been formed in the name of.

This acceptance as the leader propelled him to greater heights than just being CEO in a major influential company; Sheram became involved in politics and thanks to his interference in nineteen twenty one, the one person who could have been a major stumbling block to him was a mere small time business man instead of an important parliamentary candidate.

Sheram's rise to power was the equivalent to a runaway car; he crashed and damaged anything or anyone that even mistakenly got in his way. His ferociousness knew no bounds and scared even some of the cruellest of humans that he had befriended. The state of Earth was terrible at its best; many countries, especially those that were already quite poor were now uninhabitable because of the devastation that Sheram's army had caused. He no longer had the law enforcers he had a much more powerful army that destroyed first and asked questions later. Any humans that survived these attacks were taken into specified areas, such as, mines where they would be put to work.

Sheram enjoyed seeing their misery; this for him was revenge to the highest, a revenge that was instigated by the hate for his parents. He had never forgotten or forgiven them for his abandonment. Simsaa's vision of Sheram standing amongst burning rubble and people in agony was not too far off. Sheram was confident now that no-one could stop him as it had been quite a while since the Stonimions had last been seen on Earth; maybe they had given up and did not care as much as they liked to make out about Earth's destiny and were happy with restoring power in their own world. He had made this assumption as when he had tried to contact Imfalin there was no response. Sheram had concluded that either there were stronger powers stopping the communication than had originally protected Stonidium or that the Stonimions had got rid of her. Either way he did not care because he was succeeding in what he wanted to do and the old woman was of no use to him any longer anyway.

Sheram's over confidence would be his undoing as he had now become careless. He had removed his men from keeping vigilance on any sudden surges of power on Earth and had them all concentrating on the acquisition of the world country by country; making him stronger as each day progressed.

Thankfully Sheram's egotistical behaviour had blinded him to an important bit of information; the Stonimions had the Book of Quantime which meant that they did not have to return to Earth at this time.

It was the twenty second of July in nineteen twenty one, the day before Sheram killed Frederick Stephens. The Stonimions were at Frederick's home, on the pretence of being government officials who were carrying out a survey on the welfare of the elderly after the war. This excuse had gained them entry into his home at which point Dilyus had swiftly controlled him so that he would do as they wanted without any problems. Amaran was truly a genius, he had managed to create a replica of Frederick, although it was not made of any living breathing cells of any form, the replica looked, spoke and reacted exactly like the original. The Stonimions replaced the real Frederick with the replica and allowed time to take its course. True to form the next day they watched as Sheram came to Frederick's home and obliterated him, or so he thought.

Part one of the plan had succeeded; they had saved Frederick, however, part two was a bit trickier. They returned to Stonidium and using the Book of Quantime once again returned to Earth in the late seventies with two additional guests; Samaan and Akjam.

They had looked at the time line and found that the most vulnerable time for Sheram had been at this point. He had kept low for all those years and was just now beginning to emerge into the world, they knew that this was the point that they should act; any earlier or later would have a greater affect on Earth's original history.

Sheram was working as a farm hand, someone unnoticeable and irrelevant to the business world or politics. One day he was sitting in a field eating his lunch; to look at him you would never suspect this was a hideous evil creature, who would one day be the cause of pain, hurt and eventually the destruction of the Earth.

The Stonimions watched him from a distance, they made sure that there was no-one around and then they made their move. They had remained invisible inside Amafiz's defence shield, when they were close enough Amafiz released the shield and they stood in front of Sheram. He was taken aback and for a moment looked very confused; slowly he began to realise who these people standing in front of him were.

"Stonimions." He said as if he had to hear the word out loud to convince himself that it was really them.

Before he had any time to respond Akjam released his silvery amber rope that encased Sheram and tightened itself around him, Samaan produced his deadly vortex and Dilyus got into Sheram's warped mind, he was getting used to this now, and forced him to walk into the vortex. As soon as Sheram had disappeared into the vortex then Samaan closed it.

They had done it but there was really only one way to find out if they had succeeded; they went to the time that the Stonimions had gone to when retrieving the Keys of Light.

They travelled to each of the locations that they had been to whilst looking for the Keys. The beautiful locations remained the same, as were the people they had encountered, but there was a distinct difference in the aura of the places and the people. They also looked for Sheram's law enforcers but found that each country had their own 'normal' police. As far as they could see he was gone, or more correctly he had never been there.

There was one more test. Akjam said to Scorpicle.

"Scorpicle, really and truly, there is one more test we can do to confirm that nothing on Earth has changed because of Sheram."

Scorpicle knew exactly what he meant so Akjam took the Book of Quantime, gently opened it and as the brilliant white light emitted from it Scorpicle said "Nineteen eighty five, Basildon, Essex, England." The instant they arrived Scorpicle looked around; the shops looked the same, the local police station seemed to have 'normal' police officers and the people of the town seemed to be as he remembered them.

"It looks like how I remember it." Scorpicle said

"There is one more check I can do." Scorpicle proceeded to tune in his radio system to the local radio station.

"This is Basildon radio, bringing you the new release from Tears for Fears." The musical introduction started and Scorpicle remarked.

"Hey! Sheram's favourite song!"

"What do you mean?" Simsaa asked

"Listen."

The song's musical introduction led into the lyrics of the first verse.

'Welcome to your life,

There's no turning back

Even while we sleep

We will find you

Acting on your best behaviour

Turn your back on Mother Nature'

Then came the chorus

'Everybody wants to rule the world'

As soon as they all heard the chorus they burst into laughter.

Scorpicle grinned.

It was time to return home; the journey proved to be extremely informative for Samaan and the Four Guardians. Something had been niggling at Dilyus ever since Scorpicle took them to nineteen eighty five and he felt he had to ask.

"Scorpicle, how come you know so much about Earth, especially nineteen eighty five?"

Scorpicle looked towards Akjam, who told the young Stonimions the whole story. They all knew that Scorpicle was no ordinary car but what they did not know was that Scorpicle had been made by Amafiz's grandfather, Daaran the invincible; but the computer program that had been downloaded by Akjam, was in fact the brain pattern of a fifteen year old boy who had been killed tragically.

Akjam had noticed some unusual energy surges occurring in Stonidium and had stumbled upon Imfalin's plan to come to Earth. He was unable to stop her but he did manage to follow her, through the portal she had created. This was why Scorpicle had not been affected by the time; Akjam used his

314

bracelet and downloaded the young boy's brain pattern. He found that she had the intentions of kidnapping a human child, for what purpose he did not know. When he tried to stop her a young human teenager was injured by Imfalin's attack on Akjam. He tried to save the teenager but was too late; however, he downloaded the brain pattern from his bracelet into Scorpicle's computer system once he got back to Stonidium.

The young Stonimions were lost for words. Simsaa became a bit tearful again. "I'm sorry that's so sad."

"Well yes and no, if I was meant to die on that day then I'm glad Akjam had been there, if not then I would never had met you guys. I was an orphan and had no-one, the care home and authorities put my death down to misadventure, this way I have had a family for a long time who have given me more love than I could've asked for."

They were all quiet for the remainder of the journey home, each deep in their own thoughts, each waiting eagerly to see family and friends again in Stonidium the free land.

EPILOGUE

Sheram landed with a huge impact, creating a small crater where his body hit the ground. He got up and dusted himself off. He looked around trying to get his bearings; Sheram walked a few hundred yards at which point he had reached a small hill.

So far he had not seen any signs of life, animal, mineral or vegetable. The place was desolate. When he reached the hill he climbed over it and to his chagrin he saw two beings one of whom he was not happy about seeing the other he was relieved but at the same time disappointed that the being was here.

"Sire, you came for me!" Nadrog screamed with delight as he galloped over to his master.

"Not quite, but at least I know where you are now!" Sheram replied.

"Oh Sheram, it's good to see you again." Imfalin squealed with delight as she hobbled over to him.

"Only you would say that you old hag, yeah I bet you're happy that I'm stuck here as well."

"By the way where are we?" Sheram asked not quite sure where he had landed.

"I don't know either Sheram I was hoping you might have some idea." Imfalin said looking rather embarrassed.

"Well it looks as if we have plenty of time to find out because the way things are here I don't think time exists in this realm, nothing seems to have happened to Nadrog and he's been here for quite some time now."

"I have?" Nadrog asked looking extremely surprised by this bit of news.

"So what are we going to do?" Imfalin asked

"We are going to find a way back to Stonidium and deal with those Stonimions once and for all." Sheram smiled; making the other two flinch in the process. They knew he meant business and would not rest until he got revenge. His nemeses would regret the day that they had dared to cross him.

Made in the USA
Middletown, DE
21 June 2019